Whore

Emma L. Fenton

DEDICATION

This book is dedicated to Nick, who encouraged me to publish, to my mum, who never gave up hope of seeing my name in print, and to Kailyn and Rohyn, who provide unending love and support.

CONTENTS

ACKNOWLEDGMENTS

I would like to acknowledge my first proof readers, Alison and Linda, without whom this book would never have reached this stage. Also, all the staff at The Historic Royal Palaces and Hever Castle who provided so much help during my research trips.

Prologue

Brussels – 1513

Her first steps on foreign soil were the hardest. Whilst twelve was a normal age to be sent out into the world, to learn to be an adult in a fashionable household, it is still very young to be sent abroad, even if it is for the best education possible. And it wasn't of her education the striking young girl thought as she sat in a small parlour, waiting to be summoned before her new mistress. Instead, her thoughts were of home, of England, of her family. Her father had been ecstatic when he had come home from Brussels with a place for her at the court of the Archduchess Margaret. He had never once thought that maybe his little girl didn't want to go, that maybe she wanted to stay with her siblings in England. He thought only of the opportunity it gave him, to have his daughter raised in such a fashionable court would make her invaluable in the marriage market. He had told her she wouldn't have to go until she was ready, which was a lie. He had told her that he and her mother, and both of her siblings would be there to send her off, which was a lie. He had told her that she wouldn't have time to feel homesick and lonely, which was also a lie. So, at twelve years old, the little girl sat, feeling her whole family had abandoned her, and she was quite alone in the world.

An usher broke her reverie, opening the door in silence and gesturing her inside. The little girl stood up to her highest, and forced her mouth into a smile. Only the huge dark eyes betrayed her heartache. As she stepped forward into the brightly lit room, pretending confidence she did not truly feel, she felt so insignificant, and so forsaken, and so dreadfully alone. And

1

it was in that moment that she decided that never again would she allow fear to rule her. Never again would she depend on the presence of others to make her feel safe. From that moment on, little Anne Boleyn decided that the only person she needed was herself.

Chapter One

England – December 1521

That first smell of the air at Dover was enough to bring flooding back all the memories of the England of her childhood. Almost seven years away from home was a long time, but in that first breath of Dover air, it felt like nothing. She was home. Everything was so green, and so fresh, and so familiar. The sea breeze blew through her long, loose chestnut hair, sending it behind her in ripples. She longed to get off the boat and take off her shoes and stockings, and run barefoot through the grass, like when she was a child. But she was no longer a child. At twenty years old Anne Boleyn was a very different person to the frightened girl who had stepped off the boat in Europe all those years ago. She was tall, and slender, and although no one would describe her as beautiful, she was the most captivating woman most people had ever seen. Perhaps it was the huge dark eyes, which seemed to take everything in, and to hide so many secrets. Or perhaps it was her sophisticated style, honed by six years at the French court, serving Queen Claude. Or perhaps, just perhaps, it was that the discerning eye could just make out, behind the cool, courtly exterior, there dwelled the heart and soul of a passionate woman, just waiting to be released.

During the ride from Dover through Kent, to the family seat at Hever, Anne drank in every ounce of the countryside. She knew that when she married James Butler, the man her father had chosen for her, she would have to go off to Ireland, which everyone knew, was dour and dank and full of wild tribes. As she rounded a bend in the road, she got her first sight of the castle at the bottom of the hill, and at that, as tired as she was, she pushed her horse into a gallop, and was pulling to a clattering stop in the courtyard well before any of the others were even in sight.

Anne dismounted and looked at the house she had grown up in. It was exactly as she remembered it, every stone, and the familiarity made her feel safe and secure. The sound of hooves made her turn, to see her father and the handful of liveried grooms joining her in the courtyard.

"Oh Anne!" Screamed a voice from behind her. Anne turned on the spot to see her older sister, Mary, running towards her like a child. Mary wrapped Anne in a tight embrace, "I've missed you!" Mary whispered into Anne's hair. She pulled away. "Now let me look at you." Mary commanded, and Anne stepped back and basked in her sister's admiring gaze. She took the opportunity to look for changes in her sister. Mary didn't look any older than she had the day she had left Anne in France, six years ago. The sisters had only had a few short months together before events out of Anne's control called Mary back to England. Anne and Mary had always been like chalk and cheese. People could be easily forgiven for not realising they were related at all. Mary was plump and fair and very pretty, whilst Anne was dark and slim and unusual. Even their personalities were opposites, with Mary being so relaxed and pleasure loving, and Anne so intense and tempestuous. But the sisters relished their differences, as between the two of them, they felt there was no storm they could not weather.

"Come on Mary, let's go inside, there is so much you have to tell me, your letters were so poor! I feel like I don't know anything about what's happened here since I left!" Anne adored her sister; in the way most younger siblings have a sort of worship for their older ones, and yet saw from her life so many things she desperately didn't want to emulate.

"I know sweetheart, I'm awful, I know, but I was always much better at living life than writing about it!" The two girls giggled, and arm in arm, they strolled into the house, and up into Mary's bedchamber.

Although Anne was glad to be back at home with her sister and her parents, she missed France. And more than that, she resented being summoned back to England to marry a man she had never met, to settle a dispute their fathers had about the right to some stupid title! What did she care? She would at least like to meet a man before her father informed her that she would be expected to bear his children! She hated the idea that she was viewed as nothing more than a brood mare, despite her extensive education. But she couldn't discuss that with her sister. Dear, sweet Mary wanted nothing more than to please others, and that had led her to near ruin, salvaged only by a marriage to a lowly courtier, not worthy of a Boleyn match, which was used to poorly cover up her affair with the King of England, Henry VIII. Mary loved nothing more than the sensual side of life, and enjoying every pleasure life had to offer. It was a sentiment Anne both admired and abhorred. Whilst she wished she too could have such a relaxed approach to life, where happiness was her only goal, Anne couldn't bear the idea of being used by men the way that Mary was.

Finally, Anne asked the question which she had been burning to ask her sister since she had heard of her affair. "Mary, isn't it humiliating to be his lover, but not his wife. Don't you feel, well, used?"

"Oh Anne, I love him." Mary said, so dreamily Anne wasn't sure Mary even understood.

"But, surely you know that people are talking about you, calling you a whore? Surely it can't be satisfying to know that if you fall pregnant you won't know who the father is?"

"I love him." Mary said again, simply. "Henry Tudor is not a man a girl can say no to, he's certainly not a man I would want to refuse. And if I was to fall pregnant, it would be Henry's, there is no doubt."

"But of course there would be doubt!" Anne interrupted, infuriated by her sister's lack of humiliation at her position. "If you have a husband and a lover there is always doubt."

"But William isn't my husband in that sense, not since our wedding night. Henry gives him money and positions and he lets Henry have me."

"As if you were his prize mare!" Anne exclaimed, her temper rising.

"No Anne, it's not like that. It's never like that. Henry loves his wife, but he does not desire her. I love Henry, and my husband loves his King. I do not try to take him from his wife, and so his desires are fulfilled, and Catherine can sleep at nights."

"Whilst her husband romps with her maid!" Anne was appalled. "I'm sorry Mary, but however you justify it to yourself, I can't condone it."

"You just wait little Anne," Mary said, with infuriatingly condescending serenity, "One day, you will fall in love, and you will do anything within your power to make that man happy. I hope you're lucky, and the man you fall in love with is your husband, but that is so rare Anne." Mary stroked her sisters' cheek, which was flushed a rare shade of pink against her snow-white face. Anne's face filled with concern.

"So, do you not love William?"

"Of course I do. Very much. But he is away a lot, Henry sends him to many places to do things for him. I never ask where, or what. But just because I was lucky in my marriage, and because our parents were a love match, doesn't mean everyone's is. The King and Queen married to broker an alliance. In many ways, that's what your marriage will be too." At the mention of her own marriage, Anne flinched. Mary smiled at her. "Marriage isn't that bad Annie, don't worry yourself. You don't look as pretty when you frown. I'm sure your new husband will worship you so much you cannot help but fall desperately in love with him!" Anne couldn't help but smile at her sister.

"It's not being a wife that worries me, it's having to go all the way to Ireland!"

"I could persuade Henry to give him a place at court, if that would make you feel better. Then you would have to live here."

"Can you do that?"

"I don't ask much from Henry, but I can get things I really want. We don't leave much time for talking!" Mary grinned conspiratorially, but her slightly prudish sister didn't feel her sister's whorish antics were worthy of a smile. Anne had sworn to herself long ago that she would never ever act like her sister did with men, giving herself away at such a low price. Anne had decided that she would only give away her honour once she was married, not just to the first man who swore his love to her.

Anne did not have long in the countryside idyll that was her childhood home. Instead, after a few short days spent talking idly with her sister, and wandering around the estate she had half forgotten, Anne was back on horseback, to be presented at court.

Anne was, at first, distinctly unimpressed by the court at Greenwich. She was so accustomed to the delicate sophistication of Paris, that the bold exuberance of the English court repulsed her. Here was a court where the fight for power was brutal, where the King wished only to fulfil his whims, and the court ran in circles to supply his every desire. Anne was, however, impressed with the King, much against her inclination. She had made up her mind to despise the man who was besmirching her beloved sister's reputation, but in fact, she was comparatively admiring. She saw in him a petulant child, who had been spoiled and ruined by years of adulation, yet who was as masterful, and handsome as everyone had told her. And whilst she knew that his tempers could send reverberations throughout the whole country, she could also see that to make him laugh made you an honoured friend, whether you were rich or poor. He adored beauty, and youth, and therefore surrounded himself with the beautiful and the young, and Anne could finally, truly understand why Catherine, his Queen, was abandoned for mistresses. Catherine had the appearance of a woman who had, in her youth, been beautiful, but who had grown fat through years of failed pregnancies, and whose deep, almost masculine voice still had a detestably strong Spanish accent, making her always seem like a foreigner in the court that had been her home since she was fifteen. When they had married, Henry had not cared that his bride was older than him, but now, whilst Henry was still young and vibrant, Catherine was ageing, and pious, and this repulsed Henry. Perhaps he would have been happier if one of his sons by Catherine had lived. Perhaps then he would still worship her with the wide-eyed adulation he had felt when he had first met her, when she had come to England as a bride for his older brother Arthur. And perhaps if she was a little more relaxed, he might have still loved her, and comforted her for the loss of so many of their children. But instead, Catherine kept herself apart, and aloof, and she repulsed her husband entirely.

But as Anne got used to the court, she began to love it. And probably her favourite thing was the devoted attention she received from almost every man at the court. There are two distinct types of beauty in a woman. First, there is fashionable beauty, whereby a woman fits the figure that society deems attractive. This beauty changes, dependent on time and place. Mary Boleyn possessed this kind of beauty. Her fair hair, and plump, inviting body were the epitome of desirability in Henry's court. The other type of beauty is subtler, and yet infinitely more alluring. It is a beauty that transcends time and place, a beauty not reliant on how fair or dark, how plump or slim its possessor is. This beauty emanates from the soul. It enslaves all who witness it, in spite of the fact they cannot explain it, cannot justify it, cannot understand it. It is a beauty men would die to be near, and women would kill to possess. And it was this type of heart stopping, breath-taking and yet invisible beauty that Anne had. She was noticeable in a crowd for her French fashions, including the French hood, which showed off tantalising amounts of her thick, luscious hair. She was more intelligent than the other women at court as well, and men felt refreshed, and yet taken aback by her witty repartee, and her enlightened and informed views on world affairs and theology. Thomas Boleyn had done well by his little girl, sending her out over the seas for her education, because it became clear that she entranced every man who gazed upon her. Thomas realised that his daughter could have any man she wanted, and suddenly it seemed barbaric to marry her away to Ireland, when she could be of so much use at home. Without ever mentioning so much as the Butler name to his daughter again, Thomas proceeded to dissolve the marriage talks, to allow Anne to catch herself her own husband, one whom, Thomas hoped, had an uncontested title already in his possession.

Beauty of all forms was the most important factor to success in Henry's court, which meant that Anne was always destined for greatness. And her huge potential was first realised when the court met for its New Year's festivities that year. This, the culmination of the Christmas celebrations was an orgy of food, and wine, and dancing. Although the new Boleyn at court held no key role in the festivities, the novelty of her individuality was peaking, and she never failed to have a partner for every dance. The men of the court marvelled at her grace and style as she glided across the dance floor, whilst the women burned with envy at her sophisticated clothes, and her light, nimble footwork, which made even the most dainty and graceful court regular appear awkward and ungainly. The glares of these women were painful for Anne to feel. They also highlighted another key difference between her life in France, and the world back in England. In France, she was idolised by the women for her skills, her allure, and her intelligence. Here, the women were beginning to eye her with suspicion, as a rival. Women who were being courted by the most eligible men at court became more eager to have the flirtation sealed with a betrothal, and even those who were married were afraid of being cast aside for such a nubile young specimen. But this didn't dishearten Anne. She felt sure that once people got to know her, and ceased to see her as a threat, there was no reason for her to be disliked at all.

Chapter Two

Spring 1522

"Isn't it exciting Anne!" Mary gushed to her sister. "This is to be the most spectacular masque ever seen at court, and we are to be leading roles!"

"It is not as witty as the pageants in France." Anne drawled. Her disinterested attitude masked an eagerness she was unprepared to share, even with her beloved sister. All but Mary viewed this unconcerned attitude as aloofness. Mary knew Anne better, however.

"You, my witchy little sister, have a plan! It is a man, I am sure of it. You have set your sights on a man and you intend to ensnare him tonight!" Anne smiled knowingly, but Mary Brandon, Duchess of Suffolk and the Kings precious younger sister interrupted the sisters' chatter. Anne put on her widest court smile for the Duchess, and dropped into a low curtsey. The Duchess eyed Anne suspiciously. She disliked the striking young woman, because she knew what had happened in France all those years ago.

In 1515 the King's beloved younger sister Mary Tudor was eighteen, and the most beautiful and eligible young lady in the whole of Europe. And she was in love. She was wildly in love with Charles Brandon, the Kings best friend. It was the sort of ferocious passion that can only be felt by one so young. But unfortunately, a princess cannot marry for love, she must wed where she is bid, and Henry bid her to marry the ageing King of France. Not even the promise of being a Queen and being surrounded by luxury could make the prospect of marrying the decrepit old man appealing to the vibrant young woman. Mary begged and pleaded with Henry to reconsider, but he would have none of it, he needed to form an alliance against Spain, and marriage was, by far, the best way to form such a tie. Mary wept, and then flew into a temper, and then, finally, appeared docile, pliable and amenable. It was in this mood that she visited her brother, and begged that if she married the French King, when he died she could choose her next husband herself, and be guaranteed of her brothers blessing. Henry's response was, in reality, noncommittal, but in her desperation, Mary took it as his word. So, Mary went to France and married the King, and in next to no time at all he was dead. Henry sent his closest friend and most trusted adviser, Charles Brandon, to recover his sister from France. He was already planning another dynastic match for her, still young, still beautiful, and still the most desirable match in Europe. Mary, however, felt that her brother sending to her the man she loved more than any other was a sign that he would accept their marriage. Little Anne Boleyn, who was in the train of the now Dowager Queen of France, watched in horror, as night after night, Charles Brandon visited the bedchamber of the supposed grieving widow. After what seemed to the little girl a lifetime of creeping around, Mary and Charles announced their marriage, and, perhaps predictably, Henry was furious. Anne had never understood why Mary would risk her position as the King's favourite sister to marry a man so beneath her in status, and why she would risk falling pregnant before they were even married. She boldly asked her mistress this, and was dismissed coldly. Anne was left behind in France when Mary returned to England, and she had never forgiven Mary Brandon for her lax morals, and cold behaviour.

Mary Brandon always felt uncomfortable around Anne Boleyn. She felt that those dark eyes bore straight through her into her soul, and it terrified her. Mary straightened her sash, which bore the epistle 'Beauty' and signalled the other women to follow her out into 'Châteaux Vert'. Chateaux Vert was the masterpiece devised by William Cornish, to impress the ambassadors of the Spanish court. The eight most beautiful ladies of the court, dressed in white satin, played the eight female virtues. Anne portrayed 'perseverance', whilst her sister played 'kindness'. The virtues were being held prisoner in Chateaux Vert by female vices, played by the boys of the chapel Royal. The most handsome noble men, led by the King, besieged Chateaux Vert, and freed the virtues, and the freeing of the virtues signalled the commencement of the dance.

Very early on, Anne found herself partnered with Henry himself. He was instantly dazzled by the wit of his partner, and found her boldness a refreshing change from the softly spoken, passive young women of his court. When he asked her name she laughed a high, light laugh, curtseyed low, and stepped away from the dancing to join her brother George in a shady alcove. Henry's eyes followed her slender young body, but were quickly distracted by Mary, replacing her sister seamlessly as the King's dance partner.

Henry's were not the only eyes to follow Anne across the room. She was also watched by the son of the Earl of Northumberland, the most eligible young man at court, Henry Percy.

Anne felt his hot eyes on the back of her neck, and bit her lip, fighting the temptation to turn around and smile. If she had any chance of making Henry Percy fall madly in love with her, rather than simply admiring her, she had to be less eager than the English girls, more aloof, more unattainable, and more desirable.

"I do declare Anne, you have not listened to a word I have said to you!"

"Something about some woman or other I am sure." Anne laughed.

"Sometimes I feel you are the worst sister I could wish for," joked George. The pair laughed. George was devoted to Anne, and she to him. George was the perfect combination of his sisters; he had Anne's wit and intelligence, but Mary's love of life, bordering on the reckless. George was nineteen, and was still a wild young colt at court, desperate for recognition and respect, and yet far too flighty and strutting to really earn it. Their father continually threatened to send George to Oxford, to give him a finished education which the King so admired. Anne, however, could see all that George had to offer, and she adored him, with a passion even more ferocious than that which she bore towards her sister. George had climbed trees with her and talked of literature when they were children, whilst Mary preferred to sit and play with her dolls This shared childhood meant more to Anne than the bond of sisterhood. This shared childhood was something Anne had fantasised about constantly during her first few years away from home. And even towards the end of her years in France, when she was feeling low, it was George whom she thought of, remembering those lazy days sitting under trees eating apples they had picked for themselves, reading aloud their favourite poetry, and composing ballads of their own.

Anne and George's conversation was cut short, before George could ascertain which of the many admirers watching Anne had caught her eye. The arrival of Thomas Boleyn, their father, was enough to fling all frivolous thoughts from their minds. Anne curtseyed in a gracious manner, and her father raised her, kissed both her cheeks and beamed at her. She knew it could only be good news, which for her father could only mean wealth and power.

"I have been promoted," Thomas whispered with pride. "I am to be treasurer of the household, and am to be made a Knight of the Garter." Anne squealed.

"Father, I am so proud of you," she gushed. Her father's elevation would make her that bit more appealing in the marriage market, and as she had her sights set on the son of an Earl, this small elevation in the stature of her family would be the perfect addition to her eligibility. The Boleyns may be new money, and they may not own much land, but they were riding high in the King's favour, so the money and land would not be long to follow. And Anne shrewdly knew that any man with half a brain, which was the only type of man that appealed to her tastes, would know to snatch up this prize before her father rose too high, and far too many offers were landing at her feet. She cast a casual glance over her shoulder. Henry Percy was still watching her. She looked down demurely, but then looked up again, catching his eye, and for just a split second, he could have sworn he saw a desire in her glance to match his own.

Chapter Three

Spring 1523

Anne was still rather alone in the Queen's apartments. Of course, she had Mary, but Mary's company was beginning to grate on Anne. She wished, all too frequently, to discuss her night time adventures with the King, and Anne had no desire to be a part of that. But the solitude suited her. She had learned long ago how to keep her own council, and how to be her own friend. She did not need the approval of a group of fawning, preening, self-obsessed girls. They thought only of how to ensnare themselves the best husband. Anne smiled to herself. She knew she was well on her way to catching the very best of all the unmarried men at court, and not one of them had even noticed. She hadn't spoken more than twenty words to Henry Percy, and maybe that was why he was so enthralled. Her beauty had captivated him. If she had been like the others he may have passed it off as a passing attraction. He may have talked her into his bed and then forgotten her when the next pretty thing turned his head. But Anne was different. Anne didn't seem to want to make people fall in love with her as the other girls did, and it was that more than anything that was making him fall so hard. The idea of making this woman love him consumed his entire life. He wrote her letter after letter, ballad after ballad, and sent not one. Anne knew he was in love with her, and now came the most crucial part of her plan. To allow him to believe that she might love him in return, and not just his title, and the security being his wife would provide. This would require all the powers she had at her disposal. For once she was married to him, she would become a Countess in waiting. She would have all the power and influence she could want. And a puppet husband would suit her purposes well enough. Anne yearned for the wealth and security that the Percy match could bring her. She would be kept at the centre of a buzzing court, one of the first ladies of the kingdom. And never again would she be looked down upon as the daughter of an upstart, and the sister of a whore. She would finally have respectability, she would be an equal to the women who whispered behind their hands that if one sister was a whore the other must be, and those who laughed at the Boleyn's lack of status or history. And that, more than anything, was what Anne desired. She wanted to be accepted by the court she had come to call her home, as she had been in France.

The doors of the presence chamber opening stirred Anne from her reverie. In came a few of the young men of the court, along with the King, and a handful of musicians. "Wife, I bring you entertainment." Boomed Henry with a great show. He often did this, burst in upon Catherine's quiet reflection with music and dancing, much more to please himself with the company of beautiful women than to please his wife. Catherine, however, was the daughter of Isabella and Ferdinand of Spain, and she did not show any outward emotion, a trait which terrified most of her women, and repulsed Anne, who could not have hidden her wild and tempestuous nature even if she tried.

"My husband, how kind of you to bring such merriment into my rooms, I was just about to summon musicians for myself."

"Then, my Lady, you will have no objection to your ladies setting aside their needlework and passing some time dancing." Henry smiled, and clapped at the musicians, who hurriedly began to play. Anne was the only lady not to throw aside her work and spring to her feet in eager anticipation of a dancing partner. Instead she voiced aloud a desire to finish the seam on the shirt she was sewing, and remained by the window, head bent on her work.

She sensed he was near her before he spoke, she could hear the soft shaking of his breath, and she fought back a smile. "Mistress Anne." Said the voice, soft as honey. She looked up, and caught her breath at how close he was to her. She wanted him to desire her without a doubt, but for him to bring himself so clearly into her presence had surprised her.

"My Lord." She said with true decorum, her own voice quaking only slightly with nerves.

"Anne," he said, his voice a little choked with emotion, "I cannot tell you how long I have yearned to speak with you alone."

"With me my Lord?" she whispered. She found it hard to get the words out. She told herself that this must be the fear of his passion, rather than any of her own. After all, passion had taken her sister down a route of licentiousness, which she had no desire to follow.

"You must know that I have been watching you for so long. I have never before found the courage to speak to you. You are so different to the other girls of court, and since the day I met you I have not been able to get you out of my mind."

"My Lord." She whispered, barely audible this time.

"I am sorry, I have startled you. You have obviously been ignorant of my hopes, of my desires. And for me now to come upon you whilst you work to throw my love to you is most ungallant. I shall leave you to your needlework now, my beautiful Mistress Anne. And I ask of you only this, may I write to you sometimes?" She nodded, unable to speak. "And would you respond?" He asked, a note of desperation in his voice. Again, she nodded, scarcely daring to look into his face. "Then with that I shall leave you, my love." He said, and with that he was gone. It took a full five minutes for Anne to control her heart beat and her breathing. It was only then that she allowed herself to be taken up to dance, and to be passed from one man to another like a puppet. Everyone noticed the difference in Anne, even the King. Her usual vivacious flirtation and witty conversation was replaced with a vacant expression. The King was much more observant than many of the other men, he had seen Henry Percy approach Anne, and he suspected that the young fool had professed love. He laughed to himself. Anne Boleyn may not have titles and land and an enormous dowry, but she was far too good for a young fool such as Henry Percy. She deserved a man of intellect and learning, yet one of sport and of activity. A man who could entertain her in public, and bring her indescribable pleasure in their bedroom. She was as wild as the wind, and she needed someone just as hot and ferocious, not some wet drip like Percy. She would, of course, never accept him. He was sure the young colt would soon be curled in a corner, tail between his legs, licking his wounds before he returned to his father's estate in Northumberland to await an appropriate match. But Anne, who should she be matched with? Her father was flying high at court, and her sister brought him pleasures he had only before dreamt of, so who should he marry little Anne Boleyn off to. This, thought Henry, would require some thought.

"How often does he write you?" Mary asked her sister in a whisper a month later.

"Twice a day, sometimes more."

"Always of his love for you?"

"And of his plans for us."

"So, you are betrothed in secret!" Mary squealed with the excitement.

"No!" Anne exclaimed. "I have made no promises to Henry Percy, and you must never tell a living soul I have." Mary laughed. "Mary, I mean it!" growled Anne. Her dark eyes seemed to flash red as the anger swept across them. Mary hated that look, it scared her.

"I promise Anne, I promise. But has he asked you?"

"Every day. And every day I tell him I need another day to consider his suit."

"But why, don't you love him?"

"I suppose I must." Said Anne cautiously. "I anticipate his letters eagerly enough. And I certainly like the idea of being a Countess one day. And it would mean Father could never resurrect that dreaded Butler match."

"Oh, Annie that isn't love. That is practicality. You once told me you would never marry for such things. You were going to run off like a heroine in a story and marry your true love."

"I was six when I thought that Mary, I have grown up since then. From what I have seen, love and passion only lead to the ruining of a woman's reputation and no promises from the man. I think pragmatism in marriage is far more advisable. At least I know that if Percy should betray me I would never feel the hurt. And he would keep me safe, and comfortable."

"Annie, what has happened to you? Where has the girl intent on a heart stopping, ground breaking, breath taking love before she would even consider giving away her hand?"

"She grew up Mary. She watched her older sister humiliated, and relish in the humiliation. She has watched a devoted Queen be mocked by her pleasure-seeking husband. She knows now what she didn't then, that she will never trust a man enough to truly give away her heart." Mary stood up slowly and walked away. She didn't want Anne to see the tears welling in her eyes. She would never have wished this on her precious sister. She would never have wanted the choices she had made to kill the spirit that made Anne who she was. She suddenly felt remorse for the decisions she had made, and for the fact that she had flaunted them in front of Anne. She truly regretted turning her beautiful, carefree sister into this pragmatist, who yearned for power and adoration more than she yearned for love and happiness.

Anne watched Mary leave. She was used to seeing Mary walk away from distasteful situations. And Mary was usually accompanied by their father. Ever prepared to support his little harlot so long as she continued to bring him honours and fortune. Anne thought back to the time all those years ago when Mary had fallen from grace in France, and her father had seamlessly removed her from the continent, and placed her in the bed of Henry of England.

In the hot summer of 1516 the young courtiers of Francois I of France spent most of their time picnicking outdoors and dancing until dawn. The Queen, Claude, daughter of the late King, was pregnant as usual, and rarely took part in these festivities. Her ladies in waiting, however, joined in readily. Readier than most was Mary Boleyn still very young, and beautiful in a soft and giving way. She had caught the eye of the King. Francois made no real effort to hide his affairs, and Claude had the gracious dignity to ignore them. The whole court, therefore, knew the first night he took Mary Boleyn to his bed. He has simply whispered in her ear, "Tonight, my English rose, you shall bring joy to your King." She had curtseyed, keeping her eyes on his, filled with lust, and with that he had led her from the dance floor.

The following morning the men of the court laughed bawdily about the noises they had heard coming from the Kings chamber that night, and they speculated how long the King would keep her as a mistress, and to whom she would be given when Francois was done with her. Mary made no attempt to hide her passion for Francois, and was gloatingly proud of having given her maidenhood away to so worthy a recipient. There was giggling amongst the whole court as night after night Francois would lead Mary from the dancing, and the two would return a while later looking dishevelled. Within weeks even this vague semblance of discretion was gone. She would sit upon his lap in front of the whole court, and would allow him to kiss her there, in public. Anne was only a child, and did not truly understand. All she knew was that the whole court was laughing at the sister she idolised, and that Mary was relishing in it.

As summer turned to autumn, Francois tired of Mary, his summer love. She took this rejection better than many of her predecessors, and happily moved on to a new love. Mary fell in love easily, and was happy to give anything and everything to those she loved.

One night, when Mary returned to their chamber late as usual, Anne sat bolt upright in bed, prepared to find out for herself why her sister was now known as the 'English Mare' because all the men at court claimed to have ridden her. Mary's explanation had been lacking to say the least. "You will know soon enough little Annie what it is to be desired, what it feels like to awaken a man's lust. And then you will not turn your pretty little nose up at me. You will understand that a Boleyn can never make a good match, not really, and that the best we can do is hope that one day a man rich enough will take an interest in us, and find us husbands. That is what a woman must do Annie, find a husband."

"But who will marry a whore?" Anne spat. Mary smiled, not a little bit offended by her sister's rude response.

"Many, my dear sister, many. Men would give almost anything for my favours. Already I am offered jewels and clothes and riches, and soon I will be offered someone's hand. It may only be a younger son, or a man of little fortune, but it will be man glad to have me. And then I shall be able to find a rich husband for my pretty little sister." Mary blew out the candle to signify the end of the conversation. Her sister was never offered the marriage that would have saved her reputation. Instead her father had recalled her to England, rumour has it, after showing her miniature to the King of England.

Anne roused herself from this remembrance and noticed her cheeks were damp with angry, humiliated tears. She scrubbed them away quickly. She never wanted to be like Mary, she never wanted to give in to desire, nor to be used to slake a man's lust. She grabbed parchment and quill in a frantic hurry, and began to scribble a response to Percy, accepting his proposal and urging him to make their betrothal official, before a priest, as speedily as he could arrange it. Anne Boleyn would not rely on her sexuality to get herself a husband, she would use her brains. She would not end up like Mary, currently riding high in their father's favour because the King had chosen to name his latest ship after her, drunk with love and unashamed of her position as the King's whore. Anne would not degrade herself. Anne would marry Henry Percy, she would be adored, she would be contented and most of all, she would be safe.

Chapter 4

Late Summer 1523

"I think, my love, that it is time we made our betrothal known. It is time to bring the matter to the King's attention." Percy murmured to Anne, as they lay next to each other in a secluded spot in the palace garden.

"What business is it of the King's?" Asked Anne sullenly. The good fortune being piled upon her family by her sovereign was not enough to make her care much for his opinion, despite his power.

"Because, my silly little Anne, the King would know of the matches of all those at court, he almost never disapproves. And if we are to convince my father that this is a suitable match, and tear his thoughts away from Mary Talbot who he has his mind set on as my bride, we need the support of the King. If the King blesses the match, then not even my father would have the power to deny it."

"Maybe if your father met me?" Anne suggested. She did not feel inclined to beg to the King, cap in hand, and rely upon him for her happiness.

"My father would advise me to take you as a mistress and nothing more. It wouldn't matter how charming he found you, my love, my father's own thoughts are with his dynasty. He wants my marriage to greaten the land holdings in the North, and for my sons to do the same. I think," he dropped his voice to a whisper, "he aspires to have as much control in the North as the old Earl of Warwick had."

"And Warwick lost his life fighting to increase what he had. Why are men never content with their lot!" Anne cried.

"Well, many women are not contented either, or would you rather stay plain mistress Anne Boleyn instead of becoming my wife, and the future Countess." Despite herself, Anne laughed. She supposed she thought only of her own advancement and security, and that her sons would have something to inherit from their father other than the name bastard.

"Well, if we must go to the King, so we must." She sighed, resigning herself to the fact that she would be viewed by the court as the rest of her family was, complicit in her sister's degradation, using Mary to get what she wanted.

"Ah, but we shall not approach the King, I shall have private conference with Wolsey. As he is my master I am sure he would not deny me such a wish as that which my heart so fervently desires." He kissed her, gently at first, but with increasing passion. With difficulty Anne pushed him away.

"When we are married my Lord, but not until then." He smiled.

"My virtuous Lady. In that case I shall away to speak to the Cardinal immediately." With a final fleeting kiss, he jumped to his feet and sprinted away. Anne watched his slightly ungainly figure disappearing from her, then laid back on the grass, staring at the little wisps of clouds in the sky. How much she yearned to get this match completed, then, maybe, she would not feel so on edge every time a man looked at her. Unlike the court of France, where the affairs of the courtiers were not only common knowledge, but often paraded before the poor, cuckolded spouses, England was filled with seditious and secret affairs, conducted in quiet corners and out of the glare of public eye. Anne feared more than anything that any of these young libertines, if they set their eye to her, might decide that her protestations of virtue were a game, and might cease to give her a choice. When she was married, she would lose that fear, she hoped.

King Henry felt guilty for spying on the little lover's glen he had come across in a rare solitary stroll, but he found that he couldn't take his eyes from Anne Boleyn whenever he saw her. Of course, her sister was the more beautiful, and so wonderfully giving and sensuous. But Anne, there was something about Anne that made his breath stick in his throat, that made him both want to possess her entirely, and somehow, inexplicably, to wrap his big hands around her delicate little neck and squeeze, to see if her excessive life and energy would prevail. He wasn't truly sure why, but the thought of Anne marrying that milk sop Henry Percy was repellent to him. It made his stomach tie itself in knots he couldn't undo. In general, he preferred his mistresses to be married, it made it easier to oust any bastard offspring of the union onto the complacent husband, and saved him the worry of constant bastards thinking to seek his throne. So why did he want Anne Boleyn to remain unmarried? As he watched her lying in the sun he felt his stomach unclench. It was probably only that Percy would take his bride to the North, and he wouldn't get the chance to continually gaze upon her face. After all, Percy was a quiet country type, not suited for court. He would have the match broken, and Anne could be given a new husband, a seasoned courtier who would mildly sit by and let his wife join the King in his bed every night. He left her in peace, staring at the sky, determined to find Wolsey before Percy did, determined to put a stop to the match.

Anne felt her eyelids begin to droop as she lay in the early afternoon sun. She had cried off her usual duties, complaining of a headache, and she had no desire to return to the palace just yet. It would be alright to doze here in the sun, in this seclusion. The only person who knew where she was was Percy, and she would not mind his company should he return. With the peace that came with sensing everything she had schemed for would soon be hers, Anne allowed herself to slip into sleep.

It could have been five minutes later, or five hours, but Anne was awoken with a start. "Mistress Boleyn." Called a young gentleman wearing Wolsey's livery. "The Cardinal wishes you to join him in his apartments, he wishes to speak with you."

Anne jumped to her feet. She hurried along behind the man, whose name she didn't know, frantically attempting to neaten her hair which was wildly tangled from her sleep, and to arrange her dress to look at its most becoming. If Wolsey wanted to speak to her about her impending marriage, if he wanted to impress upon her the great honour being done to her by the heir of the Percy family wishing to marry her, she wanted to look the part. As she walked confidently into the apartment, she flashed Wolsey her most winning smile. His face remained impassive. Her eyes scanned the room, and seated in a corner was Henry. He would not meet her eye. Something was wrong. Something was very wrong indeed. Her smile faltered ever so slightly.

"You wished to see me your Eminence?" She enquired, sweeping a low curtsey and kissing his proffered hand with reverence.

"Yes, pray be seated mistress Boleyn." Anne saw only a roughly hewn wooden stool available and took it. She noted that Wolsey's own seat was almost a throne, and as he sat and folded his hands across his corpulent belly, he looked worryingly regal. "Young Percy has been to see me today about a betrothal between the pair of you."

"I believe my Lord came to you to seek your blessing, and to ask for your intercession on our behalf to the King."

"Unfortunately, madam, neither my blessing, nor my help will be forthcoming." Anne felt a coldness spread from her extremities. How could Wolsey possibly be saying no? He, himself, had risen from humble origins, indeed, much humbler that Anne's, and his aspirations were much higher.

"Might I inquire as to why, my Lord?" Anne asked, her voice steely.

"Because, as I am sure you are well aware madam, this match is entirely unacceptable. For the daughter of a Knight to marry into the family of Northumberland is unthinkable."

"My Lord," Anne began, trying to keep her anger from her voice, "My father may only be a Knight, but my mother was born a Howard, daughter to the last Duke of Norfolk, and sister to the current. Surely a niece of a Duke is worthy of the son of an Earl?"

"Perhaps, if the circumstances were different. If the said Duke had no heirs of his own body, so that the offspring of his sisters stood to inherit. But as your uncle has an abundance of heirs of his own, you, madam, are of little consequence." Anne had been prepared to take many insults from the Cardinal in order to get him onside, but at the accusation of being of little consequence Anne's sharp temper flared. She stood, pulling herself to her full, and rather formidable height. Her beautiful face was set as stone and her voice, instead of her usual silky and seductive tone, was sharp and cold as ice.

"I do not need to remind you that you harken from much meaner origins than me. You are, I believe, nothing more than the son of a butcher for all your titles. I shall, of course, appeal this matter to the King. I am sure that his Majesty will see that when two people are of a mind to marry one another without any thought to advancement or position that it is reason enough to allow it. I fear, my Lord Cardinal, that your wise judgement shall be overturned." Wolsey laughed.

"Madam, do you think I would deign to make such a decision without first consulting with the King. He is of my mind, that this match will not do, and will never have Royal approval."

"And what if we chose to marry without Royal approval." Anne spat. "For I see no reason that this marriage would not be a good one."

"Then you would commence your married life with a husband missing his head madam. And as he would have died as a traitor to his King, you would receive nothing barring the taint of treason. And who would touch you then, niece of Norfolk or not." The Cardinal sneered. Anne's anger burned white hot.

"Then you have made an enemy of me this day Cardinal. And mark my words, one day I shall be in a position to repay all of the hurt you have done me. You have ruined my life, ruined my marriage, and ruined all that I was to become. And I shall not rest until I know you have suffered from the same injustice you have just doled out to me in the King's name. For all of us here present knows who made this judgement. You shall burn in hell my Lord." And with that Anne turned on her heel with a swirl of skirts and left the apartment. It wasn't until she had marched a few corridors away that she realised that not only was Percy not with her, he hadn't spoken a word in defence of their union. Poor weak Percy. This was why he needed her. He was all heart and no backbone, and he wouldn't survive without her strength. And Anne held onto her strength until she was shut in her own chamber, when she threw herself face down onto her bed and sobbed until her eyes ached and her throat was hoarse. Even when the tears stopped falling she couldn't bear to move. She had been so foolish. If she had been like Mary, so gentle that none could deny her, or like George, the eternal diplomat, right now she could be walking away hand in hand with her betrothed. Instead she had poured venom on the one person who had it in his power to truly influence the King, and now he would not help her. Now she was his enemy. Now, all of her plans of riches and security would come to nought. She began to weep again, not the furious tears for her wounded pride, but the true, heartfelt tears that came from knowing that her future was undone, and the fear that she would be forever cursed by Wolsey.

Meanwhile, Henry Percy sat, still silent, in Wolsey's chamber. His heart was broken, there could be no doubt, but in his deepest soul he had always known that he would never be allowed to marry Anne. He knew that his father would never agree to any match other than the one with Mary Talbot, who was an heiress in her own right. Certainly not a match made for love with a girl who would have a pittance for a dowry. Marrying Anne had been a dream. He loved her with an intense passion, a passion which he was relatively sure she didn't reciprocate. But that didn't matter. He knew he wasn't the most handsome of the men around the court, and if she wanted to marry him for security and riches he wouldn't mind. He had been sure that she would have come to love him in time. But it was not to be. And now he must sit and wait. Wolsey had sent word to his father, and he must await his father's arrival, and his wrath. He was anticipating a beating. He may be a fully-grown man, but his father was much more physically imposing, and could, despite his age, give blows enough to break a nose.

The ride from court to Hever was not filled with anticipation and excitement as its reverse had been. Anne was being sent home in disgrace. She had presumed to make herself a match and had failed, and now she must face the consequences. Her father rode alongside her, his mouth a stern line, his frown emphasising the already deep lines on his forehead.

As she had expected, she was summoned to her father's presence as soon as she had changed from her riding clothes. She walked to his room with pride, almost aloof. She may have fallen at the last, but she had contracted a marriage with the heir to an Earldom, she had nothing to be ashamed of.

"What were you thinking you stupid girl!" her father exploded as soon as the door closed behind her. "To make a betrothal without my knowledge!"

"Henry Percy fell in love with me. Is that a sin now? I was sure you and my mother were a love match." Her voice was filled with the haughty disdain she had perfected in France.

"Love? Love has nothing to do with anything child!"

"I am not a child father. Whilst the whole world revolves around my married sister whoring with the King I am getting older, and if I am not matched soon I will die an old maid, for surely my looks will fade."

"You have little enough of those girl, and far too much of your uncle's pride. Thinking to align yourself with Northumberland!"

"At least I aspired to a grand match, when my mother settled so below her station for you! I thought the legacy of we Boleyn's is that we better ourselves through marriage." Anne's voice was so cutting, her comment so close to the mark, that Thomas Boleyn took a deep breath and changed tactic. With Mary, anger worked, and with George, disappointment. Anne would need cajoling, and he was not above such an action if it kept his family in the ascendancy.

24

"Annie, the match was a great one, and had you pulled it off Lord knows how proud we would have been. But you must have known that between you and that halfwit Percy you couldn't pull this off." Anne was confused by her father's sudden softness. She ignored the slight on Percy, but was a little affronted at the implication that she was not capable of such a match.

"If Wolsey hadn't decided that...."

"Wolsey? Oh Anne, you aren't a fool. Open your eyes. Wolsey was acting on the behalf of the King. The King has a wandering eye, and it wandered to you my child. If I had known of your intentions I could have helped. I could have interceded with Northumberland, I would have offered you a handsome dowry. With the Earl on our side we could have convinced Wolsey, who would, in turn, have persuaded the King. But I knew nothing of this matter until Wolsey advised I kept you under closer observation."

"You would have helped?" Anne's voice went from stone to that of a small child again. She was always so headstrong, she never asked for help, even when she needed it.

"Of course I would have helped. Like you said, it is the Boleyn way to better ourselves with our matches. Mary has married a man with no real standing, but with great potential. I had always known you would marry someone greater than we could have imagined. But perhaps this match was not to be. You would have been bored in Northumberland."

"I would have been well loved. Henry Percy has a faithful heart."

"I am afraid, my darling daughter, that his affections may be less constant than you think. After your conversation with Wolsey, young Percy was marched back up to Northumberland, and has already become betrothed to Mary Talbot, as his father wanted. They shall be married any day I don't doubt."

"What?" Anne was hurt that he hadn't even fought his father a little for her. She had hoped he would hold out against another match, that he would write her impassioned letters about running away to marry. It seemed that Henry Percy was as weak and malleable as they had all said. The affection she felt for him suddenly ran cold. A man could profess to love her so deeply, and yet at the beckoning of his father he would gladly give her up and marry where he did not love. Unwelcome tears filled her eyes and she furiously blinked them away. She would not waste tears over Henry Percy, who obviously hadn't wasted any over the loss of her. Anne, in that moment, firmed up her resolve. Not only would she hold her virtue in hand for her husband, and not only must that husband provide her with security and safety, but he must be strong. He must have a will of his own, or at least a will she could bend to match hers, with no other influences. She wanted a man in control of his destiny, not an heir. She swore to herself in that moment that her heart would be of ice. She would not fall victim to love like Mary did, she would not throw away her heart on any man who flattered her. She would never fall in love, she would only do what would protect the interests of Anne Boleyn. After all, what was love anyway. It was a word said by men to encourage women to drop their morals and part their legs. She would not be fooled by any man, just because he told her he loved her.

Chapter Five

Summer 1524

"But George, it wouldn't be right for me to be there!"

"She is your sister Annie, she needs you."

"She is birthing a bastard. I cannot approve of the child, so I cannot support her. I have never had a child myself, so I would be of no use to a woman in childbed. Why must I go?"

"Because our sister wishes it. And because in spite of your feelings about her relationship with the King, you love Mary. And because you know, whether you like it or not, that if our sister bears the King a healthy son then our star will continue in the ascendancy. He hasn't cast her off, despite her being with child, so he must love her deeply."

"I go because I am bid to. And I go because I yearn for court, for dancing and merriment and people! And because I know that you are coming to court, now you are done at Oxford becoming a learned gentleman."

"Whatever the reason, you and I are off to court Annie, and I am certain that we will set the place alight." Anne collapsed in giggles. George always made even the most abhorrent situations seem pleasant. Anne had been appalled when she had heard that Mary was carrying the King's child. And she was even more repulsed at the idea of being present at the birth as Mary requested. For a woman who was not even married to be present at a birth was very unusual. And as a virgin, Anne felt wholly unprepared for what was going to be expected of her.

The birthing chamber was dark and hot and smelt stale. Thick carpets and tapestries hung the walls and covered every window, and despite it being a gloriously warm summer the fire was burning constantly, pumping its sickening smells of burning herbs into the room, making breathing a chore. Anne felt she had been in there for a lifetime, although it had only been a week and a half. The birthing chamber was a realm of women, and there were no men permitted. Even the roles usually played by men were taken over in this world. Anne longed to steal away to walk outside, but Mary would not let her leave her side. Mary was afraid, and she would speak to no one of her fears but Anne. Anne was afraid herself as Mary spoke of her dread of the oncoming pain, and the chances of her death. She felt secure enough in the King's love that she was not concerned if the child was male or female, only that they both survived the ordeal.

"And I hear tell," Mary whispered, anxiously, "That Margaret Beaufort, the King's own grandmother, was sent by God such a terrible ordeal in bringing forth Henry VII that not only could she not bear another child, but that she swore herself to a life of celibacy."

"I do not think you were made for celibacy, sister." Said Anne. She meant the comment as a cutting remark, but it seemed to reassure Mary.

"Yes, I hear that Margaret was a very Godly woman already, mayhap she simply chose a nun's life and others have blamed her time in childbed." The smile still lingered on the corner of Mary's lips when her face went white, her eyes widened and she let out a low moan that only Anne could hear.

"Is it starting?" Anne asked cautiously.

"I think so." Mary whispered. "I have been having the pains for an hour, but they were not so bad, this was worse. They told me to expect it to last many hours, and I didn't want to make a...." As the next pain gripped her, Mary pitched forward, curling herself into a ball, and Anne panicked.

"Fetch a midwife, I think it is starting." An unknown woman came forth from the depths of the room. With no ceremony, or indeed manners, she lifted up the bedclothes and inspected Mary.

"The baby will be a long time yet I fear. But move her to the birthing bed. Someone put a pan of water on the fire to boil, and bring some strong wine. We may be up all night."

As the pains grew stronger and more frequent Anne wished nothing more than to cower in a corner. Watching Mary writhe in agony as the midwife bade her keep still and quiet so as not to frighten the child was more than Anne could stand. But Mary would not let go of her hand. Her beautiful nails were carving into Anne's flesh, and she was sure if her sister didn't relinquish her grip soon she would draw blood.

"Alright now ducky" Said the midwife. "I want you to push."

"I don't know how." Mary whimpered. But suddenly it seemed to dawn on her. Mary pushed herself up a little, gripping tight to Anne's hand and she released a noise like an animal. Anne saw the veins pop up all over her sister's pretty face, distorting it into something hideous. Her face was red, and sweating and her grip on Anne's hand tightened. Mary let out another almighty grunt and appeared to be bearing down.

"I can see a head, keep going ducky, your babe is almost here." Anne felt the blood running down her hand as Mary pushed again. "Head's out, you're almost there." The midwife reassured her. After what felt to Anne like a lifetime of pushing, Mary's grip relaxed, her whole body sank back into the soft pillows behind her, and her breathing sounded normal again. And then came the sound that almost melted Anne's heart of ice. The baby made its first cry. Not the pitiful wail Anne had anticipated, but a full bellied howl. This was a baby who was strong and lusty, and, although Anne hated to admit it, likely to be like its father.

"A girl" A voice from the sea of faces announced. Anne watched in wonder as the tiny pink screaming bundle was tightly bound, and passed to Mary. It was only then that Anne saw Mary's face. Whilst just minutes before the familiar features had been contorted in agony, making her a monstrous sham of herself, suddenly Mary looked serene, blissful, so at peace. Anne was amazed that after all that her sister could look so content. But then, looking into the face of her little niece, she understood, and somewhere in the depths of her, the parts she tried to conceal even from herself, Anne felt a soft, but clear tug of yearning to have a child of her own.

The baby, who Mary had named Catherine, was not visited by the King until she was four days old. Anne was by her sister's bedside when Henry strolled into the room.

"I hear you have borne a daughter." He said to Mary. His voice was casual, but his eyes took in every inch of Mary's beautiful matronly figure.

"Yes, my Lord. I have named her Catherine, if that is acceptable to you of course?"

"Call the child whatever you and your husband would call it." He said. For a second Anne saw the hurt in Mary's eyes. The King, it seemed, was not prepared to own the girl as his, despite her already vivid Tudor red hair, and a pout to exactly match her fathers. "And hurry with the churching my sweet," He added in an undertone, "for my bed has been cold without you." Mary blushed in a very becoming way. With one last yearning look at the much fuller bosom, Henry turned and left.

"So, he will not own the child?" Anne asked, incredulous.

"I never truly expected him to." Mary murmured, her voice honeyed by the bliss of motherhood. "He owned Henry Fitzroy, but he was a boy, and born of an unmarried woman. Why should he choose to own little Catherine, a girl born to a woman already a wife? But he still wants me in his bed Anne, he still loves me. So many others have been cast off when they fell with child, but not me. Even Bessie Blount was dismissed when she grew too big, but he has remained devoted to me. He really loves me Annie, and I love him." Anne didn't have the heart to tell Mary of the rumours flying around the court about the various liaisons of the King whilst his mistress had been in confinement. And the idea of the baby's father, King though he may be, of not owning such a perfect child as Catherine was beyond Anne's comprehension.

She was overjoyed when a maid told her that her brother was waiting outside to speak with her. Glad of the excuse to be away from Mary and her fawning adoration of the King, Anne went to see George.

Stepping outside, Anne took a great breath of the cool, fresh air of the palace. She smiled, but the smile faltered when she saw the look on George's face.

"What is it?" She asked urgently. "Tell me quickly."

"I am to be given my own manor at Grimstone." George said, sullenly.

"George, I am certain that a manor is a gift, it's a thing to smile about, and yet you look as if someone has died!" Anne laughed.

"All gifts, when they come from the King, come at a price. I thought the manor was a gift to honour the birth of our niece, the King's daughter."

"Who the King will not acknowledge."

"Of course, he won't." George snapped. "Why should he acknowledge a bastard daughter got on his whore?" He took a deep breath. "My manor is a grant, to accompany my betrothal."

"Betrothal? To whom?"

"Jane Parker." George said through gritted teeth.

"I know Jane Parker, George. She may not be the most intelligent girl of the court, but she is pretty enough, and kind and sweet. I am sure she would be devoted to you."

"Oh Annie, she is a simpering girl, hardly an illustrious match. I had hoped for an heiress, or a great beauty."

"George Boleyn that is no way to speak of your future bride." Anne said in feigned severity. George laughed.

"Oh, I know she won't be that bad, it's just that there are so many more women out there who would be more to my taste."

"Unfortunately, my darling we are not rich enough to care little for who we marry to perpetuate our dynasty, nor poor enough for it to be of no consequence but love. We must, therefore, marry where advantage shines. I imagine her father offered a fine dowry."

"I wouldn't know. The negotiations were made with father. I am old enough to have left Oxford, and old enough to be a husband in charge of my own household, but too much of a child to be able to take part in my own marriage negotiations. It's ridiculous." Anne smiled. At least her brother was getting a wife. She was older than him, and still without even the prospect of a husband.

Chapter 6

Summer 1525

"I don't understand Anne." Mary cried. "When I found out I was having Catherine, Henry was overjoyed. And now I tell him I am carrying his child again and he seems to be pulling away from me. He hasn't so much as danced with me in a week, and he has taken to calling me 'Mistress Carey' instead of 'my darling'." Mary tried to say more, but her frenzied sobbing blurred the words into something unintelligible. Anne absentmindedly patted Mary on the shoulder and made soothing noises. She found it hard to console her bereft sister on the loss of her favour, possibly because she had hardened her heart even more towards the bluff King who could happily make women pregnant without ever accepting responsibility. Whilst she still felt a level of unwilling awe towards the King who seemed to perpetually have fun, she still lived in fear of those little bright eyes shrinking into the evil glare that was becoming just a little more frequent, and that rosebud mouth puckering into the pout of annoyance which inevitably came before an explosion to make even the strongest of men quake. Henry Tudor was a man like no other, an over indulged child, and yet somehow a magnetic personality. As the years had progressed Anne could understand the love Mary felt for him, but she was so afraid of him, and of his power, that she knew she could never allow herself to care for him like Mary had. Even in spite of all of this, Anne may have been able to feel sympathy for her sister, after all, it was not so long ago that she had felt her world collapse as her marriage and all of her prospects were cruelly withdrawn from her without a real reason, except for one thing that weighed heavy on her heart. For three days in a row she had received letters from the King. Letters praising her beauty, her poise, her dancing, in fact, anything that he could think of. These letters had been accompanied by trifling gifts, each of which she had returned. The idea that her beloved Mary would be replaced in the King's affections by her was repulsive. And whilst she could not very well tell him that he repulsed her, there was no way that Anne would ever tarnish either herself or her relationship with her sister by allowing Henry to act upon his desires.

"Play." Henry commanded. "I have a desire to dance." The musicians instantly began to play, and Henry scanned the room, eyes roaming between the many beautiful young women desperate for his attention. His eyes fell, as they so frequently did, on the woman standing at the back, calling all eyes to her without being in any way obvious. The woman whose beauty was more radiant and more alluring every time he saw her. The woman called Anne Boleyn. He took her hand without asking her permission and took her into the centre of the room. They were quickly joined by a dozen or so more couples. Anne stepped the dance lightly, as if she were walking on air, and never faltered, but she managed to look haughty and disdainful throughout. As the song ended Henry held her arm, just above the elbow, and took her to the edge of the room. Panic filled Anne's heart, and the smallest of sparks that she struggled to identify. Surely it couldn't be the spark of desire. She dismissed it immediately.

"Anne, you have returned my gifts." Henry stated bluntly.

"Yes, your Majesty." Anne replied. There was no point in denying the truth.

"Did you not like them?" His face looked genuinely concerned.

"It is not that your majesty. I felt they must have been sent for me in error. I was sure that your Majesty meant to bestow the gifts on my sister, who is once again carrying your child." There was a flicker of anger in Henry's eye that made Anne flinch.

"I have been informed that your sister is going to bestow another child upon her husband. I am sure they will be very happy." Anne looked puzzled for a second, and then saw a sort of earnestness in Henry's eyes. It was almost as though he truly believed the baby wasn't his. As if somehow, he could deny what he knew to be true if he found it to be disagreeable to him, or believe a lie if it suited him best.

"Yes, your Majesty." Anne bobbed a curtsey and made to leave, but he still had hold of her arm.

"The gifts were for you Anne. Maybe now you will accept them, as we have eased the confusion."

"Alas, your majesty, I cannot accept gifts from you."

"And why not, may I ask?" Henry's voice was lilting in a half laugh, but his eyes glinted a warning. This was a man who always got what he wanted.

"Because, your Majesty, as beautiful as the gifts are, I could not accept such things from a married man, with me still, as yet, unmarried. It would be quite unseemly."

"Unseemly to accept a gift from your King?" The threat in Henry's eyes flashed brighter.

"You must forgive me your Majesty, but I am a poor daughter of a simple Knight. I have nothing to offer a man in marriage except my virtue. And there are those who would question that if I were seen to accept gifts from any man, King or no." Henry laughed outright at this. Anne breathed deeply. She had wanted to yell all manner of abuse at him, but as soon as she had seen the look in his eyes she knew that he would have punished her for it, and probably her whole family too. She discovered, in that short encounter, why men bent over backwards to give Henry his way, why husbands threw their wives in his way, why fathers had no qualms about the despoiling of their daughters. Henry was a King acutely aware of his power, and totally unafraid to wield it if he didn't get his own way. He walked off laughing, and Anne leant against the wall to disguise the fact that her knees were trembling. She closed her eyes and tried to block out the entire room.

"What did he want?" Came the voice she had least wanted to hear. Mary. She could not tell her that the man she loved so deeply was already trying to get her sister into bed. But there was no way she could look Mary in the eye and lie to her.

"He..."

"He wants you now." Mary said dully.

"What? I mean, I..." Anne felt awkward.

"It's alright, I knew it would be someone else. My sister is the same as anyone I suppose."

"I said 'No' Mary."

"Most girls do the first time he asks." Her voice betrayed no emotion, her face looked grey and tired. Mary looked like a woman who had given up the fight.

"I won't bed him Mary, I swear. Not after what he has done to you." Anne's passion rose as she spoke. "I would never hurt you like that."

"Annie, you won't have a choice." Mary said softly, and she walked away. Anne took the next opportunity to slip out of the Great Hall into the gardens. She slipped through the shadows until she found a quiet, concealed corner. It wasn't until then that the proud and haughty Anne Boleyn fell to her knees and wept. She wasn't sure if she was weeping for her sister, or for herself, but somehow Anne knew, now that Henry had set his eye to her, she and Mary would never be quite the same again.

"Wolsey." Henry bellowed. Within seconds Wolsey appeared at his side, wheezing in a very exaggerated way. His bulk had expanded much since being in the King's service, and he sometimes struggled to keep up with the King and his excessive, boyish energy.

"Sire?"

"I want to plan a great celebration."

"Yes, Sire."

"I shall make some promotions to the peerage."

"As you wish."

"My sister Mary's son shall become Earl of Lincoln, I think."

"A very wise decision my Lord. The boy is deserving of a title, as he is so close to..." Wolsey allowed his voice to trail off meaningfully. He had been subtly promoting a marriage between Henry's only surviving child, the Princess Mary, and the son of Mary Tudor and Charles Brandon. This would eliminate any question of rebellion in favour of the boy should Mary succeed to the throne, and was a wise political move.

"He is close to the throne *now*." Said Henry pointedly.

"Yes of course your Grace. But I had been led to believe that the Queen...." Wolsey had a habit of leaving his sentences drifting. It often convinced Henry that an idea had been of his own conception, rather than Wolsey's.

"Yes, yes, I am sure the whole court knows that the Queen no longer bleeds, and I no longer share her bed. And the whole of England knows that my succession lies on the shoulders of Mary. And failing her the little Earl of Lincoln to be. But I have other plans." Wolsey had the grace to look quizzical. In fact, the 'other plans' Henry was referring to had been whispered about court since Bessie Blount had presented Henry with such a perfect son, who was already growing into a strong child of almost six years. Rumours abounded that Henry intended to divorce Catherine, marry Bessie and then have their son legitimised by the Pope. And there was a precedent of course. John of Gaunt had married his mistress, Katherine Swynford, and had successfully had his bastards by her legitimised. "Little Henry Fitzroy, I shall make him Earl of Sheffield."

"A very suitable title your Grace." Wolsey said, smiling.

"And also Duke of Richmond and Somerset." Wolsey stopped in his tracks. Giving a bastard son an Earldom was not, perhaps, that much of an issue. To make him the most powerful Duke in the country, second in power and influence only to the King himself was indeed setting him up as a rival heir.

"The people would not have a bastard King." Wolsey said, evenly.

"Who is to say who will be King when I am gone. Mayhap I shall outlive Catherine and get sons on a second wife." Henry blustered. He had seriously considered declaring Fitzroy his heir, but somehow, love the boy as he did, he couldn't quite do it. He could have offered him the vacant Dukedoms of Cornwall, or York, but they were traditionally those of the first and second sons of the King. Henry could not bear the possibility that there would not be a real Duke of Cornwall, or Duke of York to challenge their bastard brother for his title. So, he had decided instead to give the boy the Dukedom of Richmond which has belonged to his father's father, Edmund Tudor, and had therefore been his own father's before he had become King, and the Dukedom of Somerset, which had belonged to the Beaufort family, last held by his mother's father. Both the Beaufort and Tudor lines were of bastard Royal blood, and Henry liked the symbolism. To him, the titles said, 'this is the son of a King, but he is not lawfully begotten.' For Wolsey to imply that he was setting Fitzroy up for Kingship made him angry. "I can promote whomever I like Wolsey, and neither you, nor any other of my advisers can gainsay me. I am King, am I not!" Wolsey bowed his quiescence. Henry calmed a little. "And I shall make Thomas Boleyn, Viscount Rochford." Wolsey did not question this, but looked mildly amused. "He is a good man with little income, and I would remedy that." Henry bounded off after saying this, in the direction of his tennis court. Wolsey smiled to himself. 'The things Henry does to celebrate his whores.' He thought to himself.

"I hear the King is to promote Bessie Blount's bastard. They say he will be made heir within the year." Anne said to George knowingly.

"Well, then *they* know nothing. Because I am convinced that the plan is to marry Mary to a Plantagenet, a son of one of the sisters of the Kings mother, or to James of Scotland. That way the line of decent will go through either Edward IV's line, or a doubly Tudor line, as James is the son of Henry's sister Margaret."

"Or she could marry the son of Mary Brandon?" Anne suggested. George dropped his voice conspiratorially.

"He is weak. Henry would only marry her to a strong man, older than her by a way I would wager, if he is intending to leave the getting of a male heir to Mary."

"Where do you get your information George?"

"Occasionally my head shares a pillow with a woman whose head is close to an important adviser of the King."

"So, you, too, are a Boleyn whore." Anne joked. Somehow George working his way around the woman of the court seemed to her much more becoming than Mary's increasing waist line and slowly drooping face as she came to accept that she was no longer the King's most beloved mistress, and was, in fact, just another whore carrying his child, with a convenient husband waiting to own it.

"A whore, my darling? If that is what you choose to call it. I would rather lie with almost any woman at court instead of my wife."

"Is she that bad George?"

"And worse. She is kind enough, just a little too enthusiastic. She wants to please me with such devotion that its off putting."

"You would rather she fought you off her?" Anne teased.

"Well, my innocent sister, men like a mistress to behave with lust and desire, but they prefer their wives to show grace and breeding. The woman is as rampant as a milk maid." Anne blushed at her brother's frankness. She could not ever imagine herself conducting herself like a milk maid, she was far too refined for such behaviour. The idea of a man making her feel desire like that scared her a little. There was silence between the two for a moment. "Is the King still after you Annie?" George asked, with genuine concern.

"Yes. Every day he sends me messages, and every day I rebuff him. And every day Mary looks at me like I have stolen her happiness. George, I am so scared."

"What of?"

"What if there is only so long you can say no to a King before he takes what he wants without consent."

"Henry is chivalrous Anne, he likes to believe he is an Arthurian knight. He would never take you by force."

"It's the way he looks at me though George. Like he desires me so much that he would rather see me ruined and broken than with anyone else. I am afraid what he will do to me if I keep saying no, but I'm just as afraid what he will do to me if I say yes."

"Then perhaps now would be a time for admirable retreat?"

"How do you mean?"

"What if you returned to Hever for a while? I know it is not as scintillating as court, but once Henry has found a new love, then you could return with your honour intact?"

"George, I think that may be the only way." Anne sighed. She blinked rapidly. Although George was the other half of her soul, she wouldn't even let him see her cry.

After a week at Hever Anne was beginning to become accustomed to the quieter life, and she was starting to enjoy the peace. There were no real obligations for her, she could simply sit in the garden from dawn until dusk and read and think, rousing herself only to return indoors for food when the lack of light was making her eyes strain. This morning, the same as the others, she settled herself at the foot of a shady oak tree and flipped open a book. She was unaware that she was not alone until the sun came from behind a cloud, and cast a huge shadow over her. She looked up, startled. It was the King. She scrambled to her feet and dipped into a curtsey.

"You left court without permission." Henry boomed. Anne was confused. Henry had no need to come in person for a missing maid of honour.

"I had permission from the Queen your grace."

"But *I* did not give permission." Henry said, in a voice reminiscent of a toddler who had been scolded.

"I did not think my presence or absence would be of any moment to your Majesty. After all, I am one of many maids in waiting to your wife." At the mention of his wife Henry gritted his teeth. Anne braced herself for the explosion.

"You are well aware that I desire your presence. Both at court and in my bed." The bluntness of this remark, made Anne flinch.

"I thought," Anne said tentatively, "that I had made it clear to your Majesty, that my virtue is for my husband and no other."

"I will find you a husband then." Henry pressed closer towards her, his voice thick with desire.

"I do not want a complacent husband who would allow another man to have me in exchange for riches. Then I would be no better than the whores at Cheapside." Henry stepped closer, Anne's back was now pressed against the tree trunk. His smile was menacing.

"There are many women who would give anything to be offered a place in my bed."

"Then I beg your Majesty, go to one of those women, and take her willingly. For you shall never get what you desire here." Henry's eyes flashed fire.

"You think yourself too good to be my mistress?"

"My Lord, I am your devoted subject in all matters but this. I will give myself only to my husband. I will be no man's mistress. And you, whatever else I may feel, are not free to marry. So, I must ask you once again to leave me be."

"You are not the first woman to throw that gauntlet down to a King. My grandmother was simple Lady Elizabeth Grey when she caught the eye of King Edward. She held out for a crown. I wonder if it is my throne you seek?" Henry's voice was cold.

"My Lord, mayhap if you had no wife I would be inclined to seek the position. As it is, you have a Queen, and I have no intention of taking the place of any woman. With all the respect I can muster Your Grace, I must ask you to leave."

"I could crush that little throat of yours Boleyn, before you could even scream. I could crush your throat and have you right here."

"And all I can do is throw myself upon your Majesty's mercy as a good and chivalrous King, and pray that you would never use me so ill." Something about the pleading in her voice, and the fact that unlike most courtiers she had looked him right in the eye throughout the exchange made Henry come to his senses. He didn't take women by force. He was shocked with himself, afraid of the feelings this woman stirred in his chest. Without another word, he turned and fled to his horse and the few guards he had brought with him. Within seconds he was mounted and galloping away. Anne sank to the ground, trembling. There had been no doubt in her mind that he would crush the life out of her. The tears that flowed were of relief, and terror. He would not leave her be. He thought she was after the crown, and he would now be set to convince her that it was, in fact, the man she desired.

Chapter 7

Spring 1526

"I have chosen a new motto for the Shrovetide joust." Henry said excitedly.

"Really?" Anne sounded deliberately disinterested. For months Henry had been sending her messages, attempting to send her gifts, and trying to steal words with her during dancing. He had been careful, however. He had never made a blatant overture towards her, and as yet the court was not aware of the growing infatuation of their King.

"It will be 'Declare? I dare not'. Do you like it?"

"It is not my place to like or dislike anything of your Majesty's choosing." Anne dismissed him. The turn of the dance separated them for a few moments, and as they re-joined Henry pressed the matter.

"Maybe you do not understand it?"

"I believe it means that you have become besotted with a woman other than your wife, and you are afraid to declare your love." Anne scoffed. Henry looked hurt. He liked to think himself subtle and witty, as that was the persona that his courtiers mirrored back to him. They laughed at his jokes, they feigned ignorance at his meanings and they behaved in every

41

way as if Henry were a glittering wit, and they nothing but dirty commoners. Not for a second had Henry ever doubted their honesty. Anne, however, was different. Anne, for some reason, did not idolise him like his court did. She riled against him, she argued with him, and she spoke her mind. It was perhaps that which was most beguiling. Maybe if she had simpered and pampered him he might have left her alone. The fact that she did not treat him as a King to be adored, but as a man, who could be refused, intrigued him. The feelings were growing stronger each day. He could not bear to be without her, even for a day. Although he knew that she had begged him for her honour and virtue, and he respected that, it was taking all of his willpower not to whisk her away behind one of the many tapestries concealing secret passages and to make her love him. Although her stubborn disrespect about his motto made him cross, he worked hard to calm himself.

"The lady in question will not have me. She is preserving her virtue for her husband."

"And she does well by it." The dance stopped and Anne walked to the edge of the room. Henry felt his fists clench. He felt his blood boil. And he felt once again the strange desire to crush her arrogant neck until she could frustrate him no more. When his vision cleared he looked for her, desperate to persuade her to another dance, to get another chance to talk to her. But he searched in vain. Anne had left the great hall, as she so frequently did after their encounters. With other women, this would mean 'follow me'. Henry knew that with Anne this meant 'this conversation is over', and despite being a King, he was also a man, and he could not deny his love something she so clearly desired. He let her go.

Henry was convinced as he walked out to the joust with his new motto emblazoned everywhere that he was the image of subtlety. Instead a whisper went around the crowd, so silently one could feel it rather than hear it, 'The King has found another woman to love. How long until this one gives in?' Anne heard the whisper and was mortified. She sat between Mary, now eight months pregnant, and Jane, wife of her brother George. Whilst this whisper made Mary look morose, it appealed to Jane, who seemed eager to discuss it with Anne. Anne looked at her coldly.

"Jane, you should know better than to discuss the private life of our King in present company." Her eyes flashed a warning. Jane looked down at her hands. She was desperate for her new family to embrace her. Unfortunately, Mary was far too concerned with Henry's desertion, Anne was far too aloof to allow easy confidences, and George, regardless of how she tried to please him, seemed to prefer the company of others to herself. Anne was seething at Henry's use of this new motto, after she felt she had made it plain that it was far too obvious. It was, therefore, even more horrific to her when Henry pulled up his horse directly in front of her.

"My Lady." He said, smiling. Since her father's promotion to Viscount Rochford, Anne had become Lady Anne.

"Your Grace." She said through gritted teeth. "Do you mean to shame me as you have my sister?" Henry looked confused. "My sister, in case you had not noticed, is now in her eighth month of pregnancy." Mary was fuchsia with embarrassment, but Anne persisted. "The entire court is aware that you are the child's father." Henry's eyes flashed with the look of warning Anne knew to recognise, but she threw caution to the wind. "And now you wear your new motto to come and speak with me. Now the entire court will presume that I am the source of your affection and will, in time, assume I have succumbed to you. Please leave me now Sir, whilst my honour may still be salvaged." Henry went in turn white, then red.

"The whole court can see that your sister is with child. But with a reputation such as hers, who would hazard a guess at the child's paternity. I am sure there are a dozen men who could claim it." Mary's eyes filled with tears, and Anne felt guilt at having brought this upon her sister in public. "And as for you madam, I think you would do well to think to whom you speak in the future, if you wish to retain the position you currently hold." Henry wheeled his horse around and trotted off, visibly shaken. The entire crowd could see the devastation on the face of pretty Mary Boleyn, and the look of horror on the face of Anne, and immediately the whispers recommenced, with much less subtlety. 'The King has traded one sister for another. Whores, the both of them.' Mary sobbed, and Anne put out her hand to comfort her.

"How could you do that?" Mary wailed.

"I only meant to caution him from ruining my reputation."

"You, Anne Boleyn think far too much of your reputation, of what people think of you. You will never be happy, because you wouldn't want to break your ice queen facade. I warrant you this Anne, I may not be the clever sister, or the one with fancy airs and graces, but I will be the happy one, and you, well I doubt a single person in England will mourn you when you die." And with that, Mary rose, and swept off with as much dignity as she could manage with the enormous swell of her belly and her vision was blurred by tears. Anne sat in shock. Mary had not bothered to lower her voice, and the entire stand was looking at her. No one spoke to Anne like that, especially not Mary, who was ordinarily so placid. Part of Anne wanted to run after her, but she didn't know if she would want to fall on her knees and apologise, or to pull her hair and scratch her face for saying such frightful things. Instead, coolly, and calmly, Anne turned to face the tiltyard again, and refused to move her eyes from the joust for the entire remainder of the tournament.

Fortunately for Anne, towards the end of the day something happened to take everyone's minds off the dispute between the Boleyn sisters, and from the King's new infatuation. In a fluke accident, Sir Francis Bryan was caught in the face by a lance, and as a result his eye was so badly damaged the barber surgeons had to remove it. From then on, the Shrovetide joust was remembered as the day Sir Francis lost his eye.

A week or so later Henry had waylaid Anne in a corridor to talk to her. Anne felt very uncomfortable about this, but it appeared the whole court knew the King was enamoured with the younger Boleyn girl, and she felt the only way to ward off rumours she was his mistress was to be seen talking to him and politely refusing.

"I ask only for a chance to make you love me as I love you." Henry beseeched.

"Your Grace, you are confusing love with lust I fear. Once you have had me I would be cast aside." Henry could see that Anne was scared by this idea.

"I would love you until the end of my life, Anne." Henry begged. Courtiers passing by suppressed their sniggers. They had lost count of the number of women they had heard Henry profess eternal love for.

"No, you wouldn't." Anne said, her voice soft. "My sister thought you would love her forever, and yet she has now been dismissed, she is in confinement at Hever awaiting the birth of another child of yours. If I let myself love you, how could I ever be safe from the same fate? You can offer me nothing except your love, which I know to be changeable." Henry touched her cheek. The fight that normally filled Anne seemed to have evaporated recently. His sources at court told him it was since her sister had left for her confinement without saying goodbye, and without asking for

Anne's company. But it was more than that. Anne was genuinely sorry for the pain she had caused Mary, and was equally sorry for the pain she caused every day, being the new object of Henry's desire. Anne was terrified of the opinion of others, despite what Mary had warned, and the idea of being known as the second Boleyn to share Henry's bed would destroy her. Anne's world revolved around what other people thought of her, it was how she knew what to think about herself.

"My love, my love, I would love you forever, if you would only open your heart to me."

"I can't." Said Anne, her voice cracking with genuine emotion. "I can never love you Henry." He smiled at the familiar use of his Christian name. "I cannot let myself love you, because you have a wife. Now I beg you, do not torture either of us any more with talk of a love that can never be."

The conversation was broken by a messenger wearing her father's livery. Anne took a deep breath and turned away from Henry for the message. It was short. 'Mary has been delivered of a healthy son. She has named him Henry.' Without a word to the King, barely stopping to hand the messenger a coin, Anne went to her room to write to Mary, with congratulations and apologies and to pour out her heart. Henry stood still, smiling, taking in his conversation with Anne. She felt tortured. That meant that she wanted to love him. A little more gentle persuasion and Anne Boleyn would be his.

Chapter 8

Summer 1526

"I think it's time to send you back to Hever, Anne." Thomas Boleyn said thoughtfully to his daughter.

"Really? I thought you would want to throw me in his Majesty's path to tempt him like you did with Mary." There was a hint of scorn in Anne's tone.

"You are not like your sister." Thomas said simply. "And your fate will be different. It appears your refusals are driving the King wild with desire. Taking you away from him will only heighten that, and protect your precious reputation."

"And what do you hope to gain from this father?"

"I am not sure yet, but myself and your uncle Norfolk agree, there is change in the wind. I am sure our star is on the up, but right now I need to make Henry want you more than he has ever wanted anyone. You must not give in to him, no matter how much he begs."

"What do you take me for?" Anne asked, astonished. "I have been refusing him for an age already."

"Yes, Anne, but remember, I am your father. I have known you since you were a child, and I can see the edges of that heart of ice beginning to melt." Anne opened her mouth in response, but no sound came out. It was true, perhaps, that she didn't feel quite the level of anger she once had towards

Henry, but she was not fool enough to love him, or to let him have what she had so fervently refused him.

"Whatever you command father." She said. Although the words were submissive, her tone implied that she was not in favour of being commanded by anyone.

Hever was beautiful in the summer. There were masses of roses in every colour filling the air with a heady perfume, and the scent of lavender was captured by every dress that brushed past. But this stay at Hever was not as pleasant as her last. There were no days spent in the gardens reading from dawn until dusk. This time, Anne spent most of her waking hours behind a small desk, looking longingly at the outside world. The first day she had arrived here, she had been followed almost immediately by a messenger from Henry. He had sent her a gift of jewels and a love note. Since that moment, Anne had been attempting to compose a reply. Despite being extremely eloquent in several languages, Anne could not find the right words to say. She did not want to positively encourage his affection, and yet, she did not feel so compelled to demand he leave her be. Her difficulties were compounded by her father's frequent questions as to what was happening, and the new letters and new gifts that were arriving daily from court. Anne felt overwhelmed, it was almost like she was drowning.

Finally, on the eighth day, she threw down her quill and ran into the garden. As she breathed in the rich, clean air she felt calmed and at peace. She took off her shoes and stockings and ran barefoot through the grass, and when she eventually reached a shady spot, she lay down on the cool grass, her hair fanned around her like a deliciously dark halo. She lay without moving for a long time, she didn't even think, other than to congratulate herself upon finally finding peace in her mind. She knew it could not last. She knew that she would have to return indoors, and she knew that the pile of letters would still be there waiting for her response. And so, she dragged her mind back onto her reply. Here, in the tranquillity of the garden she thought deeply on what she truly felt. She didn't love Henry. She knew she didn't. But she no longer loathed him with that ferocious passion. That somehow made her feel guilty, like the lack of hate was betraying Mary. Mary was fine, however, living once more with her husband and the two small children he was happy to call his own. She had barely spoken to Anne since the joust, and although this still hurt, it was no longer the same stabbing pain in her heart, more of a dull ache, and the knowledge that she had lost the better part of herself forever. She forced her thoughts away from Mary, and back to Henry. She did not desire him, she would not allow him access to her bed, but when she thought of him she felt the faintest of lurches in her stomach. Maybe it was the power that both allured and terrified her. Whatever it was, she no longer wanted him to leave her alone, and she was almost enjoying the attention. She gave herself a mental shake. She was losing her pragmatism. She was giving in to emotions. But somehow, she felt herself being dragged down a path she was uncertain of. If she really wanted to flee, she could be away to France in a few days, she would always be welcome there. But she didn't want that. She could isolate herself at Hever forever. She didn't want that either. She wanted to be at court, and she wanted, well she wasn't sure exactly, but whatever it was, she knew her only chance for happiness was at court.

Back inside Anne finally found the words to explain herself to Henry. She told him that her lack of response hadn't been through cruelty, only from being unable to think of what to say. She confessed that she was a little afraid of him, and was afraid of his wife. She was so softly, subtly encouraging, without promising anything. Her words were woven with such care that although Henry might infer from them a chance to win her heart, she never gave him any absolutes, she could deny anything. As she signed off, she felt the sudden urge to send a token to him, as he had sent so many to her. She looked through her jewel case, trying to find something that conveyed exactly what she wanted to say, and then, right at the bottom she found it.

Henry could barely breathe when the messenger presented him with a letter and a gift from Anne. He had been waiting for a response for what felt like a lifetime. As he read the letter his face lit up, she loved him, she must love him. She had ceased to deny him, and spoke only of her fear. Fears could be dispelled. After all, he was the King of England, someone beloved of the King would never have the need to fear anything. He turned his attention next to the gift. He gently unwrapped the velvet wrapping and gasped as he saw the significance of what he held in his hand. It was a tiny golden ship, with a solitary hanging diamond. Within the ship was the figure of a maiden. Henry laughed aloud. Anne, the maiden, was entrusting herself to Henry, the ship, with a devotion as hard as diamond. He had snared her. And now he would claim his prize.

It was barely light outside when the maid ran into Anne's chamber to tell her that the King had arrived and wished to see her. Anne felt that strange tug somewhere behind her bellybutton, but ignored it. The maid helped her to dress in a sumptuous gown of Tudor green, and with great poise and dignity Anne descended the stairs to meet her King. When he saw her, Henry's insides throbbed with desire. He had been with beautiful women in his time, even his wife had once been considered desirable, but the paragon of perfection coming towards him was more stunning than the rest put together. Her step was so light it appeared she was gliding rather than walking. The early morning sun glinted on her hair, making it shine brown, and then red. He swallowed the lump in his throat, and he realised he couldn't think of any words to say. Surely anything he said to such an angelic being would seem crass and insignificant. He swallowed again, hoping something, anything, would come to his mind. She curtsied low as she reached him. As she bent her head her hair parted, revealing her white neck. It took all of his willpower not to shower that beautiful neck with kisses. As she raised herself, she kept her eyes on the ground, shielded by thick, dark lashes. His hands trembled ever so slightly. He had never felt love like this, it was so intense, and so powerful he wanted to weep. She remained silent, waiting for him to tell her why he had woken her at dawn with this impromptu visit. He wanted to tell her with pride that he had ridden through the night to get to her home, that he had to see her after interpreting her coded message, that he loved her, and would protect her if only she would allow him the one thing he wanted. Instead, he opened with "Lady Anne." So formal.

"Your Majesty." She responded quietly. She raised her eyes to his. They were quizzical, but there was also almost a mocking there. She was vaguely amused, it seemed, by his slightly travel worn appearance.

"My Anne." He corrected himself.

"Your Majesty." She repeated.

"Even now it is still 'Your Majesty' Anne. Can it not be 'my Henry'?" The quizzical look intensified.

"But you are not *my* Henry. You are the Queen's Henry, you are *my* King." Her words had a touch of coolness to them. He did not want to make her angry with him, not when he had ridden all this way in the anticipation of such exquisite pleasure.

"I can be your Henry." His voice trembled a little. "The court and the world know that Catherine is my Queen in name alone, she shares my throne, but not my bed, and she has no place in my heart. I am not hers any more, not in any sense that matters, I can devote myself entirely to you."

"You are hers in every sense that matters." Anne replied. Her voice, rather than edged with the anger Henry both anticipated and dreaded, was almost a whine. "She is your wife, she is your Queen, I could only ever be your whore, and I will not degrade myself to be that to any man, King or commoner."

"But I would forsake the bed of every other woman but you. You would be the only one who had my heart and my body."

"You wish to make me your maîtres en titre?" Anne blanched.

"My what?" Henry asked, confused.

"Maîtres en titre. It is the title King Francois gives to his official mistress. She is recognised throughout the court as the sole woman whom Francois beds."

"Well then yes, that is what I am asking you to become."

"Have you never listened to anything I have said? I cannot share your bed when you have a wife. Not even if I am the only woman to do so. Not even if your wife no longer shares it. I cannot bring myself to do it." Henry sighed. He had hoped to keep his trump card to himself, he had hoped she would be convinced. He had hoped she had wanted to be convinced.

"And what if I had no wife?"

"What?"

"I am seeking a divorce from Catherine. No one knows of it yet but myself and you. Catherine and I have borne no surviving sons, it is a sign that my marriage is cursed by God." Anne looked shocked. She wasn't sure what to think. "And although Wolsey will look to the French princesses to find me a second wife, that will take months, maybe years of diplomacy and all that time I will be yours alone. And even once I was remarried, I would only bed the Queen to make a son, never for love, never for desire, that would be saved for you. There would be no wife for you to feel guilt over." Henry smiled. He was sure now she would throw herself into his arms, and that within the hour they would be in her bedchamber, and he would be enjoying that which he had so long dreamt of. It took a second to recognise the disgust on Anne's face. Ignoring all protocol, she turned her back on him and fled out of the room. In the seconds it took him to absorb this reaction, he heard the heavy bang of a large oak door. She was outside. Suddenly, he came to himself and he ran after her.

He eventually caught up with her, and caught at her arm. There were tears running down her face. He held the hope in his heart for a second that the tears were a sign of her joy at the offer he had made. He was already planning the suite of rooms he would allocate her at Greenwich.

"I thought you loved me?" She sobbed. He could see it was difficult for her to get words out. He had seen Anne give in to her rage on many occasions, but he had never seen her cry like this, like she was hurt and broken. He wrapped her in his arms. For a moment Anne relished being there, she inhaled his scent, of horses and new velvet, and felt safe in his arms.

"I do love you sweetheart. How could you doubt it?" The questions prompted Anne to pull fiercely from the embrace. The heartbroken girl was gone, replaced with the wild, angry Anne Henry both feared and worshipped.

"How can I doubt it? Because you offer me such an insult. To make me your acknowledged mistress would be to ruin all my chances at marriage, at happiness. I have told you again and again that I will not give you my only treasure."

"But Anne, I would give you treasure beyond your reckoning. And any man would be happy to marry you. I could make you a Duchess, second only to Royalty."

"Do you think I am so shallow that all I care for is a title?" Anne raged. She had stopped thinking now, the words were tumbling out of her mouth fuelled by emotion and she was saying things that were as surprising to her ears as they were Henry's. "Do you think that I seek marriage for my own security? If I were to take up this position, every son I presented you with would be a bastard. A bastard you would ignore, and fail to recognise as yours, and my husband would need to be weak willed enough to accept them as his. The whole world would know all of my sons to be bastards. That stain does not go away Henry. Rich birth or poor, bastardy taints them all. I do not want to give you useless bastards. I want to present the man I love, the man I marry, with a long line of legitimate children. Children who will not have to fight for their places. Yes, I would like money, and a title, but not for myself, but so the many children I intend to have never have to struggle, or worry about who they are to marry, how they will survive. I want what every woman wants Henry. I want children who will have a future. And you insult me by denying me that." Suddenly the fight went out of her. Anne collapsed into a heap on the floor, weeping like a child. She felt suddenly foolish for the words that had fallen out of her mouth unbidden. She had never even thought of children, of their inheritance, of how their lives would be. But now the words were out there she knew them to be the truth. She was shaking now, not just from the wracking sobs pulsing through her, but from fear. She had yelled at the King of England. And although she had done that before it had never been like this. She was awaiting the wrath of the King. But it didn't come. Henry absorbed her words, and took in the passion in which she spoke. She had mentioned the one thing that was likely to penetrate his mind, to make him think of the things he wished to ignore. Sons. She was going to give her husband sons. She would not give him sons to carry the taint of their parentage. He sat next to her on the grass and pulled her in close. There was no refusal now, she let him hold her, and let him stroke her hair, and she gradually stopped crying.

"My love." He said, in a voice so gentle and tender she could not help but look up at him. He wiped the remaining tears from her face with his thumb. "Please don't cry, my beautiful angel. I did not mean to insult you." His voice cracked, he found himself close to tears.

"I am sorry." She whispered. "I should have remembered to whom I spoke."

"Annie." He said, using the pet name her family used for her when they sought to pacify her. "My Annie. That is why I love you. Every other person in the world speaks to me as a King, and always has. You speak to me as a man, as if you are not afraid of me. And that, I think, is the only way to truly love someone." Anne didn't respond. Henry looked at her tear stained face, still so beautiful in the early morning light, and this time it was he who said words he hadn't thought through. He said what was in his heart, and once he had, he knew it was the only thing in the world he wanted. "Marry me."

Chapter Nine

Spring 1527

Now that Henry had promised her marriage, Anne was feeling a little more secure, and was a little more willing to open her heart towards him. She was feeling much warmer than she had been a year ago, although enough of her pragmatism had survived to ensure she had not allowed herself to fall in love with him. Her father and uncle had been elated when she had shared the news with them, and slowly, they had been working towards encouraging Henry's divorce from Catherine.

The divorce was proving to be hard work. Henry was convinced that because they had no surviving male children the marriage was cursed by God. Now, more than anything, he wanted someone to validate his conscience. Someone who unlike Norfolk and Boleyn had nothing to gain from the result. He was genuinely devastated at the pangs of his guilt, and he spent many nights reading his bible by candlelight attempting to find where he had displeased his God. His only solace was the company of Anne. She still refused him permission into her chamber, but she had finally consented to sometimes walk alone with him in the palace gardens, and he relished those moments with her.

It was on one of these walks that Anne gave him the information which would finally get his divorce into motion. "I know of a man who may be able to help our situation Henry." Anne smiled, her dark head resting softly on his shoulder as they walked, arm in arm, by the river.

"Oh? And who is this man?" Henry asked. He was only half listening to her words, the other half of him was inhaling the scent of roses in her hair, and wondering if she tasted of rose petals as well.

"His name is Robert Wakefield. I believe, if asked, he would be able to determine where in the Bible it says that your marriage is cursed. Once you have that, you could send Wolsey with it to the Pope."

"We could be married by Christmas." Henry said jubilantly.

"With an heir in my belly by the new year." Anne smiled. Although Henry loved her passionate rages, and her wild side, which made him think of how she might be in the marriage bed, it was the softer side of Anne he loved the most. The side that made her voice trail off lightly as she spoke of their children, and of them growing old together. He had never felt so in love in his life, and the idea that this Wakefield could hurry his happy ending into existence made his heart sing.

"Then I shall have him brought to court, and he will find my reason. The Pope shall grant my divorce and.."

"I will be all yours." Anne finished. Henry shuddered with desire. He had moved past the stage where he had urges to throw her against a wall and have her willing or not. Her determination to give him a son whose legitimacy was indisputable made him contented to wait. Or if not contented, at least resigned to it.

"What is your area of expertise Wakefield?" The King asked. Wakefield had been brought to him some weeks later after some extensive study of the Bible. The audience was extremely private, with only the King, Wakefield and Thomas Boleyn present.

"I am a scholar of Hebrew your Grace." Replied Wakefield.

"And tell me of your findings."

"In the original Hebrew, there is a passage in Leviticus which is often mistranslated. People believe it reads 'If a man marries his brother's wife it is an unclean thing. He has uncovered his brother's nakedness. They shall be childless." When translating it from the Hebrew however, it becomes clear that this should actually say 'without sons'." Henry felt his heart skip a beat. "If you would pardon my abruptness your Highness, I feel this passage applies to yourself and her Majesty the Queen, as she was first your brother's wife, and God has given his punishment by denying you male issue." From slightly behind Henry, Thomas Boleyn nodded his encouragement. Even when he had been instructed what to find, and had been assured of the King's receptiveness, telling his Monarch that he was a sinner was a daunting task.

"But what about in Deuteronomy, which says a brother must marry his dead brothers widow?"

"My Lord, if once again you will forgive me, I firmly believe that that section is only applicable to Jewish people. As your Highness is of the Christian faith there is no obligation for you to follow that reading." Wakefield was terrified by the silence that followed. He had been told by the Boleyn family to find anything at all which would invalidate the Royal marriage and to present it to the King. He was now afraid that he had gone too far, and that he had insulted his sovereign. The tense silence was broken by Henry's booming laugh.

"It appears that my conscience and the will of God are one and the same." Henry smiled. "I shall have my divorce! Now Wakefield, you will write all of this down, and you will sign it. And if needs be you will swear it under oath do you understand?"

"Yes, your Majesty."

"And you speak to no one of what has gone on here today. Not a single word or I shall have your tongue cut out, do you understand?" Henry looked so threatening Wakefield was unsure if he was joking or not.

"Yes, your Majesty." He repeated. Henry waved a hand to dismiss him.

"And then, Thomas, I shall make you my father in law." Henry laughed heartily, with real joy. He could practically feel the papal declaration in his hands.

The next day in the gardens Henry went down on his knees before Anne. "Wakefield has the proof. I will speak to Wolsey immediately, and I shall have my divorce. Now I ask you again Anne, as a man soon to be free to marry, will you be my wife?" Anne smiled jubilantly. Henry truly meant to marry her. It was not another ploy to get her in bed, if he was speaking to Wolsey, it was to happen. She nodded. Henry stood again, and taking her in his arms he kissed her, their first kiss. Anne had expected to remain detached, much as she had when Henry Percy had kissed her all that time ago. But somehow, she found herself pulled in by the kiss, by his desperate desire for her. He pulled away gently, and left her. As Anne stood there, trembling slightly, she realised that if he had tried to lay her on the grass and have her there and then she would have had no power to stop him. She wouldn't have wanted to stop him. Suddenly she was feeling that which Mary had told her of so often. Anne suddenly realised she may be falling in love with Henry.

"Wolsey, I have something important, and highly private to speak to you about." Henry said, beckoning his chancellor into a private chamber away from prying ears. "For years now I have wrestled with my conscience on a matter which is of upmost importance to my happiness, and to my realm. My marriage." This was not news to Wolsey. He had long known that Henry, so filled with his own self-importance, could not conceive of any reason why his mistresses presented him with babies a plenty, but his wife had given him only one child who had survived infancy. "I have received a signed statement from a scholar of Hebrew, Robert Wakefield."

"Yes?"

"He has found Biblical support for my long-felt surety that my marriage has been cursed by God." It was not often Wolsey was blindsided by Henry, in fact he prided himself on always knowing what the King was doing, and who he was doing it with. So, news of this statement was a little surprising. "he argues that Leviticus 20:21 states that a marriage between a man and his brother's wife is incestuous, and that the marriage will bear no sons."

"Now I am sure your Majesty has also read Deuteronomy which clearly states that..."

"Deuteronomy is only relevant for Jews Wolsey, surely the whole world knows that." Henry scoffed. He liked feeling superior over his minister, who often behaved like an indulgent father.

"Well, yes Majesty, of course." Wolsey faltered.

"And so, you will take this statement to the Pope, and you will ask him to issue me with a divorce."

"You wish to divorce the Queen?" Wolsey was a little shocked. Despite the perpetual rumours, he had always hoped that Henry would remain with Catherine until she died. She was much older than him, and not of robust health, and so he was sure within a decade Henry would have a new young wife to give him sons. But Wolsey was ever the diplomat, and if Henry wanted a divorce, it meant a break with Spain. This could only be managed by a treaty with the French. A treaty signed and sealed by a marriage of the English King.

"Yes." Said Henry impatiently.

"Then of course, your Majesty, I shall do all in my power to bring this to pass. I would advise, however, caution. To go to the Pope with this immediately, with one man's word against a Papal dispensation would be folly if you truly wish to be rid of Catherine."

"Well, what would you suggest?" Asked Henry sulkily.

"Let me convene an ecclesiastical court. All the bishops of England will attend and we will discuss the matter. I am sure they will all agree with your Majesty, and I think perhaps the signed agreement of the entire upper level of your clergy will go down with the Pope much better than the word of one scholar."

"Very well." Henry pouted. "Have your court. But I want my divorce Wolsey, have no doubt about that."

"Of course, Sire." Wolsey bowed. "And perhaps, if you are so inclined, I can start some enquiries about the marriageable princesses of France. Divorcing the Emperors Aunt will surely bring the wrath of Spain upon us, and so an alliance with France would be most advantageous." Henry had anticipated this.

"If you think it best Wolsey." He said, in a very plausible imitation of boredom. Wolsey backed out of the room. Henry had no intention of marrying a French princess. There was no one in the world now who could tear his heart away from his Anne. But he did not want Wolsey to know that. Wolsey would not approve of Henry elevating a subject to the throne. In fact, Wolsey disliked the raising in position of anyone but himself. So, whilst Henry trusted Wolsey implicitly to do what he had been asked, he thought it wiser to keep his true intentions concealed, to ensure that Wolsey devoted himself fully to the issue. Henry congratulated himself on his intelligence. Then he sent word he wished to see the Royal goldsmith. It had been at least a week since he had sent Anne jewellery, and he was desperate to send her some more without delay.

Wolsey, of course, knew of the King's infatuation with Anne Boleyn. He knew, as the whole court did, that she refused to sleep with him, and held him wrapped around her little finger. He was sure she was just like her sister, keeping Henry in her thrall with whore's tricks learnt in France. But a nobody woman around court was far too insignificant for someone as important as Wolsey to spare more than a passing thought about. Maybe if he did he would see how in love the pair were. Maybe if he listened, he would hear the promises Henry made to his beautiful beloved. Maybe if he could look past a person's station in life, he would see that Anne Boleyn was the rising sun, and that the only chance for future success was to align himself with her. But Wolsey was sure he knew best. Kings would have their concubines, and they had foreign princesses as Queens. And that was simply the way of the world.

"I call Henry, King of England to court." Said Wolsey, his innate pomposity satisfied with the excessive formality of the court he had created. Henry came into the room and sat on a throne in front of his assembled bishops looking every inch the penitent. "Henry of England," Wolsey proceeded, "this court charges you with unlawfully marrying your dead brother's wife." There was a little ripple amongst the gathered men, many had simply not been told the weighty matter they were set to discuss.

"I accept these charges. It is my belief that I am guilty of living in sin all these years with the Dowager Princess of Wales." The tension was palpable.

"And why," Wolsey continued, "is it that you have only come to this conclusion now?"

"For many years I have ignored the pangs of my conscience because of the love I have in my heart for the Queen, or for the woman I have wrongly called my Queen." It was then that the whispers began. Did Henry truly meant to separate from Catherine? He certainly seemed genuine. His face really did seem wracked with guilt. His brow definitely appeared to be furrowed in pain. "If it is found that the marriage is a true one, I should happily spend the rest of my days with Catherine, but I know in my soul that I have offended God, and that he has cursed me. I know that I will not get legitimate issue without repudiating my marriage with Catherine and marrying a woman whom God deems worthy."

"But, Sire," Came the tentative voice of Bishop Fisher, "you have legitimate issue, the Princess Mary."

"A woman cannot rule Fisher." Snapped Wolsey. "In as far as this case requires, only male issue is relevant."

"I beg your pardon Cardinal," Fisher replied silkily, "but the Princess *is* relevant. If she were wisely married she could have many sons to continue the line of the King."

"That is not the point." Henry interjected. "My dear Bishop, my sleep is plagued with nightmares of God's wrath. I have committed a sin, and I must be cleansed and forgiven. I have married a woman who could not be my wife."

"The Pope gave a dispensation." Bishop Gardiner put forward, tentatively.

"Not even the Pope can dispensate for a marriage which is against Holy Law." Argued Wolsey.

"That is exactly what a Papal dispensation is for." Fisher asserted.

"Well, in this case," Wolsey declared, his voice imperious and cold, "the Pope was wrong. Your Majesty, unless you have anything else to add to your statement you may leave the court." He wanted Henry to believe that the Bishops agreed with his principle, that his conscience was their concern. He didn't want him to see the lengths of bribery and bullying that would need to be descended to in order to convince these stubborn old men to give their King his way.

"They said what?" Exploded Anne, her face contorted with fury.

"They said they could not come to a verdict. They said the matter was too weighty and that we would have to refer the case to Rome."

"They are prepared to deny the King his wishes!"

"Yes, my lamb, but I am sure that the Pope will consent."

"Wolsey said without this court the Pope would deny you. And Wolsey promised you the verdict. Wolsey knows nothing." Anne scoffed.

"Careful, my love. Wolsey does his best. And maybe this is a case for Rome."

"No, Henry. This could have been settled if Wolsey had done his job. If Wolsey and your Bishops served you as devotedly as they claim. How can they be your loyal and devoted subjects if they deny you this?"

"Because they, like I, have their consciences to consider."

"And because they are more afraid of the Pope's authority than your own."

"Now Anne, you go to far." Her pretty face crumpled. She had learned that

Henry couldn't bear it when she cried. She didn't even need real tears, the threat of them was enough. She loved him, she knew that now, but she could not shake the need to be in control of the relationship. Henry still scared her, and she was still afraid he would throw caution to the wind, and she would end up pregnant, with Henry still married to another woman. She bowed her head and allowed her shoulders to shake in such a way that silent sobbing was implied. "Oh Annie." And he folded her into his arms, cradling her close to him and rocking her gently.

"I am afraid." She whispered into his doublet.

"Of what?"

"That Wolsey will not get you the divorce, and that you will tire of waiting for me, and that I will end up with my heart broken."

"I will never tire of waiting my love, because I know Wolsey will do all in his power to get me this divorce. You will still be my wife by Christmas."

"Do you promise Henry?" She looked up at him, her big eyes wide, and glinting with tears.

"I promise." He kissed her. Anne sank into the kiss, and abandoned herself and her worries for the few moments when it felt they were one. "Now my love," He whispered, pulling away from her, "let's have dancing tonight, and no more tears. For I shall send Wolsey to Rome just as soon as we go on our summer progress."

"Must we wait that long?" Henry saw the hints of genuine desire in Anne's eyes for the first time.

"My love I am afraid we must. I need Wolsey here with me whilst there is council business to attend to. Once we have closed council for the summer he can go to Rome and be there as long as it takes to get my divorce." He kissed her again, delighting in the hunger of her response. He resisted the urge to start unlacing her bodice. Somehow, he felt sure she would not refuse, he was sure she would in this moment give him all he could desire, but his longing for their love to produce an heir made him stop. He stepped back. Without thinking, acting purely on instinct, Anne moved towards him, and kissed him again. He felt his desire rising to a point where he wouldn't be able to stop himself. He put his hands on her shoulders and pushed her away from him gently.

"Henry. My love." She whispered.

"No." He said, unable to believe he was denying her. "As much as I love to see you like this, so deliciously wanton, I will not take now that which you have so long held back. I shall wait until our wedding night, and we shall make a son." Before he could change his mind, he turned and left. Anne found herself panting with desire. She had never felt anything like this before. His refusal had guaranteed her love for him. That he would deny her when she was yearning so desperately told her one thing. He really was deeply in love with her. Her words the year before about legitimate children had stayed with him. He was giving her what she wanted ultimately, instead of what she wanted instantly. That was a love that was real. She was truly his now, she would do anything for him.

A week or so later, disaster struck. The court was at dinner, and the noise in the Great Hall was deafening. Although Catherine sat at Henry's side, his eyes never left Anne. The whole court could see what Henry pretended was hidden, he was madly in love. The soft pink glow on Anne's cheeks and the little smile playing at the corners of her lips told the world that she felt the same. The first thing that Henry noticed was the sudden silence. There was not so much as the sound of knife on plate. He tore his eyes from Anne and scanned the room. There was a messenger in the doorway, he was filthy from the road, and looked fit to collapse with exhaustion. His guards well knew not to admit any man into his presence looking like this unless the news was dire. Henry stood and wordlessly beckoned the man forward. He looked like the walk would finish him off, and silently, George Boleyn appeared from nowhere, put his arm around the man, and led him to the dais.

"Speak." Said Henry, his mind filling with dread. A fleet sighted off the coast? A rebellion? His mind flooded with unpleasant scenarios and he needed the man to unburden himself with as much haste as possible.

"Sire, I come from Rome." He paused.

"Go on." Henry urged, his impatience clear.

"Sire, I regret to inform you that three days ago Imperial forces stormed Rome." There was an audible gasp from those near enough to hear these words, and the message was repeated in whispers throughout the room. "There has been sacrilege, many killings, many rapes, and much theft." The man went on.

"And his Holiness? What of the Pope?" Asked Catherine, urgently. Henry had forgotten she was even sitting there.

"He escaped, and has barricaded himself with a few Cardinals into the Castel Sant Angelo. He is the prisoner of the Emperor now."

"Surely, this was not done on the command of my nephew?" Catherine asked, her voice no more than a whisper.

"I believe he was there in person." The messenger reported, and suddenly looked as if he might faint.

"Get this man food and wine." Henry ordered. It was only then he let his eyes lock with Anne's. The words they didn't say aloud were swimming through both of their minds. The Pope was in the hands of Catherine's nephew. How could they ever hope to get their divorce now?

Chapter 10

Summer 1527

"Catherine." Henry said tentatively, as he entered his wife's bedchamber for the first time in three years. Catherine sat up eagerly. Although she was ageing, a fact not helped by years of disappointed hopes and doomed pregnancies, Catherine still had a look of girlish delight in her eyes to see her husband coming to her bed once more. "I had to talk to you about something Catherine." Henry started, unsure what to say. He had realised that despite having held an ecclesiastical court, and despite preparing dispatches to go with Wolsey to Rome in the morning, Henry had still not told Catherine of his plans. He was determined tonight to have all out in the open, and to be able to show to the world that Henry of England would not live as husband and wife with a woman who was once married to his brother.

"What is it husband?" Catherine asked. The word 'husband' prickled on him. His intention to approach this gently ebbed away.

"You may not call me that." His tone was cold.

"Why not?" Asked Catherine, genuinely confused.

"Because I have reason to believe that I am not, nor have I ever been your husband in the eyes of God." Catherine was dumbfounded. "You were my brother's wife, and I went against scripture to take you as mine."

"Your brother?" Catherine flushed crimson. "My Lord, you know that he never was my husband in that sense."

"I know no such thing madam." Henry riled. Catherine clasped his hand desperately.

"Why are you saying this?" Catherine asked. Henry was repulsed by her. Whilst Anne's tears made him desperate to give comfort, Catherine's made him feel sick.

"Catherine," He began again, hoping to sound reassuring, and loving. "This has nothing to do with the love we have shared. I still love you, deeply. My heart has long fought my head on this matter. But there is no getting around the fact than in my deepest soul, I know that this is no true marriage. I must ask you to stop calling me husband, and I will live with you as if you were my sister, which as my brother's widow is fitting." Catherine sobbed and Henry backed away towards the door.

"Who is she this time?" Catherine spat, her emotions rising. Henry couldn't help but contrast her with Anne. Catherine, composed, regal Catherine seemed to demean herself by giving in to her emotions, but Anne was defined by her passions and rages.

"There is no other woman Catherine. This matter is being referred to the Pope, and I will live apart from you until the Pope has given his decision."

"You live apart from me anyway." Catherine struck with venom. "You share your bed with my ladies, but this is the first time in years you have come to my chamber."

"Because, madam," Boomed Henry, pulling himself up to his full height and looking at his most intimidating, "I have long known our marriage to be condemned by God. And if it were not for love of yourself and our child I would have had this matter settled long ago. And as I am in fact a single man, I can take whatever lady I deem fit to my bed."

"Like the Boleyn whore!" Catherine yelled. That remark stung for two reasons. Firstly, because in almost twenty years of marriage Catherine had never once mentioned any of his affairs, and had taken them all with grace, and secondly because the slur on the woman he loved so deeply was inexcusable.

"Lady Anne Boleyn conducts herself with both grace and dignity madam. And she is not my whore, I have not taken her to my bed, and nor shall I." He stormed out of the room, slamming the door behind him. He could hear Catherine's anguished wails down the corridor as he stalked to his own apartments.

When he arrived in his rooms, his gentlemen knew exactly what to do to pacify his moods. A goblet of wine appeared in his hand, and a plate of fruits was at his side, and at the table before him was a letter from Anne. They had decided that it would be best if Anne left court for a while. There would be an inevitable backlash when word got out that Wolsey had gone to the Pope to petition for the King's divorce. Catherine was popular, and although Anne was much admired and envied, they both knew it would be a struggle to get many to consent willingly to a commoner Queen. The letters between the pair were flying at such a rate Henry was amazed they could find enough messengers. Reading his letters from Anne always calmed him. She spoke to him as a wife in so many ways, recommending books to him, advising him on his diet and chiding him for riding too hard, or working too late. But she also spoke to him as a mistress, speaking of her yearning to see him, of the depth of her love, and of her desperation for an end to their troubles. This letter was much the same as the others, but it was such a soothing balm. By the time the wine was drunk, the fruit devoured and the message responded to with love and devotion, Henry was calm and content enough to go to bed. His men had jovially offered to bring him a wench to expend his energy on, and though ordinarily Henry would have delighted in this sort of one off dalliance, he had no desire for such now. He had Anne. She was pledged to him body and soul, and he had promised her that by the years end they would be married. He could no longer imagine entwining himself with any woman but her. She had totally bewitched him, he was sure it was something to do with those dark eyes. It was those eyes that haunted his dreams.

The following morning Wolsey reported to Henry for his final orders before his trip to Rome. Henry reiterated his need for a divorce, and he wished it to be quick. Wolsey was going to try to convince the Pope that Henry leaving Catherine would pave the way for an Anglo-Franco alliance that would immediately come to the aid of the Pope and his Cardinals. Wolsey set off, determined that he would get Henry the result he wanted, but with the leisurely grace of an older gentleman going for a ride for pleasure. Twenty minutes after Wolsey had left, Dr Knight and Mr Barlow entered the King's presence, bowing low. Both men were friends of the growing 'Boleyn faction' at court, and they were determined to get the King his divorce.

"You are prepared to ride to Rome at all speed?" Henry asked, with a little urgency.

"Of course, your Grace." Dr Knight replied, bowing low. Henry was entrusting these two men with a much more delicate task than the one given to Wolsey. Anne had reminded Henry that even once he had his divorce, canon law required a dispensation for Henry and Anne to marry, as Anne's sister had been Henry's mistress. This was painful for both of them to think about, and Anne's dreams were haunted by images of her love and her sister romping with wild abandon. A second dispensation was also needed, because Anne had previously been contracted to both the Butler heir and Henry Percy. As neither of these contracts had been consummated there was no fear on that count, but it was still necessary, and whilst Henry dismissed the need for dispensations, Anne was not yet quite trusting enough to marry Henry without them. She was watching him bring down a daughter of Spain in his quest to obtain her, and she knew it would be much easier to tear down a commoner, unless she had God on her side. And so, this expedition was Anne's idea, and to please Anne, Henry had ordered it as his own desire.

When Dr Knight and Mr Barlow set off, they could barely be seen for the cloud of dust surrounding their horses. They reached the coast hours before Wolsey, and they were fated to reach the Pope days earlier.

Whilst Henry wished to dwell on his lover in Kent, and their servants on the continent, serious matters at home kept his focus on London. The country was battered with excessive rain, which caused the rivers to burst their banks and many people to be flooded out of their homes. The waters ruined the crops and the people of England were going hungry. In towns up and down the land there were riots, people protested the elevated price of grain, and were begging more and more from their landlords. These landowners were then lobbying the King and court for money to feed their tenants. When news of yet another riot worryingly close to Greenwich reached Henry, he headed straight for the chapel and fell to his knees. Henry spoke to God with fervour, but as was his habit, he spoke as an equal. Henry had always felt himself to be close to God in a way no other man could be, being almost divine himself. He felt sure that God was punishing England for having a King who had dared to try to marry the wife of his dead brother. It was as if he had married his sister, and God was raining punishments down. Henry told God he was seeking to rectify the situation, he told him he planned to marry Anne, who was good and virtuous. And he was unsure why God seemed slow to respond to his pleas for a respite for his people.

Chapter Eleven

Spring 1528

Henry and Anne felt like they had suffered a lifetime of disappointment. Wolsey had failed to get the dispensation for Henry's divorce, and so, despite Anne having a dispensation saying she was free to marry, and one being in place to permit their marriage, they were still being kept apart. The agony of this separation was causing both of their famously short tempers to fray. People began to comment that the King would soon tire of his tempestuous mistress, and settle instead for a woman who was calmer, and more placid. Henry felt sure that his tension would dissipate the moment he took Anne to his bed. But after all they had gone through so far, he could not risk getting her pregnant, and he had no desire to tarnish her reputation, as any whisper of impropriety would hinder his chances at a divorce. Anne raged at her brother in the privacy of his rooms. Night after night his devoted wife found herself shut into the public rooms, as her husband and his sister shared the inner sanctum. Anne went in there every night looking furious, after a few hours with George she came out calm and self-assured again. Neither of them bothered to tell Jane what they were talking about alone every night. She tried once to listen at the key hole, only to discover that it had been blocked by cloth. Jane still desperately wanted to please her husband, and as a consequence she trailed behind Anne constantly, like a puppy. Anne was infuriated by the insipid woman, but mostly managed to keep a veneer of courtly calm. She was, after all, a Queen in practice, and howling at every annoying sycophant was not regal in the slightest.

Finally, in early June, Henry and Anne heard the news they had been so desperate for. Finally, the Pope was giving them a chance. He was sending out a papal legate, Cardinal Campeggio, to try the case formally. If Campeggio found the marriage to be invalid, Henry would have his divorce. The happy pair danced late into the night, and fuelled the rumours that Anne was surely about to submit, and that Henry's desire would soon be slaked.

Far away in Rome, the Pope was speaking in confidence with Campeggio before he set off on his journey.

"I have here a dispensation, giving you the right to declare the marriage of the King of England invalid, and a second permitting his remarriage if you feel it to be the will of God."

"Holy Father, surely if I make this declaration the Emperor will continue his assault against us."

"That, my son, is very likely."

"And if we refuse King Henry's wishes he may well invade himself. I hear the King is desperate for his divorce."

"That is also true."

"So how can I decide Holy Father, if either course leads us into war?"

"Do you think God does not have a plan Cardinal?"

"I am sure he does, but I could not decipher it if I tried."

"How is your gout Cardinal?" The abrupt change of topic confused the old man momentarily.

"It gives me great pain Father, but I would never allow a personal infirmity prevent me from doing God's work."

"Ah, but God would never permit you to hurry so much in doing his work that you would do yourself more harm than good." The look in the Pope's eyes was filled with deeper meaning.

"I suppose," ventured the Cardinal nervously, "I could take a slower pace to reach England than I originally considered. For my health, you understand."

"I think God would approve of that plan my son. And if you were not to reach a verdict by the time the Vatican enters its summer recess?"

"Then I would be obliged to close the court and return to Rome until the autumn. When of course, the political situation may have changed."

"Yes, indeed my dear Cardinal. I think it would be unwise to speak to anyone of the dispensations you hold. At least, not until the Emperor has been defeated, and we are once again at liberty."

"I agree completely Holy Father. These papers will remain for my eyes only until I am sure that you are safe. Or until I am obliged to return for the recess." The Pope smiled, and with a gesture of his hand he dismissed Campeggio. He had much younger, stronger men who could have been sent to preside over this court, but he was sure that sending old, gouty, Campeggio would be the ideal solution. After all, England was a long way away, and he had heard it was frightfully cold and wet. Campeggio suffered famously bad gout and his health was fading with his increasing age. It seemed unlikely that a verdict would be needed until at least October, and maybe even longer. If needs be, he would trade King Henry's divorce for military intervention against the Emperor. He may be the voice of St Peter on earth, but he was a realist. When one is caught with ones back against the wall, certain unpleasant decisions must sometimes be made.

The days ticked by in England since the notification that Campeggio was on his way. Frequent reports had him making an excessively slow pace, travelling by litter for much of the journey due to a severe case of gout. Henry was growing impatient, but Anne counselled caution.

"If you fly at him upon his arrival about the time it has taken Henry, we will never get what we want. He will side with Catherine to spite you."

"It is just preposterous that he hasn't even reached the coast yet."

"But he will Henry. We have waited for so long already, so what if it takes him a few weeks to arrive, if we get the divorce."

"I know you are right." He sighed. Anne cut him short with a brief kiss.

"And when he arrives we must give him lavish accommodation at court, and fete and celebrate him."

"And here was me thinking you disliked Cardinals."

"Henry, I would dance with the devil himself if it freed you from her. You know how desperately I love you." She found she meant those words. Anne, like Henry, was used to getting her own way. She was petted by her family, who always gave in to her, and a short rage followed by tears sent Henry into such a panic that he would offer her anything. And so, it was novel being deprived of the one thing she had decided she wanted, Henry. And the novelty made the passion that bit more ferocious. The knowing it could not be satisfied made the desire that bit more intense. But Henry's increasing impatience and foul temper was making her fear of him that bit more tangible. His rage was rarely directed at her. Even if it was for the merest second she was showered with apologies and gifts. But she saw the dark side of him rearing more frequently. She was praying for the divorce, not only for her own happiness, but also for the sake of everyone around her and Henry. If his temper kept escalating in the way it was, she was unsure what he would do. All she knew for sure was that Henry Tudor was capable of tearing the whole country apart to get his own way, and that if he did, the golden King would never be blamed, it would be the raven-haired woman by his side.

Chapter Twelve

Summer 1528

As spring blossomed into summer, the dreaded sweating sickness hit London. No one was sure what caused it, only that it was brought over from Brittany when Henry VII and his band of mercenaries had landed to fight King Richard for the throne. The sweat was a terrifying disease. A family who were all well at breakfast could be dead before dinner. The victim felt a slight headache, and was sometimes a little sick, and then suddenly their entire body was burning up, and before the day was out, most who succumbed had died. There were many remedies, but nothing conclusive, and the only sure escape was to flee. And flee the court did. They scattered to their country estates, to anywhere they could go that was out of London. Henry was whisked away quickly, as a King with only a daughter and a bastard son as declared issue needed to be protected. Anne went to Hever, along with her brother. It was as they were nearing the edge of the Boleyn estates that disaster struck.

"George, I feel unwell." Said Anne in barely more than a whisper.

"Oh Annie, you worry too much."

"George, my head has been hurting since we left London. And I can barely hold myself upright." At this George looked properly at his sister. Her naturally pale skin looked almost translucent, and she seemed somehow to have lost her glow. Her face looked like a skeleton on top of her shoulders, which he could now see were beginning to shake with the fever. Acting without thinking George pulled over their horses, and dragged Anne onto his. Whilst holding tightly to his sister, who felt increasingly like a rag doll, George pushed his horse to a gallop, far outstripping the rest of the party in his haste to get Anne to their home. Once there she was taken immediately to bed, and a physician was sent for. George immediately procured a quill and parchment and scribbled a note to the King. If Henry wasn't informed immediately then his fury would rain down on the Boleyn family. And if she died, well that didn't bear thinking about. Note written, George searched for a messenger, and paid him handsomely to get to the King as fast as lightning. As he watched the man's horse shrink until he became a small cloud of dust on the horizon George raised his fingers to his temples, and pressed firmly. His head had been pounding now for over an hour. He put an uneasy finger round his collar, he felt suddenly hot and sticky.

The clatter alerted a servant that George had fallen, and he was hurriedly put to his own bed. The physician was informed there was a second case of the sweat in the house.

Upon receiving a messenger in Boleyn livery Henry was overjoyed. He had been hoping to get a letter to Anne that day, but had been tied up in matters of state, but this message would ease his mind. He was so pleased to have this note that he paid the messenger a gold coin without even looking at the panicked expression on his face. He broke the seal and saw, not Anne's beautiful flowing hand writing, but the sharper and more stilted text of George Boleyn. The letter fell from his hands as he finished it. Anne sick. Anne with the sweat. He had sent away the woman he loved more than his own soul, and she was dying. How could he let her die without kissing her one last time? But as much as Henry loved Anne, as violent as his passion was, he was also terrified of sickness, and the idea of death. He could not sit at her bedside as much as he might wish to, because he was far too afraid. But he must do something.

"Send for Doctor Butts." Henry bellowed to the room at large. Everyone remained still, no one knew to whom he was bellowing. "God's blood, one of you get the Doctor!" The Duke of Norfolk stepped forwards and spoke softly to the King.

"Are you unwell Sire?" Henry allowed his eyes to meet Norfolk's. They were swimming with tears.

"Anne." He half whispered, his voice filled with a profound agony. Norfolk stepped up immediately.

"You." He ordered, pointing to a young man whose name he did not know. "Get Doctor Butts now. Tell him he must be ready to travel within the hour." The man ran off. "And the rest of you, do you have no other business to attend to?" The arrogance and authority combined in Norfolk's voice to make his words followed instantly by all. All, that is, except one man. Charles Brandon stepped forwards to the King. Norfolk disliked Brandon. Whilst he could trace his family back in the annals of the aristocracy, Brandon was new blood. He had been made an orphan at the Battle of Bosworth Field. As his father had gone down the standard bearer of Henry Tudor, the boy had been brought to court, and was eventually set up as a companion to young Henry. The two had been firm friends ever since, and once he had gained the crown, Henry had lavished honours on his old friend.

"Your Grace, what can I do?" Charles asked Henry, ignoring the infuriated look in Norfolk's eyes.

"Charles, its Anne." Henry choked. "They think it's the sweat." The tears began to flow. Charles put his arm around Henry and led him to a chair in a gesture that was more reminiscent of father and son than of subject and monarch.

"Anne is a strong woman." Charles soothed. "There are many who come through the disease with no harm done at all. And you are sending Doctor Butts, you could do no more."

"Charles, what if she? What if she's already?" Henry couldn't even bring himself to speak of Anne's death. Charles made soft soothing noises as he did to his children when they were upset.

"Her fate is in God's hands Henry." He whispered. "If he wills her to live, she will live." Henry's sobs subsided enough to allow him to stand.

"I am going to chapel to pray for the deliverance of the woman I love. Woe betide anyone who disturbs my prayers unless they bring me good news of the Lady Anne." And with that Henry swept from the room. Norfolk and Brandon stared at one another with cold eyes for a moment, and then both went about their own way.

As Henry had wished, within the hour Doctor Butts was riding full pelt to Hever to see what could be done. He was concerned for his own fate more than that of the Lady Anne. He knew that which Henry could never understand. There was nothing medicine could do. If she survived the first night she would probably live, although some supposedly never recovered their full strength. But if God willed her to die, then she would die, regardless of anything he did. But if she were to die, then the King would hold the Doctor responsible. He shuddered, and urged his horse to speed up, silently praying that the haste wasn't in vain, and that he would find the Lady alive, at least, when he arrived.

Thankfully for both Doctor Butts and Henry, Anne was alive when he arrived, but weak. Her skin was clammy, and her breathing rattled. Despite the panic in his mind at seeing how close to death she was, he sounded both convincing and practical.

"Her only chance now is to release this heat before it damages her mind. Cover her in as many blankets as you can spare, if we can break this fever out of her, and she is still breathing at dawn, I think she will be saved." The same treatment was given to George, who, fortunately, did not look as close to death as his sister.

Many miles away, however, there was no Doctor Butts to advise the third Boleyn sibling. Mary sat at her husband's bedside, dabbing his brow with a cloth dipped in water and mint leaves in the hope it would cool his burning flesh. His breathing was uneven, and ragged. Mary had never watched someone die before, but she felt certain that William was dying. She didn't know what she could do. She had dismissed the servants as soon as he had shown signs of sickness, and the children had been sent away. She, alone, remained to nurse him, with just one woman who refused to leave her side. As the night progressed his breathing seemed lighter and lighter, until suddenly, without any warning, it stopped. Mary sat for a full five minutes, her hand on the still chest, just in case she felt a flutter of breath. She remained in silence for a further hour before she called her woman to fetch someone. Bodies of the victims of the sweat must be disposed of quickly, as it was believed the corpse could still pass on the disease. As men roughly wrapped her husband's body in sheets and bundled him down the stairs, Mary threw open the windows to release his spirit. The night air felt deliciously cool on her cheeks. Her hair was loose, and fluttered lightly in the soft breeze. She was a widow. Now what would become of her and her precious children?

As the dawn broke at Hever, the inhabitants breathed a sigh of relief. Both Anne and George had made it through the night. They had both broken their fevers within hours of each other. Anne was now sleeping peacefully, the colour returning gradually to her pallid visage. George was awake, and was propped up with a series of pillows, being spoon fed a weak broth. Doctor Butts wrote to the King that Anne appeared to be over the worst, but that they would know little else until she awoke. And that may take time. For hours Anne lay in a sleep that looked to the casual onlooker like death. It was only upon close examination you could see her chest rise and fall softly. Her face, so often contorted in anger and frustration recently, looked as peaceful as a child having a pleasant dream. But as the hours dragged on, people began to worry that the peace in her face was not a sign of an end to the discomfort of illness, but as the relaxation of one waiting for death. It wasn't until sunset the she stirred a little, and managed, with much help, to be raised to sitting. She was asked a few questions to test her mental agility, and after her telling the Doctor in a cold but dignified way that she would not speak to him any further until someone had helped her bathe he wrote again to Henry, telling him that he was convinced that Anne had come through her ordeal unscathed.

The same could not be said for Henry. The few days he had faced the possibility of losing the love of his life Henry had veered dangerously between vulnerability verging on mental incapacity and a rage unlike any that had been seen before. He funnelled his rage towards Catherine. Anne's illness must somehow be her fault, because as far as Henry could see the only person who could seek gain from her death was Catherine. Henry's desire for the divorce was fuelled by his new hatred for his wife. And upon hearing that his beloved had been saved, Henry had gone down on his knees to thank God for the sign he had desired, a sign that God favoured Anne Boleyn and wished her to be Queen. A sign that his divorce was God's will. And after such an incontrovertible sign, Henry was prepared to do whatever it took to make Anne his wife.

It was many weeks before Anne was strong enough to return to Henry's side. The court was still scattered, and the more intimate setting made Henry and Anne more relaxed, they felt a little like a couple on their honeymoon. Their reunion had been intense, but fractured. Each in turn moving away from the tantalising temptation of their embrace, unsure they would be able to control the urges which filled them. It was unspoken between them, but they stopped seeing each other alone, as there lay too much temptation in solitude, and they had come too far to allow their future to be shattered by a bastard baby when they were so close to a chaste union.

Anne had been back at court ten days before anyone told her that her sister had lost her husband. Thomas Boleyn was very grudgingly giving support to his older daughter, and his granddaughter, but young Henry Carey had become a ward of the state, as the sole heir of his father. Wardships were bought and sold at Henry's court to the highest bidder, and there were many who wished to buy Henry Carey. Although he was as yet not acknowledged, no one who looked at the small boy could deny his parentage. He was Tudor through and through. And someday that boy's marriage would be very beneficial to whomever had the power to arrange it. As many men jostled to be given the honour, Anne felt a surge of compassion for the nephew she barely knew. She begged Henry on bended knee for the wardship of her sister's son, beseeching him not to tear the boy from his entire family. Henry could deny Anne nothing, and the wardship was granted. In actuality Anne had no intention of playing a large role in the boy's life, or keeping him at court. He served as a constant reminder that she had no son, and that her sister had borne her beloved two perfect children. Instead, Anne now had the power to keep Henry in the country, at one of the small estates the King had granted her. He was well provided for, and his education was second to none, but he was out of the sight of the people, and it was not long before the second bastard son of the King was fading in people's memories. After all, he was never owned by his Majesty, maybe he was, in fact, the son of William Carey. Anne had, whilst appearing the loving Aunt, extinguished a threat to any children she may have. The only person unhappy with this arrangement was Mary Boleyn. She was mortified that her son should be given away like a prize, and devastated that she was not awarded his care. After all, she had carried him inside her for nine months, she had loved him and nursed him. And Anne didn't even want him. But somehow, despite it all, Mary struggled to blame Anne. She couldn't believe her sister had taken her son for anything other than to protect him from those at court who would have sought to manipulate him. She laid the blame, instead, on Henry. He had the power to have given her their boy, but instead he had attempted to make as much profit as he could. She was struggling sometimes to see in this King the young, carefree and passionate man she had loved so deeply. Instead, she was increasingly seeing an impetuous and malicious boy, acting selfishly and stubbornly to benefit only himself. She was beginning to feel pity for Anne being in love with this man who was so rapidly degenerating into a tyrant. She knew that Anne would no longer be able to extricate herself. She knew that Anne would have to cling on to the loving man and hope she could save him from himself. Mary shuddered to think about what would happen if Anne could not keep Henry's dark side under control.

It was once Anne was back at court that Wolsey himself succumbed to the sweat. Anne was torn. She knew that Wolsey was against her. She knew that if he died from his disease that Henry would listen to no one but her, and that she and Henry would be happy. But she was far too shrewd to have missed the fact that in spite of this, Wolsey was the only one who could truly control Henry. Without the guidance of the older man, Henry would become too powerful, and he would want to test his powers. He may well cripple England just to show his own might. Wolsey could manage Henry in a way that Anne never could. She hated to admit that she needed Wolsey to keep Henry happy, but she did. Perhaps now was the perfect time for reconciliation. But it would have to be on her terms. She knew that Wolsey was feeling the pressure of Anne's increasing influence. And she knew that when he was in his weakened state he may be prepared to come to some form of truce, whereby he retained his political power and wealth, but Anne got Henry. This may be her only chance to sway the Cardinal's allegiance to her side from Catherine's, and she must show him that more than anything this was also Henry's desire. And so, she wrote to him, a letter filled with warmth, and a letter from one victim of the horrendous disease to another. She wrote to him of her prayers for his deliverance, and of her devotion to him. This made a show of friendship clear enough for the Cardinal to understand, and yet ambiguous enough that Henry would not see the hidden threat. The threat came when Anne asked Henry to write a post script to the letter. When Wolsey read this, he knew that Henry had written in response to Anne's supplication, and not of his own volition. This was a clear sign of where power lay, and with whom he must align himself in order to retain his own power.

As court began to come back to its normal self, with nobles flocking back as the weather cooled and the disease dissipated, Henry presented Anne with a gift. Durham House, a magnificent home on the Strand. This may have seemed like a little gift on the surface, simply a house, nothing excessively extravagant, but it sent a very firm message. Anne Boleyn was no longer at court as one of Catherine's Ladies, she was living independently in London, able to come and go to court as she pleased. And perhaps more pertinently, able to entertain whomsoever she desired. And the company she desired was Henry's. By this simple move Henry deprived his wife of his company many nights of the week. He would simply hop onto one of his many Royal barges and spend his evenings with Anne. Some nights were spent in lavish entertainments, with gluttonous amounts of food and wine, almost as though it were a miniature court. Others were more intimate, with just a few close friends, sitting informally around a smaller table, with interesting discussions. Those nights were the ones Henry and Anne preferred. They were also the nights that Anne must resist the ever-growing temptation to invite Henry into her rooms. Despite her many promises to herself to retain her virtue, and to never be ruled by lust, or love, Anne felt her resolve weakening with every visit. She was beginning to worry that Henry, infatuated as he was, would not wait for her forever. She was beginning to fear that another woman, less guarded of her virginity would soon be warming the bed of the man she loved. She was beginning to be afraid she would lose it all.

During one of these intimate suppers Anne broached a very difficult topic with Henry. She had become very interested in a wave of new religion sweeping the continent. Being interested in a new trend was not, of course, unusual, nor was it a crime. However, Henry was very conventional in his religious beliefs, and with the support of Wolsey had enacted many laws prohibiting the practice of any forms of this new religion, including the reading of certain books. One such book, 'The Obedience of a Christian Man' was in Anne's possession. Or, more correctly, it had been in Anne's possession. And it was the issue of this book which Anne needed to talk to Henry about.

"My love." She began, in a sweetly devoted voice. "I have a serious issue I would like to discuss with you. I need your help."

"Ask and it shall be granted sweetheart." Said Henry. He was at his most magnanimous after a few goblets of wine, and there was little he could deny Anne, even sober.

"The Dean of the Royal Chapel has confiscated a book of mine. I so desperately want it back, as I had marked some passages I had a desire to read to you. I thought that they may be pertinent to our 'secret matter'."

"Then what right has the Dean to confiscate it. Of course, it shall be returned to you, and he shall be punished. On whose authority does he think to take the books of ladies!"

"On yours, Sire." Anne said, softly. "It is a book by William Tyndale." Henry looked at Anne questioningly.

"Then possessing that book is against the law, madam." His tone was warning.

"Have you read it, my love?" Anne asked, her voice silky and seductive. She ran her fingers over his hand casually.

"Of course, I haven't, it is prohibited." Henry blustered.

"Then I must beg your indulgence my Lord. It is not a woman's place to lecture a man, let alone a King, but I simply must insist you read it. Tyndale makes some very convincing and useful arguments."

"Tyndale, madam, wishes to destroy our Holy Church." The warning in his voice was fading, and the anger was beginning to show through.

"I beg your forgiveness, my Lord." Anne sounded humble, almost penitent, and she bowed her head. "I am, of course, a simple woman. I just wished you to read a few passages in the book concerning the Pope, and whether or not he should be able to dictate to Kings, Kings who are anointed by God. The book simply poses the question, the Pope is an elected leader, all be it a leader who represents God in Rome, but as a hereditary King, shouldn't you speak for God in your own realm?" Anne looked up, a small glint in her eye as she whispered her final plea. "Should a King have to bow down to the authority of anyone besides his God?" She had hit the perfect note. Henry could not bear the idea of his authority being usurped by anyone, even by the Pope.

The very next morning Anne and Henry sat in the gardens, reading the Tyndale book together, and debating whether, perhaps, he was right, and maybe Henry should be the sole master in his realm. And maybe, just maybe, Henry might not need the Pope to decree his marriage invalid.

Chapter Thirteen

Autumn 1528

Henry and Anne heralded the arrival of the papal legate, Cardinal Lorenzo Campeggio as if their desires had already been fulfilled. Neither of them could see any reason for the papacy to deny them what they wanted, especially as the case was being tried within Henry's realm. Unfortunately, Campeggio was so old, and so crippled with gout, that following his arrival at court he needed to spend several days secluded in his rooms resting and recuperating. This was, however, more than the ailments of an old man, this was a strategic move. Campeggio's men could then assess the grounds at court, they could put out feelers and they could establish the mood of the people. The information gathered was, however, mixed. There was a strong, and growing, faction at court in favour of the divorce and the marriage to Anne Boleyn. However, there was an equally powerful faction in favour of the Queen. Campeggio realised that this would need delicacy in order to resolve the issue without causing a dividing rift, not only through the English court, but throughout the Christian world. France would side with Henry, Spain with Catherine, and the tiny papal states would be crushed by the ensuing battles.

And so, with this knowledge at the forefront of his mind, Campeggio begged an audience with the Queen. He had, he believed, a solution which would suit everyone. Henry would get his new marriage and his heirs, Catherine would not have to concede to a divorce, the Princess Mary would avoid bastardisation and would retain her place in the line of succession, behind any half-brothers that may be born of her father's remarriage. It was, in theory, an easy option. But Campeggio had thought this before he met with the formidable will that was Catherine of Aragon.

"I will not consent to a divorce Cardinal, and I will be appealing to Rome."

"Madam, the Pope has sent me personally, to be his representative."

"I respect you, Your Eminence, but you have no authority in my eyes. This is a decision for His Holiness alone, not one to be passed on to a Cardinal." Catherine turned her back, she was indicating that the audience was over. But Campeggio stood his ground. He had not suggested the proposal which could solve this issue yet, and he would not leave until Catherine listened.

"With all due respect, your Majesty, I come with a suggestion that would prevent the divorce, and the slur on the names of both yourself and the Princess Mary." Catherine turned, looking suspicious.

"In what way, Cardinal, can you give my husband the divorce he wants so he can marry a harlot, without branding me a whore and my daughter a bastard?" Her tone was cool, but Campeggio could tell that he had at least gained her interest.

"Madam, if you were to elect to retire to a convent, to take the cloth, your marriage would become void in the eyes of the law, allowing your husband to remarry. However, this would verify the fact that you were indeed married before God, and the legitimacy of the Princess Mary would not be questioned. His Highness would, I am sure, agree to this condition. Your daughter would retain her position, both at court and within the line of succession, replaced only by any sons your husband should go on to have." Catherine looked, momentarily, like she might jump at the opportunity. Then she turned away. As the daughter of the great Isabella of Spain she had been raised to conceal her emotions at all times. The anguish in her mind, however, was too difficult to bury, and so instead she looked out of the window at the cold, wet palace gardens, and thought. She would never have to speak of her first marriage, she would never be degraded and called a whore for laying with her dead husband's brother, her daughter would retain her title and her place in the succession. And as a naturally pious woman, a trait which failed pregnancy after failed pregnancy had compounded into a fervour, the idea of retiring to a life with God had its appeal. But there was one sticking point. She had not been raised for the church. She had been raised, since a girl of five, to be the Queen of England. Her mind was filled with politics, and with strategy, and she was not sure how she could suppress that instinct. And although she and Henry had barely even retained a friendly relationship in recent years, she loved him devotedly, and therein lay the question. Was it better to give the man she loved so intensely what he wanted, even if he would be sure of damning his eternal soul by marrying such a harlot, or should she refuse him, making herself an unnatural wife, but save him for eternity. And then Catherine decided. Her fear of God was more intense than the fear of her husband. If she had to bear on her conscience until the end of time guilt for this situation, she would rather know she had done all she could for Henry's soul. She slowly turned to Campeggio.

"It is well known that I am a religious and devout woman." She said, in a very measured way. Campeggio felt a growing sense of elation, he may have just saved himself the ordeal of the trial which would have followed, given the King of England what he wanted and all without saying that the Pope had been wrong to dispense for the marriage in the first place. "However," Campeggio's heart sank, "I am, and always will be, a wife, and a Queen and I shall not give up those titles for any man, including the King. You may leave me." She sat in a heavily padded and embroidered seat. As Campeggio bowed, she began to stroke the beautiful needlework. She had become accustomed to the beauty and decadence of Henry's court, and she would not like to taste the relative poverty of a nunnery. It was then that a thought came to her. "Cardinal?" He raised his head to look at her. "perhaps when you have the time, and with the blessing of my husband, you might hear my confession. There are matters pertaining to this issue which I would wish to discuss with a man of the cloth." Campeggio nodded his assent, and backed out of Catherine's presence.

When Henry heard of Catherine's refusal to join a nunnery his anger exploded. He had convinced himself, under the persuasion of Campeggio, that she would retire away, like Queen Jeanne of France, when she had allowed her husband Louis XII to marry Anne of Brittany, as her lack of offspring threatened the stability of the French throne. And now his plan was being ruined by the woman he now despised.

"If she thinks that she will change my mind about ridding myself of her simply because she is too stubborn to give in, then she will be very disappointed. That woman will give me what I want or she will face the consequences. No one defies the King of England, I will have absolute control in my realm. No one has the right to gainsay me." His face was bright red to match his hair, and bubbles of spittle were forming at the corners of his mouth giving him the appearance of a rabid dog. "She will not defy me again. I shall have her thrown in the tower, in a dungeon, if she will not give me the damned divorce. I offered her a way out, and she refused it, and now I will bring her down to her knees, begging for my forgiveness." His voice was filled with malice, and the spittle was dribbling down his chin, making him look crazed. Anne, the only person present for this insane rant, had backed herself against the wall, and she was trembling. She had never seen Henry filled with this anger before, and it terrified her. "No one says 'no' to the King of England and gets away with it." He bellowed. Anne felt the saliva rain down on her face, and the tears filled her eyes. Seeing her fear suddenly, Henry seemed to come out of a trance. "Oh, my love, you have no need to be afraid, it is not you who have angered me."

"I know." Anne said, barely above a whisper. "but maybe next time it will be."

"Oh, my Anne, my love, you will never face my anger. I love you so much, you could never enrage me so much."

"But I say 'no' to you Henry."

"But I love you."

"Henry, they say you loved her once. They say that you married her against the advice of your council because you loved her so madly that you simply had to have her."

"I never loved her like I love you. I married Catherine because it made sense diplomatically, and because she had been so poorly treated, and because I was seventeen, and I thought myself to be her knight in shining armour. And then God cursed our union. He will not curse ours."

"Maybe he already has. Maybe the fact that we have not yet got the divorce, that Catherine continues to fight for you, maybe it is a sign that God is against us." Anne began to cry in earnest now, and Henry bundled her slender figure into his arms, and let her sob against his broad chest. He stroked her hair absent mindedly, and whispered meaningless platitudes. Anne's sobs eventually subsided to sniffs and she pulled away from Henry.

"I am sorry to have scared you." Henry said softly, his own eyes watering. "You must know I have no desire in the world to make you cry." Anne nodded silently. She pulled herself up to her full height, wiped her eyes with the back of her hand, and held her head aloft. She swept from the room with all the dignity she could muster. She could not be so near to Henry right now, when the sight of him terrified her, but she could not let the rest of the court, the rest of the world, know that she was sobbing behind closed doors. If people, even for a second, suspected that things were not perfect happiness, their support system would start to fracture, people would begin to flood back to Catherine's side. After all, it was all well and good to abandon the Queen in favour of the most beloved mistress, but for a mistress with whom the relationship was turning sour? People would prefer the Queen they knew to the woman they didn't, if both would make their King unhappy! She barely noticed the fawning courtiers she passed as she made her way through the corridors, but they noticed her, and they noticed that their Queen in waiting didn't even have time to bestow a smile upon those who wished her well.

"Your Majesty", began Thomas Howard, Duke of Norfolk, "the council has been attempting to come up with a solution to your delicate matter." His voice was a little tentative. Lately, more than ever, the King's moods had been excessively erratic, with him one moment calling a man his 'dearest companion', and the next threatening to have his head cut off, without any real cause. Henry nodded his assent for Norfolk to continue. He was a wily old fox, and Henry suspected if there was a way to persuade Catherine to accept the divorce, Norfolk would be the one to find it. "Perhaps, your majesty, if you were to deny the Queen access to the Princess Mary until she has seen sense in this matter, it would allow for a speedy resolution. After all, the Queen writes to her daughter every day they are not together, and the enforced silence would be such punishment that within a week she is sure to bend to your will." Many members of the council nodded their assent. Henry looked thoughtful.

"I see the logic in your proposal, and I agree that it would be likely to work. However, once it had, there is no doubt in my mind that Catherine would attempt to poison Mary's mind against me, and I will not have that. She must be made to step aside without this." He paused for a moment. "But if another route cannot be satisfactorily found, then we shall revisit this suggestion. You have done well." Norfolk seated himself, and tried to look calm. That was about as well as that could have gone, so why did he find his insides filling with an icy dread? "I do, however, have another course of action I wish the council to pursue. The issue of my divorce, though now well-known enough at court, is passing through the country as rumour and speculation. I think it is time that there was an official proclamation. I wish my people to know I am not casting aside a wife for a mistress, but that the validity of my marriage is questioned, not just by myself but by many, and that should these doubts be found to be truth that I intend to separate from Catherine and to remarry in order to produce a male heir to inherit my realm." Without giving the council time to question this order, Henry waved his hand to dismiss them. It was only once he sat alone, at least, as alone as a King could be, that he began to think more carefully about the council's suggestion. No doubt it would work, and it would be an ideal punishment for the woman who was determined to destroy his hopes, and to pull his country into civil war after his death. After all, many would not stand for a female heir, and there would be a hundred men from families whose blood was tinged with royalty who would appear to fight Mary for her crown. What sort of unnatural mother would wish that upon her daughter! But the separation would hurt Mary as well. For in spite of Henry's genuine affection for his daughter, her love and devotion was tied most fervently to her mother. The lack of contact for even a few days would crush the girl, and would incur her hatred of her father. As yet, Henry was not prepared to endure that. But he knew he was reaching the end of his patience, and he knew that it would take very little to tip the scales.

Chapter Fourteen

Winter 1528/9

"Are these apartments to your liking my love?" Henry asked Anne. He had brought her from her residence at Durham house to court for the Christmas festivities. As Anne was no longer one of Catherine's ladies in waiting, it was only fitting that she be given her own apartments. Whilst Catherine still occupied the Queen's rooms, the next best in the palace were given over to Anne. They were ostentatious in their decor, as was to be expected, and they were also distinctly separate from the King's own apartments. This made it much less likely that rumours would begin of covert night time visits, as the pair would have to travel across half of the palace in order to meet, and for that to be done, without attracting the attention of anyone, was so unlikely it wasn't worth thinking about.

"Oh, Henry they are beautiful." Anne gushed. Henry's devotion to her had been increasing by the day, and perhaps without her intending for it to happen, Anne's love for Henry was growing. She put her fear of his anger to the back of her mind, feeling confident enough in his love that she thought she needn't fear him. He clasped her to him and kissed her. Neither of them wanted to break from the embrace, but both knew that they got precious few seconds alone, and that any moment they would be surrounded by courtiers.

Anne, it seemed, as the ascending star, had her own court of young ladies, without having looked for it. These ladies would follow her around, desperate to become a favourite of the Queen to be, and they often brought with them the most handsome men at court. Henry was, of course, a part of the world revolving around Anne, and this left Catherine, although Queen in name, and in her position in ceremony, with a mere handful of devoted ladies and gentlemen to frequent her rooms. While Catherine's rooms were devout and prayerful, Anne's sang with music, and bounced with the many heavy footfalls of dancing couples. There were those who turned their noses up at Anne's invitations, thinking her rooms to be a den of licentiousness, but once they spent a few moments there, they realised that any inappropriate behaviour between the guests was quickly stopped by Anne herself. It seemed, although Anne Boleyn loved fun and gaiety, she would have no immorality or lewd behaviour in her rooms. Gradually, even the more conservative members of court found themselves frequenting Anne's apartments. As the only place to have an audience with the King was in the presence of 'the Lady', even those who planted their loyalty firmly with Catherine were to be seen entering Anne's rooms daily. Catherine, of course, maintained her quiet dignity, but those who cared to look would see her needlework had become shoddy, and her face was suddenly looking every month of its forty-three years. Perhaps, even then, if Catherine had looked young, and had been filled with vitality, she could have persuaded Henry to love her again. But she did nothing to entice his feelings but pray. They sat together at the high table during every evening of the twelve night celebrations, but Henry never spoke so much as one word to her, his eyes were fixed for the entire time on the beautiful young woman sat with the other ladies of her rank, attracting the attention of all.

"I have received a letter from the Pope." Henry told Anne in confidence two days after Christmas. They were walking in the frosty gardens, followed at a discreet distance by what seemed to be half the court. They spoke in whispers in the hope that they would not be overheard.

"You do not look happy my love. Should I then assume it is not his consent for the divorce?"

"You would assume correctly my dear." Henry said, cautiously. "But he does give us a suggestion."

"Which is?"

"That we marry in January. If we are married then we can deal with the legalities later, but the Pope implies that if I were to have two wives, then both of their claims on me would be equal, and it would be easier for him to decree in your favour because of my two wives you would be the most likely to bear children." Anne paused, taking in this information.

"The Pope has consented to us marrying, and has suggested we do it next month?" Anne could not hide the excitement in her voice. It was one of the things Henry loved about her, that she had not been brought up a Princess, to hide all emotion, but that she was a free spirit, who felt things so intensely that she could not help but display it.

"Yes, that is what he has said." Henry sounded dubious.

"Then what is the problem?" Anne asked, a little more forcefully than she had perhaps intended.

"The problem, my love," Henry began, in a pointed whisper, "is that it is a sin to take two wives."

"But Henry, Catherine is not your true wife." Anne's voice was a little cool. "Or had you forgotten?"

"Of course, I haven't forgotten." Henry said, a hint of sulkiness in his voice. "But as far as the church is concerned, until my marriage is deemed invalid I would be breaking a church law."

"Oh Henry, the Pope himself suggested it, of course he will grant you forgiveness for any transgressions you make along the way."

"But Anne.."

"But nothing Henry. Don't you want me to be your wife? Your true wife? In every sense of the word?" She pressed herself against him. "Don't you want to take me to your bed and.."

"You know I do." Henry's voice was cracking with desire. "I cannot even describe how much I do. But what if you were to fall pregnant, before the Pope has chance to grant me my annulment."

"Then I shall bear you a son, born in wedlock, an heir for England."

"But would he be? When you and I are gone, and we leave our son to inherit, wouldn't there be those who would say he was conceived in a bigamous union. Wouldn't there be many who would want to see his half-sister on the throne instead. Once we are gone Anne there would be no one to fight for our marriage, and the naysayers would have their way. I want to marry you, and I want to have sons, but I want to be totally free of

Catherine before that, I do not want there to be any doubt that our sons have the right to rule." Anne's eyes flashed, just for a second, and she looked as if she might scream and argue right there in front of half the court. There was a second when Anne herself, filled with passion and the desperate yearning to be Henry's wife, thought she was going to explode at him, make him give her what she wanted. But then the logical part of her brain clicked in. The part of her brain that would not allow her to be Henry's mistress, the part of her brain that had wanted to keep her from falling in love, because love made you foolish. She nodded her head deferentially.

"Whatever you think is best my love." She said softly. She raised her eyes to meet his, with a hint of coquettishness. "Just don't make me wait too long."

Henry smiled. To have this beautiful woman clearly quivering with desire made him even more determined to give her what she wanted, the divorce, the marriage, and him.

Chapter Fifteen

Spring 1529

"Wolsey, I have a new position for you." Henry beamed with pride, and squeezed Anne round the waist as he spoke to his adviser. Anne was present for all of Henry's audiences now, and people understood that if they wanted to have a case heard favourably by the King, they should first gain the approval of Lady Anne.

"Yes, your Majesty?" Wolsey was curious. He had ever been a grasping man, having been born into such a low station in life, and was eager for a new position, with new revenues.

"I received intelligence not twenty minutes since that the Pope has died. You, my dear fellow, shall be the new Pope. I shall set about ensuring the votes of enough Cardinals to bring it about. And when you are Pope, you can, of course, grant me my divorce, and bless my second marriage, and there will be nothing that Catherine will be able to do about it." Henry looked truly jubilant, and Anne was glowing. The possessive way in which Henry was holding his future bride was enough to tell Wolsey that the moment he was made Pope, Henry would be possessing this woman entirely. Although he was still not in favour of this marriage, and although he still felt that Anne was working against him, and indeed sending him to Rome would certainly break his power in England, he could not deny the appeal of the Papal crown. He would head up not only a city state, but the entire Roman Catholic church. He would receive allegiance from all the Kings of Christendom. He would control vast wealth, and live in opulence that he could only dream of. In short, Thomas Wolsey couldn't care less if this position was given to him as part of a plot to get him out of England, and to get Anne into Henry's bed, he would not turn it down. After all, he was hardly known as a man of principles. Wolsey bowed his way out of the apartments a quarter of an hour later feeling secure in the knowledge that he would receive his summons to Rome to place his vote at the Papal elections, and that by the time he arrived, Henry would already have guaranteed that the Papacy would be offered to Wolsey. If he hadn't been so corpulent, and if he didn't have the early signs of gout appearing, he thought he might have skipped down the hallway to his own chambers.

Alone for a brief few moments, before Henry summoned in the next man he had business with, Henry turned to Anne.

"Give it two months my love, and we shall be married."

"And in three there will be a baby growing inside of me, a Prince for you and for England." Anne was beaming with pride. Henry kissed her greedily. His hands began to roam over her body, and against her better judgement Anne didn't stop him. her mind was mingled with the desperate desire to ensure that there was no question about the legitimacy of any children she bore, and the intense desire she felt bubbling to the surface as Henry's hands ran over her. He was rough, and grasping, and had he been gentle, she would probably have given in entirely, and let him have her against a wall like a common kitchen wench. Instead, in his heavy-handed desire Henry forced down her bodice. The sudden cold chill on her breasts made Anne jump, and broke the spell he had her under. She pulled away from him, panting with passion. She adjusted her gown to make herself presentable, and, her whole body shaking, she left the room. Henry cursed inwardly. He was conflicted. He wanted to wait until they were married, because he was sure Anne would conceive easily. But the way she had given in to his touch had increased his ardour, and that touch, however brief, of her pert breasts through her thin linen shift had ignited in him a flame he was unsure he could quench. Part of him wanted to follow her, and to make her have him. But she would never forgive having her honour forced. Another part wanted to storm to the kitchens, and find the first willing woman to slake his lust upon. But the betrayal would have destroyed his relationship with Anne. Instead, he took a long drink of wine from a jug on the table, steadied his shaking breath, and called in the next supplicant. Surely, if there was anything to cool desire it was hour upon hour of listening to the petty problems of lesser men.

The next week, however, both Henry and Anne were glad of their, albeit reluctant, restraint. News reached the court that although the Pope had indeed been seriously ill, he had, in fact, recovered. Rumours of his death had been abounding since he had fallen ill a month previously, and many messengers and spies were given this misinformation. However, the Vatican's own messengers bore the news that God had saved his son for further work.

This news had been a blow to Henry, Anne and Wolsey in its own way. For Henry, it meant an end to his imminent plans to get Anne with child. For Anne, it meant that she would need to find another strategy to break up the Royal marriage, because her own desire to invite Henry into her bed was alarming her. For Wolsey, it meant a postponement of his elevation. He felt sure that this Pope would die soon enough, and he was sure that it would still be in the King's best interest to have an English Pope, so for now he must bide his time.

Over the next few days Henry's envoys in Italy began to send alarming news. Since his recovery, the Pope had been in peace talks with Charles V. The two were agreeing on the terms of a treaty, and there were rumours that the outcome of the English Royal divorce proceedings were intrinsically involved in these negotiations. Whilst this news made Henry livid, with him flaring up in fits of fury worse than ever before, it brought in Anne an intense melancholy. Since the day that Henry had promised her marriage, she had been convinced she would get it. She had cast off even the suggestion of other suitors, because she had obtained that which no woman could aspire to, she had made a love match with the King. But suddenly, she felt as if the ground had been pulled from beneath her. If the Pope was making peace with the Emperor, then the chances were that the divorce would never be granted. Although Henry was interested enough in the new religion, he was unlikely to ever truly forsake the Roman church, and eventually he would be compelled to cast aside his mistress and return to his wife. At that point Anne would have a choice. She could give in to the intense physical desire which was growing within her, and become Henry's true mistress. She could give him a castle full of bastards, but would always be the King's whore. Or she could retire away, admit defeat. If this had happened to her ten years ago it would not have been a problem, she could have found many a rich and handsome man to marry her. But now, she was rapidly approaching her thirtieth birthday. It was rare to become a first-time bride this late as it was, and a first-time bride sullied with the reputation of attempting to have the Royal marriage dissolved would make her even less appealing. After all, she still had no great fortune, no name, no title, and her looks, which had been her only chance at a secure marriage, were fading. There were tell-tale grey hairs appearing in her beautiful thick mane, and there were fine lines showing around her eyes and mouth that were refusing to abate. She was trying every tincture, and ointment available to help slow her ageing process, but to no avail. If Henry didn't, or couldn't, marry her, no one would. She had no vocation for a convent, but she could not expect to be kept by her father or brother either. She was also terrified that after her years of proud boasting that she would give Henry a legitimate son, she was getting older, and women past thirty rarely conceived, and when they did, the pregnancies were notoriously tough, the complications were manifold, and the chances of dying in childbirth increased tenfold. What if after all of her fighting, she couldn't give Henry a son, or if she died giving him a worthless daughter. Then all of her hard work would be in vain. Henry had ruined her. He had loved her, but he had destroyed her. When she had met him, she could have had her pick of men. If he hadn't pursued her with such vehemence, or if she had given in, spent a few nights in his bed and then faded from his life, she might now be married with children, maybe not in such an elevated position, but maybe at peace. The passion she felt for Henry scared her, because in moments like this, when she thought of all she had sacrificed for this relationship, the intense passion seemed to flicker into passionate hate. It only happened for seconds, and then she recalled the taste of his kiss, or the feel of his hand in hers and she melted back into the dream of love. but for those few seconds, she truly hated him for ruining her chances, and she was sure that it was not so much love that she felt, but infatuation. Anne looked at herself hard in the mirror. With her face stripped bare, and without her fine adornments she was no longer beautiful. She was tired, and she was getting older, and she, like Catherine, was starting to look every year of her age.

"I did not want to trouble you with this Your Majesty." Began Norfolk gently. "But I thought you ought to know." He handed the King a letter, which had been expertly opened, leaving the seal intact.

"Ah, so you are working as a spy now Norfolk?" Henry joked. Norfolk smiled half-heartedly. When Henry read this letter, his cheery mood would evaporate.

"I find it to be in my best interests to know when certain members of the court are sending letters abroad." He said gently.

Henry unfolded the letter and began to read. Norfolk watched as his face blanched white, and then turned red, and finally purple with fury. He spluttered, unable to articulate the intense rage encompassing him. Norfolk felt his insides clench. It had been a gamble giving this to the King personally. He could have sent it with someone else, because there was always a chance that the King would punish the messenger. But, in balance, the news coming from him was the best course of action. After all, if he could show Henry some compassion at this point, it would reinforce his favour of the Howard family. Of course, Howard ascendancy was tied with that of Anne's, and this letter may in fact help Anne's cause. But Norfolk was clever. He had survived this long because he thought things through. Henry may still tire of Anne, but if he relied on Norfolk for truth, honestly and support, he would retain the uncle when he fell out of love with the niece. The letter was from the Queen, and it was to the Pope. The intonation implied, but never explicitly revealed, that this was not the first desperate missive sent to the Vatican. The letter was begging the Pope to recall Cardinal Campeggio, who she was in constant terror would conclude his preliminary observations and call an ecclesiastical court any day. Catherine was pleading to have the case heard in Rome, begging that the verdict be found by his Holiness himself, and not by a representative. And finally, she beseeched the Pope to oblige Henry to attend the court personally. When Henry reached this part of the letter the fury in his eyes looked fit to burn through the parchment. Henry had been suspicious of Catherine for years. He had always wondered whether she was first a wife of England, or a daughter of Spain. And this, as far as Henry was concerned, was proof of whose side she was truly on. Why else would she want Henry out of the country to sit and be judged by the Pope, but to make it much easier for her nephew Charles V to invade Henry's land, to marry Mary off to a Spanish noble, and to set Mary and her new husband upon Henry's still warm throne. This was tantamount to treason and Henry was determined that Catherine would pay.

"Speak of this to no one." Henry growled through gritted teeth. "You will find a man to send to Spain, a man you trust. I wish English eyes to look upon the original Papal Bull for my marriage that the Spanish have been so reluctant to part with. We have only a copy, and there is no proof that what it says is the word of the Pope. I want to know exactly what the original one says Norfolk. Do you understand me?" Norfolk nodded, and bowed. He backed out of the room. Although his exterior was his usual courtly calm, inside his heart was racing and he felt like he might vomit. He had never seen the King so angry. He set about making arrangements for one of his men to go to Spain.

"That woman thinks to go behind my back to the Pope. She thinks to make him tell me what to do. She can go to hell!" Henry bellowed. Half the court could hear what was going on between the King and Anne, despite the fact that the heavy doors of his private apartments were closed, and the two of them were alone, apart from George, Anne's brother, there for the sake of decency. "I may not be her husband but God damn it I am still her King." He was pacing like a caged lion, and every syllable he roared he emphasised by pounding his fist into his hand. Anne gripped the arms of her chair so hard her knuckles were bleached white. She bit her lip so hard she felt the gentle drip of blood in her mouth. She daren't speak until the tirade was finished. "She thinks that she can set up our daughter as a puppet Queen, she thinks to rule England through Mary, as a vassal state of Spain. She thinks that she can get away with this, but I will not allow such treachery in my realm. I care not who her nephew is, I am not so cowardly as the Pope, I will not bow down to that ugly little man simply because he has inherited half of Europe." Anne reached out a hand to touch his sleeve, he batted it away absentmindedly. She blinked rapidly to suppress the tears that had sprung to her eyes as his hand collided with hers. Almost instantly her white hand was stained with a steady trickle of dark red, where one of Henry's elaborate rings had caught the delicate skin. She refused to cry out, she was too scared to cry out. And she daren't look at George. She knew he would be just as terrified, and her darling brother would be, without doubt, desperately trying to get her out of this room, out of this court, and out of the life of the man who was in such a rage. Henry was foaming at the mouth as he continued to rant furiously. Anne tried to block it out, she tried to think instead of the times when Henry was happy. "Are you even listening?" He thundered. He punctuated this remark by throwing a goblet of wine. It missed Anne's head by an inch, and crashed into the wall behind her. She felt the wine spatter the back of her gown, and cover her hair. It took all of her dignity not to react, although her vanity was screaming at her to rinse the wine out of her hair before it began to grow sticky. But there must have been something in Anne's face, maybe the way her features were distorted with the effort of not yelling, maybe it was in the eyes that were clearly fighting back tears, or maybe it was simply the fact that she was devoid of any colour at all, and looked like a death mask. Whatever it was, Henry somehow knew that he had scared her. More than scared her. He knew she wanted to run away from him now. But he didn't know what to say to make it better. He was still so angry. His chest hurt from the furious beating of his heart, his throat felt ragged from yelling, and his head was pounding. He wanted to cry, but he couldn't cry in front of George. He wanted to bury himself in Anne's arms, and have her kiss him until he felt better, but he was unsure she would ever want to kiss him again. The second that thought crossed his mind he felt that recurring desire to put his hands around her haughty throat and squeeze. It was that image, the thought of squeezing the life out of Anne with his bare hands that snapped him out of his downward spiral. After all, he loved Anne. Why would his mind fantasise about murder if it wasn't getting out of control, and giving way to madness? And for a King to be mad was not a good thing. Henry took in several long breaths to calm himself, and then knelt at Anne's feet. There was an apology in his mind, but somehow, he could not bring it to his lips. He wanted to apologise for scaring her, but he did not want to voice it. Somehow, admitting he had scared her, out loud, would make it more real. If there was one thing Henry Tudor was good at, it was ignoring uncomfortable truths. "I did not mean to alarm you." Henry said, somewhat stiltedly. "it is only that I am so infuriated by that woman. All I want is to marry you, and she is constantly making it difficult." Anne nodded. She did not trust herself to speak, she was far too afraid of bursting into tears. "But once she has been silenced and we are married I shall never again need to feel such anger." Anne nodded again. These bursts of anger were often started by something Catherine had said or done, but Anne felt acutely aware that she could start them too. Henry kissed her hands. He tactfully ignored the blood smeared across the one he had struck. He turned her hands palms up and kissed them passionately. His anger was rapidly turning to desire, a pattern Henry found all too frequently. Anne seemed a little distracted, and so Henry moved to kiss her neck. At first, uncomfortable at her brother's presence, and still terrified by Henry's rage, Anne sat rigid, allowing Henry's advances, but not responding to them. But he knew her too well. He knew how to make her melt inside, and in a few short seconds Anne felt her body relaxing into the kisses. As he moved to her mouth she forgot that there was anyone else in the room. She allowed his hands to roam freely over her body, and for the first time, did not stop him as he lifted her skirts just a little to touch her bare calves. Her entire body was desperate for him to continue. She could hardly breathe she was so inflamed by him. She was, this time, barely aware of the dichotomy in her mind, she wanted to give herself to him, right there, right then. But then, the slightest of noises made her recall that George was in the room. It was only then that she became acutely aware of Henry's head buried in her bosom, and her skirts bunched up around her knees. She gently pushed Henry back and hurried to rearrange her dress. Henry looked confused and hurt for a second, and then looked over his shoulder at George. George was ever the courtier, he had sat whilst the King attempted to take his sisters virtue, and whilst she, by all appearances, was willing to surrender it, and he hadn't made a move. Only when he saw Henry making that tell-tale move that said within seconds things would have passed the point of no return had he subtly adjusted his position. The slight movement had been just enough to alert his sister to his presence and stop the embrace. He did not much care if Anne made a whore of herself or not, it was common enough at court for women to do so, and for lesser men than the King. But George knew what was at stake here, and hoped that Anne could hold out a little longer. Although he feared for his sister after having seen the tirade of Henry's anger, he also knew that Anne could give just as much back, and was probably the most equal match Henry could ever find. He was unsure why Anne hadn't flared up back, but he supposed that her silence had allowed Henry to burn his anger out, and her receptiveness to his advances had chased thoughts of fury out of his mind. Henry smiled at George, a knowing smile often shared between men at court when discussing the women. George smiled. He expected to be dismissed. He expected Anne to nod him out of the room, and he expected that his sister would give up her principles that very afternoon. But instead the King turned back to Anne, and said in an audible whisper, "Once we are married we will no longer need to be chaperoned. And then, my love, the fun we shall have." Anne smiled. Only George noticed the smile never reached her eyes. Only George knew the mild panic that was probably erupting in Anne's soul as she had once again almost given way to passion over reason. And only George knew that once they were married, rather than the fun Henry envisaged, there could just as easily be disaster.

Chapter Sixteen

Summer 1529

"I wish you didn't have to go my love." Henry sulked, as Anne watched the last of her belongings being piled onto the cart.

"Henry, I am only moving to Durham House, I will be so nearby. And it looks a lot better when your marriage is finally being tested, if your wife to be isn't sat at court doing her needlework. I need to be discreet Henry, there are enough whispers about me."

"Whispers?"

"That I am a whore, a witch. I have to appear pristine, else the country will not accept me as your wife."

"I care not what the country says!"

"Yes, Henry, but you will care when they won't accept me as Queen, and when they question the legitimacy of our heirs." Henry pouted. He knew Anne was right, but he didn't want to admit it.

"If you feel it is in your best interests." He said, slightly dismissively. Anne sighed. A year or two ago this was where she would have tried to placate him, with kisses and cajolements. Now kisses were a bad idea, as they always threatened to lead to disaster. She loved Henry desperately, but was starting to lose her tolerance for his showy tempers. She was forcibly reminded of a young child stamping his foot and sticking out his bottom lip to get his own way. This side of him didn't appeal to her. And it seemed inextricably linked with the part of him that flew into unnecessary anger at the slightest provocation, the part of him that scared her right to her soul. Now satisfied that her belongings were properly stored, Anne turned from Henry to go and mount her horse. She expected him to call her back, and try to steal a kiss before she left. It was not until she was riding away that she felt the icy fear in the pit of her stomach. What did it mean that he had let her walk away? She dismissed the idea after a few seconds. Henry loved her, he was just sulking. She was sure he would send her a loving letter within a few hours to tell her he already missed her. With this thought, she spurred on her horse to Durham House.

Meanwhile, at Blackfriars, Campeggio was struggling to call the legatine court to order. The old man was so small and frail, and his voice so reedy and heavily accented, that he could not make himself heard above the din. It wasn't until Wolsey bellowed for silence that it finally fell. Henry looked around the courtroom. He was convinced he saw a room filled with supporters, those who would add weight to his assertions that his marriage to Catherine was invalid. In fact, though he would never see it, the room was filled with a combination of sycophants trying to gain his approval despite their own misgivings, those desperate simply to observe the momentous event of their King being brought to trial, and only a handful truly devoted to the cause of the divorce. Though even these were not devoted due to love of the King, or real belief in his cause, only to the fact that they were sure Henry would bring about vast religious change to put Anne on the throne. After all, the only way that he would be able to marry Anne would either be through bigamy, or by claiming, as many were now whispering, that the Pope had no authority in England. This would be tantamount to overthrowing the Catholic Church in England. The English supporters of this were few, but they were powerful, and they had already aligned themselves with Anne and her family, in the hope that when the change was commenced, they would profit the most from it. Henry, though, saw none of this. Henry was blissfully unaware that despite his appearance of power in his realm, he was subtly swayed this way and that by those who had his ear. And he had no idea that the people who surrounded him extolling Anne's virtues were, in fact, the ones hoping that she would be able to persuade him into changing the whole country.

Anne knew little about these plots. She was devoted to her evangelical faith, and she wholeheartedly believed that Henry should have ultimate authority in his land. She was relatively convinced that she would still feel this even if she didn't love him. She was convinced of the inherently corrupt nature of the Catholic Church, and was sincere in her desire to see reform. But she didn't view this change considering what it would bring her, although she could see the benefits. She was utterly assured that whatever happened was God's will, and that change was the only way to the salvation of the eternal soul of her beloved. She was, possibly, the most pure hearted in her beliefs and her supplications to Henry in the matter of faith, and the most genuine in her devotion.

"Catherine, Queen of England, come into the court." The bellowing voice shook Henry from the slight reverie into which he had slipped as the croaky voice of Campeggio had explained to the bored masses why they were there.

Catherine sailed into the court, head held high, looking every inch a Queen in a gown of scarlet and yellow. Many in the audience noted to themselves that she was wearing the colour of a martyr, maybe even then Catherine knew her cause was lost, and that she would have to nail her colours to the mast. The court as one held its breath as Catherine strode past the seat which had been allocated to her and presented herself directly to her husband. She sank to her knees. She begged Henry as a wife, and not a Queen, to end his persecution of her. She assured him that she had come to his bed a maid, and that she had never been the true wife of his brother. She then painfully reminded him that she had borne him many children, and protested that it was not her fault that God had called them from the world. Henry was taken aback. He had expected his wife to meekly submit to his wishes when presented with something as formal as a court. He had expected her to retain her dignity to the last. Instead, she had prostrated herself in front of the entire court, pleading eloquently and with true passion. She had made herself into a victim, and Henry knew it would be an uphill struggle to make Catherine bend to his will. When she had finished her speech, she abruptly rose and swept from the court. In the split second before she turned her back on him, Henry saw a glimmer of defiance in her eyes. It was not until this point that he truly understood what it had meant to marry the daughter of Isabella of Spain.

Catherine was recalled to the courtroom several times in vain. She refused to acknowledge the court, she wanted the case to be tried before the Pope.

"Carry on without her." Henry bellowed. "If she absents herself from court she loses her right to hear the accusations made and to offer a response." The court was silent. Henry looked into every face, almost daring one of them to stand in support of Catherine. Of course, no one did. They all saw the blood burning in his eyes and they all knew that the first person to cross Henry would face the entirety of his wrath.

"We hold Catherine, Queen of England, in contempt of court, and all proceedings will continue without her." Wolsey commented smoothly. The court remained in silence, everyone too afraid to even make eye contact with another. Henry was breathing heavily as if he had run for hours, and his eyes were barely visible in his reddening face. This was their King, and he looked like a monster.

As the summer progressed Henry was feeling increasingly infuriated. Campeggio kept wanting more evidence, more time to consider, and kept waiting to hear further advice from the Pope. Henry was convinced they were stalling. He commissioned Wolsey to hurry up proceedings, to put pressure on the old man. Unfortunately, this was to no avail. After yet another long day in court where there was no progress made, only old men prattling about the boasts Prince Arthur had made the morning after his wedding, Henry visited Anne at Durham House.

"I sometimes wonder if Wolsey is even on my side." Henry whined. Anne bit back a cutting remark, and instead stroked Henry's hair, as if she was thinking. "To my face he seems all in favour of the divorce, but as soon as he is with that weakling Campeggio he cannot persuade him to find in my favour."

"It must be difficult for him my love." Said Anne, carefully, afraid she would inflame the anger bubbling under the surface of Henry's slightly pathetic demeanour. "After all, he must be simultaneously your devoted subject, and a dedicated child of the church. I am sure the Pope is applying equal pressure to him to stall proceedings." Henry was silent for a moment. His face slowly drained of colour and Anne was mortified. She wanted to run, but her legs wouldn't move. She braced herself for what she was sure was the oncoming tirade. Any criticism of Wolsey Henry took as a criticism upon himself.

"That damned Pope." Was all Henry could say, he was spluttering with rage but seemed incapable of forming words. Anne made soft soothing noises, but Henry was not to be so easily calmed. He began to pace like a caged animal. "My people, devoted to me, only me." Henry mumbled to himself, his speech becoming a mere trickle of thoughts, rather than coherent sentences. Anne sat, rigid. She had started this. She should have told him Wolsey loved him devotedly. She should have told him Wolsey had a plan.

Instead she let her animosity for the man who had ruined her first chance at marriage and had dismissed her as insignificant, rule her better judgement. She daren't speak. She didn't want to inflame him further. Suddenly Henry stopped, and looked at her. His eyes were filled with tears. She held her breath. The first tear fell, unbidden, from Henry's eyes. It seemed to take a second for this to register with Henry. When it did, the tears began to flow in earnest and he sobbed like a child. Anne ran to him and held him close. As the sobs subsided she began to make out words. "They are my people. All of England. They are all my people."

"I know Henry, I know." She soothed, more like a mother than a lover.

"But then why is the Pope trying to take their devotion." Anne sighed, a little exasperated. She had spoken to Henry many times about the divided devotion of a Catholic man, and he had laughed at her supposed ignorance. Now that it was having an impact on his happiness he was finally starting to see her argument.

"The Pope is the head of the Catholic Church my love, and he demands allegiance from all of his followers."

"But surely a man is an Englishman first."

"I don't think the Pope sees it that way Henry." She said softly. It was when Henry was weak like this, on the rare occasions he removed his head from the sand and admitted that there was a problem, that Anne could gently persuade him to listen to her more radical views. And more often than not, be it from conviction or devotion, he agreed with her.

"But they are my people Anne, I am their King."

"I know, and it should be that you are their only Lord, for all matters. But where God is concerned, a man must turn to the Pope."

"And God," Henry said coldly, "has dominion over everything. So, the Pope can claim authority on the whole Christian world."

"Only if you let him Henry." He looked at her, his eyes pink from crying, full of confusion. "Henry, England is your country, and you can say what happens here. A man cannot serve two masters."

"I wish there were no Pope." Henry wailed, then clapped his hand over his mouth, his eyes wide in the shock of what he had said. Anne gently moved his hands and stroked his cheek.

"You have said nothing wrong Henry. You did not speak against God."

"But the Pope is God's representative."

"The Pope is a man, he is elected by men. Were you not given your crown by God himself?" Henry looked a little confused, but nodded. "Then how can the Pope claim to be closer to God than you are. He was chosen by man, your appointment as King was divine." Henry nodded. Anne decided at that moment not to push things. He was starting to come around to her point of view, and she was sure, in time, that he would become a true believer, and his soul would be saved. But until he was ready it was foolish to push her beliefs further. For, after all, Henry was only even considering this one because it might get him his own way. She could see the cogs turning in his mind, if there were no papal authority in England, if his word, and his alone, was law, then who was to say he needed papal assent to have his marriage dissolved. Who was to say he couldn't marry Anne right now. She had opened the door for him, but he had walked straight through it, into a world with no Pope.

Campeggio stood in front of the court. He had spent the past two weeks in his bed deliberating and fighting off another nasty attack of gout. He was far too weak to be standing long, and he was desperate for the heat of an Italian summer, rather than the mild, bright, but still crisp English weather. The men and women sat in the seats before him were awaiting his judgement. The court had been in session for a little over a month now. He had heard all the evidence twice. He had spent days on end in seclusion considering things. He had written frantically to the Pope for advice. And all he was told, over and over, was to stall proceedings. The Pope was sure if Henry saw he wasn't going to get his way easily he would give up on Anne. The Pope, Campeggio thought, seriously underestimated the power the woman had over her King. He was not among the party who believed she was his mistress. On the contrary, he was quite convinced that Anne Boleyn was clinging on to her virginity like a medal. After all, surely a man who had slaked his lust would soon tire of such a woman. The only thing that could still be driving Henry was desire for that which he had been deprived. Campeggio hoped that the news he was going to give to the court would cause, after the initial frustration, the lady to give in to her King, and eventually to cause the entire question of divorce to fizzle away. He had been bullied and browbeaten by Wolsey to give in to Henry's demands. Wolsey had begged him on bended knee, but he could not disobey an order from the Pope. He knew his fellow Cardinal was in despair, but he could not change his mind. Silence fell eventually over the waiting crowds, and

Campeggio began.

"I have heard all of the evidence brought before this court. I have considered it all very carefully. However, I must inform the court that today is the beginning of the Papacy's summer recess. No decision can be brought from a legatine court until the Papacy is back in session in the autumn. It is with deepest regret that I must close this court until September, when this matter may be tried again." He sat down. Wolsey looked mortified, Henry was livid. The crowd erupted into conversations amongst themselves, but it was the voice of Charles Brandon that echoed above the rest.

"There never was any good done in England whilst Cardinals were among us." Wolsey paled. The comment was clearly directed, not at Campeggio, but at Wolsey. Brandon was one of Henry's closest advisers, and if anyone could influence the King against him at such a time, Brandon was the man. Wolsey felt a fear he had never felt before. It was as though an icy finger slid across his throat.

Two mornings later, at first light, the court began to move off on progress. This summer was different to all the others previously, however. Catherine was not invited. She was not even informed. Henry decided to not even take his leave of her. Catherine watched from a window as her husband rode off with another woman, and he didn't even look back. Anne turned, to see Catherine in the window. She looked at her with pity, but from Catherine's great distance, the look seemed to be of arrogance. The Queen, usually so regal and refined, threw herself back on her bed and cried. Anne, whilst outwardly so composed, was a little concerned that a husband who had once been so devoted to his wife, could ride away from her without so much as a backwards glance. The moments where she feared the future were becoming more frequent. The moments where she considered giving up the fight and running away were increasing too. She brushed these thoughts aside when they hit her. She laughed louder, danced faster, and smiled with more gusto than ever before to chase the thoughts from her mind. After all, she was not like Catherine, she was vivacious, and wild, and compelling, and Henry might become angry at her from time to time, but he would never truly think of discarding her.

Anne had promised herself to avoid the topic of religion until Henry brought it up. She knew that a seed had been sown, and it would take next to no time for him to have a need to discuss it. And she was right. About a fortnight after their progress began, Henry, Anne and a few close friends were gathered around under an apple tree in the grounds of a small country house.

"I have been thinking," Henry began, "That there is no need for a Pope in England." No one spoke for a few moments. "After all, am I not appointed by God to protect my people. Should that not apply to their souls as well as their bodies?"

"Of course, Your Majesty." George Boleyn said, just managing to keep his face straight. He was always amused when Henry took someone else's idea and then presented it as if it were his own.

"I mean, the Pope is all well and good, but he was elected by men, whilst I was appointed by God." Henry declared with growing conviction. There were murmurs of assent, which fuelled his fervour. "And how can a Pope claim to have the right to tell a King what to do. My orders come from God alone." More assent. Henry's speech was beginning to show the zeal of a convert. "And if I do not need a Pope to tell me what to do, do I have any need of Cardinals in my realm? I think not. It is wrong to divide a man's loyalty between two masters. All men, be they clergy or lay people, should have only one ruler, and that is me. I am governed by God, I can speak to God on the behalf of my people. I have no need for the church to mediate for me." It was clear that Henry's mouth was running away with him, as it so frequently did. He picked up on an idea, and then kept talking, without thinking. He then, of course, always agreed with what he had said, regardless of whether it was intentional. George Boleyn caught his sisters eye. The split-second glance conveyed all he needed to say. Henry was on board with the reformation of the religious system in England. It would take just a few gentle nudges to persuade him to accept the altered doctrine of the evangelical faith Martin Luther had started, and a few more to persuade him to start culling Catholic corruption, and to replace the religion of the country with the new faith.

Chapter Seventeen

Autumn 1529

Campeggio resented having to take his leave of Henry. He had wanted to slope away, and to avoid the wrath of the temperamental monarch. But diplomacy was important to the Vatican, especially with the wave of Lutheranism sweeping the continent. The niceties must be observed. As he dismounted from his mule beside Wolsey, he could think of nothing but changing into clean robes, and soaking his feet in warm, scented water. And then, by this evening, he hoped to be well on the road to Dover, to the sea, and to Italy. A liveried retainer met him, and led him wordlessly to a small, whitewashed chamber with a narrow pallet bed and a small dresser with a cross and candles. He asked the boy to bring him hot water, and he sank onto the bed. He wished sleep would come to him, but in this cold and dismal country he found it eluded him frequently. At least he had a little time before his audience with the King to rest and recuperate.

Wolsey, meanwhile, was still stood, quite alone, in the courtyard. No retainer had come to escort him to his lodgings, and he would undoubtedly be spending the night here. He felt it a little beneath his dignity to search for a servant to take him somewhere, and so he waited, aching to his bones, and desperately thirsty, until someone came to him. It was over an hour before someone passed him and spoke. It was Henry Norris, a close friend of the King's.

"Do you need assistance, Your Eminence."

"It appears the youth assigned to show me to my rooms has been delayed." He said, with all the dignity his aching body could muster.

"It seems there may have been an oversight." Said Norris, carefully. "It appears, Eminence, that no rooms have been prepared for you." For a split second, the anguish he was feeling showed on Wolsey's face, and Norris hurriedly continued. "You may use my chambers, if you wish. I can obtain a room at one of the taverns in the village. It is nothing much, but the bed is comfortable, and the fires are already stoked." Ordinarily Wolsey would have turned up his nose at the rooms of a lowly courtier, but today, after the long ride, and the long stand, he felt every inch the old man he was. He nodded his assent, and followed Norris to his rooms. When the door swung shut and he was alone, he took the Cardinal's hat from his balding head, sank his once corpulent, now rather drawn body onto the narrow bed, and wept the tears of an old man, who has lost everything.

The next morning Henry and Anne rode off early for the hunt. Anne was still half asleep when Henry had half dragged her out and onto her horse. It was not until they stopped at midday to eat that Henry explained. Wolsey had begged an audience with the King in the morning. And as a deliberate snub to the man he had once loved as a father, Henry had not only denied him lodgings, but had ridden out instead of speaking with him. Anne knew, at that moment, that she was safe as long as Henry said goodbye to her. She sensed that he wouldn't see Catherine again now, and she was sure he wouldn't see Wolsey either. And she suddenly understood that once the King decided he was done with a person he didn't say goodbye, he simply left, and pretended that they had never been.

Back at Grafton, Wolsey had watched as the King, Anne, and their favourites had ridden off. He had known that the King was finished with him. He had cursed the name of Anne Boleyn for coming between him and his King, him and his power. Gathering up his remaining dignity, Wolsey ordered his belongings collected, and moved in great procession to his house at Esher, there to await Henry's pleasure.

Wolsey accepted the charge of praemunire, of recognising an authority higher than the King, with good grace, and he handed over the Great Seal of England into the hands of its new keeper, Sir Thomas More. He felt if he was compliant, subservient, and meek, the King would eventually forgive him, and although he may never again live the life of power and extravagance he was used to, he may be allowed to live out his days in relative peace and ease, in one of his many homes on the outskirts of the city. But the punishment Henry wished to exact of his former favourite minister for failing him was greater still than that. Men were sent to inventory all of Wolsey's belongings, and they were confiscated, piece by piece. He sent Henry the keys to his beautiful Palace of Hampton Court, in the hopes of pacifying him. Henry took the keys, and ordered Wolsey to his diocese of York. The journey was a long and arduous one for a man of Wolsey's age, and it took its toll on his health. When he arrived at his home there, the roof was leaking, and there were major repairs in order. Wolsey berated himself for not visiting York more frequently, for not knowing that the house was in such disrepair, and for not seeing to it when he had excessive wealth. Now, he limited himself to living in a few rooms, those which were the least damp, and the least draughty, and he spent much of his time huddled under blankets, trying to fend off the increasingly cold winds the north of England had to offer him.

Back at court Henry was acting as if nothing were amiss. He began vast rebuilding projects on Hampton Court, to make it a fit Royal residence. He took meetings with a young theologian from Cambridge, Thomas Cranmer, who convinced him that the divorce should be tried by scholars and not priests. Cranmer and George Boleyn went forth into Europe to gather support. Henry seemed to be totally blissful, once again convinced that the divorce was just within his grasp. Anne smiled, and laughed, and danced with the rest of the court. But at night she was plagued with nightmares of Wolsey, cold and alone in York, and of Catherine, shut away from court, and of demons dancing around her, beckoning her to hell for her treatment of such good and holy people.

Chapter Eighteen

Winter 1529/30

The smile had not left Thomas Boleyn's face since he had been told the news. Now he knelt before his Sovereign to receive his promotion. The humble Viscount Rochford was being made Earl of Wiltshire. Not only was this a compliment to Boleyn's excellent statesmanship and his diligent service of his King, it was also an opportunity to promote Anne as well. Giving Thomas this new title passed his previous title to his son George, and it allowed his unmarried daughter Anne, to style herself as The Lady Anne Rochford. This minor promotion moved Anne up in the ranks of the women at court, where precedence was hugely important. This, was the formal promotion. The next day, Henry showed his cards before the court, offering the informal raising of Anne's position.

As the court filed into the Great Hall for dinner, Henry took Anne's arm, and lead her towards the raised dais where the King and Queen were usually seated. Since Henry had removed Catherine from court, the Queen's chair had remained empty. Today, however, Henry felt it was time that seat was filled. When Anne realised what he was doing she stopped. Henry looked at her. "I can't." She whispered.

"My love, you are soon to be my Queen, and I wish the court to see the high esteem in which I hold you. It will quell those who whisper that my only interest in you is physical." Anne remained frozen.

"That seat is the Queen's seat Henry. And until I am the Queen it isn't my right."

"It is your right when I tell you it is your right, my angel." He cajoled. In Henry's eyes, this was a treat he was giving his love, and he was confused as to why she would refuse it. The whole court could see the King and The Lady in whispered conversation. Many speculated as to its topic.

"Henry, my place is among the ladies. If the Queen's seat is to be occupied, surely your sister, the Duchess of Suffolk should be accorded the honour?"

"I do not wish my sister to behave as my Queen."

"I am the daughter of an Earl, your sister is the daughter of a King, and the wife of a Duke. She has much greater rank than me, and I could not take a seat which would be rightfully hers." Henry's eyes darkened. Although at state occasions he was as pedantic as any that the strict rules of etiquette and precedence were obeyed, in his own court he had the final say. It didn't matter to Henry what people said, he was their King and they would bow down to him. He could only see things from his perspective. He didn't understand that if Anne took the Queen's seat, the criticism of the masses would fall not on him, but on her. He couldn't grasp that the people of his court and his realm, particularly those who were firmly devoted to the Catholic faith, already saw Anne as the destroyer of the realm. It never occurred to him that her demure attitude in public was the only way to gradually persuade the nay sayers that she might be an adequate Queen, and that any appearance of pretension, or any dissension from court protocol would reflect badly upon her. Instead, Henry thought of wanting her company, of wanting to display to the world the woman he loved so fervently, of proving his love to Anne.

"if you will not consent as my companion, I order it of my subject." Henry's tone was not to be trifled with. There was a steel to his voice that Anne had learned to fear. She looked at him with pleading eyes. He glared at her, and then led her to the dais, and seated her in that fateful chair. The court had not heard the whispers, they didn't hear Anne beg to be seated where her station determined. Instead, they saw Anne's eyes begging the King, they saw him anger, and then take her to the Queen's chair. It was the opinion of many, if not most of the courtiers present, that Anne had begged or bribed the King into affording her the greatest honour he could. It seemed that she could persuade him to break even the most clearly defined rules of the court. The Duchess of Suffolk was amongst these people. Secure in her position as the King's beloved sister, she whispered the words that many were thinking, but dare not voice.

111

"She must be a witch, she has my brother under her spell. There is no other explanation for it." Maybe Mary, who had made such a lowly match for love, when she could have been a Queen once more, should have understood what it was to be so deeply in love with someone you would forgo almost anything to make them smile. She couldn't understand how a woman who had once been a child in her service could have ensnared her mighty brother without a spell. After all, the girl wasn't beautiful, she wasn't special, and she certainly wasn't worthy of a throne.

After that night, Anne was always seated with the King. He led her to the seat at every meal, and she resisted as much as she dared. She understood how it looked, she felt the whispers behind her back, and the evil glances across the hall. She felt scared. She had only Henry's love to protect her from the infinitely powerful nobles of the land, and their ladies, whose wrath she could feel bubbling just beneath their polite and deferent smiles.

After Christmas, Thomas Boleyn received the one honour he had coveted for years. He was created Lord Privy Seal, a position which brought with it a place on the Privy Council, and this finally gave him an opportunity to influence policy and help in the governing of the land. He already had an ally in the council, in the form of his bother in law the Duke of Norfolk. He also, however, had enemies. The Duke of Suffolk, perhaps a natural ally as a fellow newcomer to position, hated Boleyn for his influence over the King, and for his daughter usurping the place of honour from his wife. Men from old families despised Boleyn as an upstart. He would have a lot of work to do to gain their respect. But at his first council meeting he had one thing to bring to the table which he knew would cement his position in the King's good graces. Wolsey was still in disgrace, and now Thomas had the proof that he was plotting against the King. He would play his card at just the right time.

Chapter Nineteen

Spring 1530

"How can he do this to me?" Henry bellowed.

"I doubt this was a move against you personally." Anne murmured, half conciliatory, half antagonistic. She was beginning to get infuriated by Henry's insistence on making everything that happened, not just at his court but in the entire of Europe, about him personally.

"He made Charles Holy Roman Emperor. Catherine's nephew owns half of Europe, Anne." He raged. "How can it not be personal? Now I will never get my divorce."

"Henry." Anne was losing her patience. "This is more to do with a weak Pope giving in to the man who held him captive. He already had Spain and Austria, all he has really gained is the German states and his new title."

"Either way you don't get your crown madam!" Henry roared, showering Anne with spittle as he did so. Anne trembled. She had not intended to divert his anger towards herself.

"I never asked for a crown, Henry." She said softly. "I would marry you if you were a common man. I would rather you were a common man, then being in love would be all that mattered. As it is we must battle with the Pope and the people, and bow down to both for permission to marry."

"You would have me give up my crown?" Henry took a large step forwards, backing Anne against the wall. His breath was hot and smelled of wine. Anne pushed her body hard against the cool wood panelling to try and disguise the uncontrollable shakes that had encompassed her body. Henry grabbed her shoulders, his fingers digging painfully into her flesh.

"No, Henry." She took a deep breath. She was about to take a gamble. "I would have you bow down to no man." She closed her eyes and held her breath. After a second that felt like an hour, Anne felt Henry's grip slacken. She exhaled, trying to seem in control. But there was a nagging doubt in her mind. Henry was in love with power so much more than he loved her. Right now, when the acquisition of power was in the interest of them both she would be in the ascent, but as soon as Henry had that power he would never give it up. And what if his love for her failed, she would have brought down anyone who might have had the power to save her. She blinked, trying to force the thought from her mind. If Henry ever fell out of love with her she would be the mother of his son and there would be no question of her being cast aside. She just had to focus on gently nudging Henry along the right paths to get her wedding, and then she just had to succeed where Catherine had failed, she had to give him a son.

"All men bow down to the Pope Anne."

"But you are a King, Henry, how can he tell you what to do?"

"I agree with your feelings Anne, believe me. Don't you think that if I could live without the Pope's approval I would." He abruptly turned and left the room. Anne had no idea if he was still angry at her, or at the Pope, no idea whether what she had said was going to change anything. She felt the tears spring to her eyes, tears of fear, of desperations, of self-pity. She slid down the wall, and hugged her knees to her chest. She buried her face in her skirts and allowed the tears to fall. The silent guards stood near the door ignored her, they pretended ignorance, but both of them had heard every word, and both was silently questioning how much longer this romance would last, with such intensity with no release.

Henry stormed into Charles Brandon's apartments. His doublet was cast carelessly on a chair, and he was sitting with a pile of papers, seemingly absorbed in work. He didn't even raise his head as the door banged shut behind Henry.

"Brandon." Henry barked. At his words, his friend jumped up, bowed low, and looked up quizzically. He was becoming accustomed to his King's tempestuous moods, and wondered what little thing had set him off today.

"Sire." He murmured silkily. Charles Brandon had risen so high at court not just because of his position as Henry's closest friend, but because of his exquisite manners. His emotions were so masked that sometimes even his wife struggled to decipher his true feelings.

"I want to see the council, immediately. Summon them." He left. No indication as to why he wanted this task done, no questioning whether Charles would do it. Mary, Henry's sister, Charles' wife, emerged from the inner chamber.

"What does he want the council for?" She asked.

"How should I know?" He asked. "Now please, Mary, go and rest." Mary had been ill for some time, but she was keeping this to herself. Henry was terrified of illness, and the idea that his favourite sister was becoming sicker and sicker would not have elicited sympathy, but disgust.

"Do you think it's about that woman?" Mary refused to even mention Anne's name. She was staunchly supporting her sister in law Catherine, and she defended her to Henry as vociferously as she dared, for even the most beloved sister of the King cold only go so far.

"I would imagine so. Isn't everything?" Said Charles dismissively. He hated Mary talking about Anne, firstly because it made her so angry, and he was sure she needed to remain calm to fight off the ever-progressing illness, and secondly because although he had no great love for Anne Boleyn, he also had no true animosity towards her either. Brandon was a consummate courtier, all he cared about was making sure Henry was happy, and Anne made him happy, for now at least. In the past, he had frequently helped procure mistresses for the King's alarming appetite, and he was sure Henry would marry Anne, and soon tire of her as he always did the women in his life.

"You must tell him the rumours Charles."

"Why?"

"Because he should know."

"Mary, you and I both know these rumours are spiteful whispers and that is all. Why tell him something that isn't true and would only serve to hurt him?"

"Charles, it may be true. And Henry has a right to know what people are saying about his whore, and then he can discard her like she should have done years ago."

"He won't." Charles said flatly.

"If you persuade him he will."

"You have much greater confidence in my powers than I have Mary. He loves her more than air, he would sooner stop breathing than give her up."

"But..."

"If I tell him then I will be blamed."

"No. He loves us too much Charles. And besides, if he hears it from someone else and finds you concealed it he will be furious and you know it." Charles sighed. Mary was a lot like her brother. Angry, uncontrollable, and always convinced that they were right. Sometimes it was better to simply give in gracefully, he didn't have the energy to fight with her and he would feel so guilty if she felt worse after a screaming match. At the beginning of their marriage he picked fights with her for fun, and as like as not the most blazing rows led them directly to the bedroom. They had such passion. But now, after being significantly weakened by child bearing and illness, fights would exhaust Mary so much she would take to her bed for days, alone.

"Fine. I'll tell him. Prepare for the storm." He left before she could disagree with him.

The council met an hour later, all looking at one another, searching for a face that seemed less confused than the others. But none of them knew why they were there, not even Brandon who had summoned them. Henry stormed in with a face like thunder.

"Am I King, gentlemen?" He asked, petulantly. There was a murmur of assent. No one wanted to commit themselves to a long answer, as they were still unsure what Henry was leading towards. "If I am King, then why must I bow down to a priest in Rome?" Silence met this statement. No one was quite sure what response he was expected to give, and all opted for wait until the King had revealed more. "The Pope, sat in his palace in Rome, has deemed that I may not have a divorce." A wave of realisation washed over the assembled men. This was another tirade about not being given his own way. "Why, I ask you, does he have the power to tell me what I may and may not have." The silence was now beginning to feel awkward. Someone must venture an opinion. Someone must say something. But who? Eventually, after an age of silence, Charles Brandon cleared his throat.

"Your Majesty, he is the Pope, isn't he responsible for the immortal souls of all men, commoner and King alike?"

"I think not Brandon."

"Of course, your Majesty. My apologies, I have made a mistake." Brandon murmured smoothly.

"I am the ruler in this land. And no man has the power to tell me what to do in my own country." There was a general nodding and murmur of assent. "And therefore, gentlemen, as representatives of my people, I am recommending that you write to the Pope, telling him that it is the will of the people of England, as well as their King that my divorce is granted and I am free to marry Anne and to finally have a living male heir." Henry stood and left the room. There was a stunned silence. Not for a moment had the King considered that any of his people would disagree with him, that they wouldn't feel comfortable with writing in that vein to the man who controlled whether they got their place in heaven. Charles Brandon rose, appearing calmer than he felt.

"Well, get to it." He left the room, hot on Henry's heels. If he didn't tell him now, he wouldn't do it, and he didn't want to deal with the fall out if he didn't do as he had been bidden. "Your Majesty!" He called out down the corridor. Henry didn't turn to his friend but stopped, allowing Charles to catch him up in a few long strides. "Might I speak with you, in private?" He asked. Henry nodded, and waved the small crowd of hangers-on away.

"Speak." Henry said. His temper was still inflamed, this was a bad idea. But he had to deal with the anger of one of the Tudor siblings, and he would rather for once it wasn't his wife's.

"There have been some rumours Henry." He said softly. "Rumours about Anne. And I thought you ought to know."

"Oh, what now?" Henry asked, exasperated.

"There are people saying that she has taken lovers in the past. Specifically, Thomas Wyatt. They grew up on neighbouring estates and there are those who say they were lovers from a young age."

"And you credit these vile whispers by speaking them aloud?" Henry asked, anger piqued.

"I simply wanted you to know what people are saying. The truth or falsity of the rumours are nothing to me."

"We were once friends. I gave you everything, including my sister, and yet now you betray me by speaking such lies about the woman I love." Henry was infuriated, and Charles backed away.

"Leave my court. You are to go to your country estates and take your wife with you. Don't think I don't know that it was her behind this malicious act. She shall be punished, and you shall join her for allowing your wife to dictate to you. You will not return to court until I summon you." Henry stormed off. Charles began the slow walk to his apartments to tell his wife that they were once again banished from court. It was not a punishment for Mary, who loved their peaceful country life, but for Charles it was agony. As much as he loved Mary, having just her for company was grating at the best of times, unbearable at worst. He must regain Royal approval. And he would do it, even if he had to grovel to Anne Boleyn herself.

Anne, meanwhile, was back in the King's good graces. He had gone straight from his meeting with Charles to beg her forgiveness for his cold words on his knees. She, of course, forgave him readily. She needed to make a grand gesture now, Henry had made his and she was expected to apologise in turn for saying things which had made him angry. Anne couldn't quite bring herself to apologise. She had poured her all into this wild and furious relationship, getting little in response, and she was running out of things to give.

"I have a new motto Henry." She said softly.

"What is it?"

"Groigne qui griogne. It means, grumble those who will. It's because..."

"It's because it doesn't matter what anyone says, you and I love each other and will be together regardless." He smiled and kissed her. He interpreted her racing heart as lust, rather than fear, and left her then. He didn't want to inflame her too much, after all.

Chapter Twenty

Winter 1530

Wolsey's rise to power had been gradual. He had accumulated offices and wealth slowly, so slowly that by the time the high-ranking members of the court realised what he was doing, he was already far too powerful to stop. He had made himself indispensable to Henry by a million tiny acts, each one perfectly calculated to elicit a little more trust, a fraction more dependence, and a touch more power. The biggest mistake of Wolsey's life had been to fall foul of Anne Boleyn. Anne could forgive the breaking of her planned match with Henry Percy. Despite what others said, she was so dangerously in love with Henry, that the feeble emotions she had felt for Percy had fallen by the wayside long ago. But Wolsey had insulted her. And he continued, as meticulously as he accumulated power, to disparage her. He didn't want the divorce. And he didn't want Anne to be Queen. And he was fool enough to think that because once he had held the King's ear so exclusively that he could have claimed the head of any man he wanted, that he still held it, and that he could dissuade Henry from this course. But Henry's passion was even more intense than Anne's. He no longer cared who got in his way, he was King, and Anne was showing him how much power was due to a King. He would get what he wanted. So, when he was presented with some of Wolsey's letters to the Spanish court, betraying him in favour of Catherine and Mary, Henry's blood lust bubbled to the surface.

He sent Henry Percy to apprehend Wolsey, to have him dragged to the tower, and there he would be executed as a traitor. Anne struggled with these decisions. On the one hand, there was no love lost between her and Wolsey, and to get rid of him would certainly remove a thorn from her side. On the other hand, however, it scared her watching Henry so eager to spill the blood of the man he had once loved like a father. These days his temper was more changeable, more violent, more passionate. She adored his intensity, and yet shrunk from it. There was a sense of foreboding deep within her, a fear that the man she loved was warping into a monster. Of course, this emotion was kept buried. All she had to do was keep his love, and then she and those around her would be safe. But she couldn't help but flinch when Henry's eyes glittered at the prospect of displaying the head of his beloved adviser as a traitor.

Henry Percy took great pleasure in the job he had been given. He would happily have dispatched Wolsey himself given the chance. The world perceived him as weak, as delicate, and as changeable. Henry Percy was none of those things. He was a skilled courtier, and he disguised his true feelings so adeptly, that not even those who knew him best knew his strength. He had fallen deeply in love with Anne. A love that never left him, although he hid it. He was almost instantly married away to a woman of his father's choosing, a woman whom he loathed. Mary knew that her husband had been in love with another woman, that he loved her still the day they said their vows to one another. At first, she attempted to make him love her in that way. She tried to entice him to her with tenderness, which failed. She prepared to degrade herself however she could to make him love her. But when that too failed, and when she found, wrapped in silk, a lock of hair she knew to belong to Anne, she began to hate him. The Percy marriage was a poor one, she blamed Anne, but he blamed Wolsey. He still loved Anne with a passion, but he never tried to make even the slightest contact with her. She had chosen her path, as he had allowed his father to choose his. He had no inclination to do anything to ruin the Royal romance, because firstly, he had nothing to offer Anne, as he had a wife already, and secondly, because just one glimpse of the pair at court told him that she loved the King with a fervour that she had never felt for him, despite her protestations of love. He watched his love rising high without jealously, but with a growing venom towards the man who denied him the chance to make that wilful, wild, wonderful woman his own. He enjoyed presenting Wolsey with his arrest warrant, and he smiled as he told him he was sure that a trial was a mere formality, as no man in the country would find in favour of the priest who denied the King his wishes, and then plotted with the Spanish behind the Royal back. He felt no pity as the poor old man, already stripped of his fine attire and luscious surroundings, fell to the floor in tears. He was not moved by his pleas for an audience with the King. He did not show any signs of sympathy as Wolsey told him of his many infirmities. He had no wish to hear the old man's begging, he bundled him into a cart, bound hand and foot, and set about the long journey to London. He felt nothing when he was called to the old man's cell in the monastery they had spent the night, and found him dead. It looked from his body like he had poisoned himself. Percy resisted the urge to spit on the body, contorted as though in agony, lying on the cold stone floor. At least now he would get his eternal punishment. The souls of those who took their own lives were set to burn in hell for all eternity.

At the news of Wolsey's death Henry collapsed to the floor in a fit of grief. His body convulsed with sobs so violently his ushers called for a physician. No man could console him. And so, they sent for the only person who could, Anne. Anne's heart shattered when she saw Henry so crippled. He clutched at the hem of her skirt like a child, pushing the fabric into his face and soaking it with tears. Anne cried for pity of him, so broken, so crushed. She needed to make this alright again, and she wasn't sure how. She was treading a tight rope yet again; one wrong move could send her plummeting to her doom. He was devastated by the loss of a loved one, and had chosen to forget that this man was to die on his own orders. She knelt with him, and cradled his head in her lap like a mother with a child. She soothed him softly, with whispered nothings and gentle caresses. In time, the engulfing sobs subsided into shuddering gasps, and then into pitiful moans.

"How could I do this to him?" He almost whispered into Anne's skirts.

"You didn't do anything." She soothed.

"He is dead Anne. That is my fault. I had him arrested and now he is dead!" He shouted. Anne flinched.

"Yes, Your Majesty, he is dead. He is dead by his own hand. This was the last act of love for you he could give." Anne was thinking on her feet, she wasn't sure this was going to work, but the fact that he was quietly listening for her to continue emboldened her. "He knew that there was no jury in England who could find him innocent. He knew he was a traitor, and he knew that once he was found to be you would have no choice but to execute him." The two of them skilfully ignored the fact that Henry had been gloating just two days previously that he would have Wolsey's head on a spike. "He took his own life, and damned his immortal soul, so that you wouldn't have to give the order. So that you wouldn't need to feel responsible for his death. He did this, Henry, because he loved you." Henry looked up, his eyes met hers. She tried to fill them with honesty. She couldn't let him believe what she suspected to be true. That Wolsey had not wanted to be forced by torture to betray his fellow conspirators. The old man had taken the cowards escape. But Henry seemed to believe her. He smiled a shaky smile.

"Then this must be seen as proof of his guilt?" He asked. She nodded. "Then he was indeed a traitor, and deserved to die. And now he cannot make himself a martyr from the scaffold. Now he is just another dead old man who will never be received by his maker." The vindictiveness of this sentiment took Anne aback. Just moments before he had been sobbing inconsolably about the loss of Wolsey, now he was positively gleeful that the man would never be at peace. "You, my angel, shall arrange a masque to cheer my spirits."

"As you wish."

"Make me a masque about Wolsey, and about what happens to traitors and cowards who take their own life." Anne felt a little nauseous.

"Perhaps your Majesty would prefer..."

"Do as I ask." He barked. He stood rather quickly, towering over the still seated Anne. Anne lowered her eyes. Henry reached out his hand and raised her. Her finger tips were like ice. He dismissed it as worry about him, he had no idea that his erratic change in temper had frozen the blood in her veins.

Anne stood before the gathered courtiers and directed an elaborate dance, filled with steps she had devised herself, showing demons pulling Wolsey to hell for his bad deeds. George, her brother, sidled up to her.

"Anne." He said pointedly, putting his hand on her arm. She casually waved at the company to continue, and allowed her brother to lead her away to the corner of the room. "What the hell is this Anne?" He asked. "It is in the most appalling taste! I many not have liked the man, but he is dead and worthy of some compassion."

"I know." Anne replied, her court smile so firmly fixed it hurt her cheeks. "But this is what Henry asked for."

"Henry bends to your will and you know it Anne. You should not be so gleeful to dance on Wolsey's grave."

"I am not." She whispered. The smile was still painted on her face, but her eyes told the truth. "George, you didn't see him. You didn't see him go from collapsed in grief to gloating in seconds. George, I am scared he might be a little mad. And now I must make him happy, I simply must, or the next masque will be him celebrating cutting off my head, and then what will happen to all of you, you have all risen so high. And I am so afraid George. But I love him so much. And I don't understand half of it. But I have to make this masque. And it has to amuse him. I have to amuse him." Anne's whisper became more and more frantic, she barely paused for breath. She was clearly raving. George clasped his sister's hands and kissed her cool, slender fingers.

"Anne Boleyn. You will calm down right now. He would not chop off your head, you foolish girl. He loves you too much. He can be a tyrant at times, I will grant you. And sometimes maybe he does seem a little.." George mouthed the word 'mad'. "But Annie, you darling thing, he loves you. And after all, doesn't love conquer all?" Anne breathed shakily.

"Of course. Of course, you're right George. I haven't slept much recently, I think it is starting to have an effect on me. I need wine. Get me wine."

"You are not Queen yet sister, you cannot order me about." But he laughed and went to find her wine. She returned to the company, still dancing frantically, her smile still firmly in place. No one could see her heart racing, or hear her ragged breath. Her last encounter with Henry had scared her, and logic was starting to tell her to get out. But her heart wouldn't allow logic to take a hold. She loved him far too much to leave. Besides, where could she go? He would always find her. It was safest to stay, it was safest to pretend all was well, it was safest to ignore logic. Surely.

The masque was, in due course, presented to the court. Henry roared with laughter at every line, and congratulated Anne on her clever dances. The bishops of England were mortified. The sensible amongst them kept their feelings to themselves. The more outspoken, or the more conscience driven, protested loudly at the disrespect shown. They were sure that their high position in the church would protect them from Henry's ever-increasing temper. They were wrong. Henry took a hard line with the entire clergy, they were charged, en masse, with praemunire.

And amongst all of the commotion, no one noticed a young lawyer, once in the service of Wolsey, begin to make himself indispensable to Henry. This young lawyer undertook more and more of the day to day ruling of the Kingdom, allowing Henry to get back to his favourite pursuits of hunting and hawking. This young lawyer kept himself under so many people's notice, but his ideas were high above his station. This young lawyer, was named Thomas Cromwell.

Chapter Twenty-One

Spring 1531

Insert chapter ten text here. Insert chapter ten text here. The clergy of England fought for as long as they could against Henry's charge against them, but eventually they conceded. They were required to pay an obscenely high fine, which Henry took great pleasure in. Everyone knew that the Church was richer than the King, and this was his opportunity to level the playing field. But Henry was determined to take it even further.

"They shouldn't be allowed to continue to take the Pope's orders over mine." Henry blurted out over an intimate dinner with a few close favourites.

"My Lord, if I may?" Spoke up the silky voice of Cromwell. Henry nodded his assent. He was amused by his oily lawyer companion. He had ingratiated himself into Henry's inner circle with ease, and it was amusing to watch him grovel. It made a stark contrast from Wolsey, this man gave himself no airs and graces, he was from humble stock and he owned it. "I agree with your position. It is absurd that the King of England should not be the upmost authority in the land." He let this statement hang in the air. He saw the anger bubble in Henry. He was ready to explode. "I believe that no man has the right to gainsay his King." He added quickly, and he saw Henry's anger dissipate slightly. "But I think the churchmen of the realm have forgotten that it is their God given obligation to obey their King." Henry smiled at this.

"But surely after this fine they will bow down?" Suggested Henry Norris.

"Ha!" Barked George Boleyn. "Those pompous windbags? They probably asked permission from the Pope before they paid the fine."

"Then what is to be done?" Asked Cromwell.

"Well they must acknowledge me as more powerful than the Pope." Said Henry, as if it were the simplest thing in the world.

"But how?" Asked George.

"I have a suggestion." Said a quiet voice. All heads turned to Thomas Cranmer. "They must simply declare is Majesty the Head of the Church in England." There was a stunned silence. "After all, I am a man of the cloth, and yet I happily acknowledge that my King is my ruler in all things. The Pope is simply another man of the Church. He is in charge in Rome, but not here." All eyes were on Henry. Maybe this was a step too far. Anne was the only one who was sure that this wouldn't cause anger in Henry, but elation. Anne's worry was how far Henry would take this.

"Of course. Of course." Henry whispered to himself. "Then if any of them should take it upon themselves to hold the Pope in higher esteem than their King they would be guilty of treason, surely." No one dared interrupt. "And then that Pope, that, that, that Vicar of Rome, can say what he likes about my divorce, I will be able to grant it for myself!"

The assembled higher clergy of England were debating their King's latest request. Some, more progressive members were less concerned by this new oath they were to swear. Many of them were unsure about their feelings on the Papacy. In recent years the church had been filled with scandals and huge numbers of them had occurred in the Papal courts themselves. After all, the rumours surrounding Pope Alexander and his Borgia offspring were still being whispered, perhaps the Pope was simply a man, maybe he was elected by men, and not by God. And God seemed to have chosen the house of Tudor to rule England. The older, more confirmed Catholic bishops were outraged by the liberties they saw their King taking with their faith. Surely part of obedience to the Church was obedience to the successors of St Peter. Even a King must pay homage to the Holy Father, and for him to claim supremacy was blasphemy at best. The arguments abounded between the men, and it was apparent that no consensus would be come to. So once again, the softly spoken but dangerously charismatic Cranmer let his voice be heard.

"Perhaps, gentlemen, I can make a suggestion?"

"Why Cranmer? We all know that you are the King's favourite clergyman, you must be in his pocket." Scoffed Bishop Fisher.

"And it is precisely because I am high in the King's favour that I make this suggestion. I am sure I could persuade the King to make a concession."

"You could convince him to drop this nonsense? I was under the impression you had suggested it. I hear you are a follower of Luther." Fisher spat.

"No man could convince him to drop the matter, nor do I believe he should have to. I believe that each man is responsible for his own soul. But my beliefs are not the matter in question. What I could offer is simply an addition to the oath. Perhaps it would be more agreeable to agree to the King's supremacy if we added the phrase 'As far as the law of God allows'. Then no man will have to either perjure his soul or betray his King. That will satisfy His Majesty, and you can choose to interpret however you wish." In the stunned silence that followed, many men thought to themselves that Cranmer would be better suited to a life as a lawyer than a priest, thanks to his snake's tongue. In truth, Cranmer was staunchly Lutheran. He didn't believe in transubstantiation, he didn't believe the Pope held responsibility for his soul, and he didn't believe he could get into Heaven simply by saying an arbitrary number of Hail Mary's and repenting on his death bed. Cranmer believed that the most important part of faith was to understand it, and interpret it yourself, and he was convinced that the doors to Heaven would only open for those who had true faith and not for those who paid a corrupt priest for them. The men continued in their debate, but they all knew that regardless of their personal feelings, if they wanted to keep their heads on their shoulders they would have to comply. And they did not know the one vital fact that Cranmer did. The opinions of the theologians of Europe were back. And the majority of them shared Henry's opinion, his marriage was invalid and he should be given a divorce. So, nothing was going to stop Henry belittling the power of the Pope now. Even now he was planning to challenge the right of the Pope to elect English bishops, so he could replace the 'old guard' with men of his own camp as the older men died, and after some encouragement from Anne he was about to send out men in secret to view the church miracles, and remove any of those deemed to be fake. The English church was on a precipice, and any man of the cloth with any sense would be making sure he was on the right side of the line.

Chapter Twenty-Two

Summer 1531

The sun was just rising over what promised to be a glorious summer morning as the cavalcade left the palace. It was, once again, the time of year when the Royal Court went on progress, and Henry and Anne led the nobles on horseback. As they trotted leisurely through the idyllic countryside, Anne was reminded of her return to England ten years previously. How things had changed! Then she was the younger daughter of a Knight, with an impressive European education, and a lowly match with a distant cousin in Ireland. Now she was riding alongside the King, preparing to be his second wife, once his first had been divorced.

Henry was jubilant, almost boyish. Anne felt indulgent towards him, this was the Henry she loved, the one whose smile beamed and brought joy to all who saw it. They moved on at a leisurely pace, their horses so close they could have each held the others reins. "I am never going back to her." Henry stated, plainly. Anne looked bemused. "Catherine. I'm never going to see her again. I have told her that by the time we return from our progress I expect her and her household to have moved to The More in Hertfordshire. She will be treated with all the dignity accorded to the widow of my brother. I will never see her or speak to her again." It was not so much the sentiment that rankled Anne, but the tone of glee he used to discuss it. After all, he had once loved Catherine so deeply, and yet there was not even a hint of remorse in his words.

"Do you not feel a little sad?" Anne asked.

"Why would I be sad? I don't love her, I don't want her, and she is standing in the way of our happiness. I thought you would be pleased my love."

"I...Well." Anne was conflicted. "I am glad that I will no longer be forced to feel her eyes on my neck every time I am at court, but it saddens me that you do not feel at least a little loss."

"Why would I feel loss?" Henry was genuinely bemused.

"Because you once loved her so deeply Henry. You worshipped the ground she walked on, and now you have taken her world away from her and do not even seem sorry for it."

"I am sorry for her." He said, in a casual, offhand tone. "For after all, she has lost the love of her life. But the love I felt for her is nothing compared to that which I now feel for you." In spite of herself Anne beamed. She always felt so reassured by his passionate declarations of devotion.

"But what if you cease to love me one day, would you discard me with such ease?"

"Oh Annie, my foolish love, I could not stop loving you if I tried. When I fell in love with Catherine I was a young man, barely more than a boy. She seemed to me everything a Princess ought to be, and I loved her for it. But you, you have shown me what it is to be so completely in love with a person it makes the soul burn. You are the other half of me Anne, and I am unsure if I could exist without you now I have you in my life." Anne blushed slightly, but her own passion met his own.

"I love you so much that it scares me." She confessed. "Because I am not sure if I could survive if I ever lost you. You are the reason that I breathe."

"Then it is a good thing that I could never leave you if I tried. You have me under a spell Anne Boleyn, a spell I cannot break."

"Don't say that." The attractive pink blush disappeared, Anne was suddenly pallid. She sat up rigidly, and her mouth was pulled tight.

"What?" Henry reached over and touched her suddenly icy fingers.

"Don't say I have you under a spell. There are men enough who would vilify me as a witch without you providing them with ammunition."

"Oh, Anne it is only a saying. I only mean I cannot control my love for you."

"Witchcraft terrifies me." She whispered. "I have been made to watch so many burnings, and it scares me. I have nightmares for weeks after, I dream about the flames licking at my limbs, about the intense pain, and the smell of burning skin. Henry, I have made so many enemies in order to be with you, and I am so scared that they will cry witch and I will have to endure that." She was shaking now.

"My love, my sweet love. I am here to protect you. People can say what they want about you, I know you are no witch."

"I am sure that hardly any of the women burned for it are truly witches Henry. They are just alone, or strange, or deformed. And out of fear people point and shout witch, and an innocent woman must endure that most horrendous of deaths."

"But any woman burned by man who did not deserve it will be taken straight to the bosom of the Lord. And the real witches will face more torture, burning in the endless fires of hell." There was a finality to his voice that indicated the conversation was over. Henry began chattering idly about the hunting in the area, and about the first stop on the progress. Anne rode in silence, feigning attention to her King. Her mind was elsewhere however, imagining the feel of the flames creeping up her body, the smell of burning flesh and hair, the acrid taste of the smoke filled her eyes and mouth and she struggled to breathe. If Henry ever lost love for her, there were many who would cry out witchcraft and force her to endure that end. She must marry him now, and she must produce a son, she had gone too far, and if she didn't now complete what she had set out to do she would die in the attempt. Even if Henry didn't believe the truth of this, she knew it beyond a doubt. It filled her with a steely resolution. Henry might scare her, she might see the shadows of evil behind his eyes, but she must ignore that. She now needed his love and protection more than anything else in the world, and she would do anything to maintain it.

Chapter Twenty-Three

Winter 1531/2

The New Year's festivities were always the most extravagant of the whole year, and this year they were set to outshine all the previous ones. This was the first year there would be no official Queen for the celebrations, and Henry set Anne up as his Queen for the season. Unlike previous attempts to make her take centre stage, this year Anne threw herself into the role. She had handed out twice as much in charity as Catherine ever had, and she gave ostentatious gifts to favourites. She was, finally, truly acting like a Queen. There were many whispers about a Knights daughter acting above her station, as there always had been, but there were also many more people stating plainly that they had never seen a couple so in love as Henry and Anne that year. The pair were truly inseparable, and even when in company they seemed to have eyes only for each other. He whispered in her ear, and presented her with new jewels every day. The only problem was that the whole world knew that she was not Henry's wife. Anyone who had not known would have been impressed to see the King of England so devoted to his Queen, and the Queen so besotted with her King. And although no one felt happy to admit it, Catherine was not missed. In fact, her dour face and lack of humour often made the court feel restrained, and Anne's wild exuberance made them drink more feely, dance more wildly, and perhaps behave in a more cavalier way than would ever have been acceptable before. Although Anne did not fully agree with the behaviour of all, the drawback to being a Queen in all but name is the lack of any true authority. Whilst Catherine could silence a group of giggling girls with a glance, Anne knew that she had no power to make anyone do anything. And for once she relished her position, rather than resenting it. She had given up worrying about the path Henry was going down, for as long as they traversed the path together all would be well, as long as she married him soon, and gave him his heir she did not care if they had to dance with the devil. All caution was gone, she had mentally freed herself, and she was finally unleashing the full extent of her wild nature. She danced longer and later than anyone else, she barely rested, she hardly ate, and she seemed to be full of a gaiety no one could quite describe. Only George was worried. He watched his sister cast off her scruples, and relish in the role of mistress, even if it was not in the bedroom. And, as would always happen at Henry's court, there were those who whispered that the change in the woman Henry loved was because she had given him that which she had so long withheld. They were convinced that the joys in the bedroom had released the joyous woman from the constraints of her aloofness. This was not the case, and the matter of consummating their union was no longer even discussed. Both Anne and Henry had grown even more intense in their desire for one another, and they both knew that even the mention of it, let alone a stray hand, would lead them into bed, and they were both sure that that would lead almost instantly to a pregnancy and they were so desperate for their child to be a legitimate heir.

The Brandon's were back at court for the festivities, and Mary was disgusted at the behaviour of her former maid in waiting. Anne Boleyn sitting on a throne, acting as if she were Queen was simply intolerable.

"Why does my brother degrade himself so?" She asked her husband under her breath. "Does he not see he is a laughing stock, cavorting with a harlot and parading her as if she were Queen."

"I do not think it is his fault." Charles whispered in response. "He doesn't seem himself at all. It is almost as if he were under a spell."

Thomas Cromwell moved from his place behind the Brandon's to the edge of the room. He stored the comment in his mind. Charles Brandon had been raised very high by Henry, and there may be a time when he needed bringing down a little. A flippant comment about the King's deep love would definitely serve to provide the Brandon's with yet another banishment.

Anne sat beside Henry, seated on the Queen's throne, to receive the New Year's gifts with the King. There were a few raised eyebrows at this, but no one dared comment on the impropriety of the situation. There was, however, an audible intake of breath when a man wearing Catherine's livery stepped forward. Henry's eye twitched slightly, and his lips pursed. He was ready for a fight. The man wordlessly opened a box, revealing a jewelled cup.

"From Her Majesty with her love and best wishes for the season." The man stated plainly.

"Send it back." Henry said quietly.

"Excuse me, your Grace?" The man was taken aback.

"I said. Take. It. Back." Henry bellowed, punching the arms of his throne with every syllable. "Tell that woman I have no desire to have gifts from her. And you may also tell her that since I do not believe she is my wife, I wish her to return her jewels to me, as they are the rightful property of the Queen of England. She had no right to wear them and I want them back." The man blinked, and looked for a moment like he might respond, but thought better of it. He bowed and backed away from the King's presence. In the deathly silence that followed this outburst, all that could be heard was Henry's ragged breathing. Anne clutched the arms of the Queen's throne. The reaction had been so disproportionate to the situation. There was no need at all for Henry to refuse the gift, given in kindness from someone who loved him. And there was no need to demand the jewellery back. After all, he would probably give it to her, and he had already given her more jewels than she could ever need. His anger had momentarily scared her. She chose to ignore it, however, and laid her hand causally on Henry's sleeve.

"Shall we dance?" She asked, her voice artificially loud, and slightly tremulous. He turned to her, and his cold eyes melted.

"Yes, my love. Yes. Music!" He called to the room at large. Almost instantly the musicians struck up a volta, and Henry lead Anne out to the dance floor. Anne smiled. She felt confident that she would never fall into the same trap Catherine had. She could not lose Henry's love, there was far too much at stake.

When the message reached The More that not only had Henry returned the New Year's gift she had sent, but that he wanted back her jewels, Catherine flew, uncharacteristically, into a rage.

"The jewels are mine by right. There is no other Queen in this land than me. I am his wife, blessed by God, and there is nothing he can do to change that. He cannot make that whore Queen, even if he puts St Edward's crown itself on her head. Nothing can make her my equal. He has had his mistresses before, and I have borne it as a Queen must, but this I simply cannot abide. That I am being cast aside, barred from my own court and asked to give up my jewels for a woman who once served me. This is just too much of an indignity." The men and women of Catherine's household stood in stunned silence They had only ever seen their Queen as regal, composed, and placid. She showed no more anger than she did elation, it was all concealed beneath a mask. They knew she cried every night, as her pillows and furs were damp every morning, and her eyes were so frequently rimmed in red. But to see her lose control like this, to rant and rave like a mad woman was unnerving. "He is bound to me, God blessed our marriage with so many children. It is no fault of ours that God called them to him so soon. Apart from our blessed Mary. And he would disinherit his daughter, my daughter. That will never happen. I will fight with every breath in my body for my girl's right to the throne. Nothing else matters. Not even the jewels." She wrenched the elaborate necklace from her throat and threw it, pearls and rubies skidded across the floor as it broke. It was as if her knees went from beneath her, so quick was her fall to the ground. There was silence for a moment, before Catherine let out the howl of a wounded animal and sobbed like a child. "Let him have the jewels. Send him them today. Just tell him that all I want in return is his love." And then the grief of her situation overtook her and the ever-composed Catherine of Aragon, daughter of Isabella of Spain sobbed into her skirts until there were no tears left to cry.

The jewels and the message were delivered promptly to the King. His response was laughter. There was no love left in him to give Catherine. Everything he had, everything he was, belonged to Anne Boleyn.

The news that was to change the face of England was brought to Henry at the end of a long list of other important things, as an afterthought. Warham, the aged Archbishop of Canterbury died. This left the seat open, and Henry was adamant that the place would be filled by someone he approved of. Anne suggested Cranmer, a man who was clearly in accordance with Henry and Anne on all important points. Henry, unable to deny Anne anything, agreed readily. It was the man himself who, however, proved to need convincing. Cranmer didn't feel he was competent enough to take on the role, the leading Churchman in England. He could suggest at least twenty men who were better qualified for the job, and he was reluctant to accept. Henry, however, was immovable. Anne wanted Cranmer, and Cranmer she would have, whether he liked it or not.

Chapter Twenty-Four

Autumn 1532

Henry looked at Anne's delicate neck. She was knelt low before him, her long dark hair was loose, and parted over her shoulders to reveal the snow-white skin on her slender neck. He held the ceremonial sword in his hand, and for a split second he wanted to draw it down hard on that beautiful neck. He wondered if the flesh would yield to the metal, if it would be difficult to do. Then he blinked the thought away, he had no desire to hurt Anne in any way, why did he fantasise about it at moments like this? This was Anne's greatest moment so far. Henry was taking another trip to France, and he wanted to take Anne. He could not yet make her his Queen, but he could promote her, give her land and titles in her own right, make her a peer of his realm in her own right. He had elected to give her the title of Marquis of Pembroke, the male title, instead of Marchioness, the wife of a Marquis. This male title automatically gave Anne precedence over every woman of the court, as they had all gained their titles through their marriages or as the right of a daughter of a peer. Anne now even outranked the King's sister, who despite being a Princess by birth was now ranked as a Duchess by right of her husband. As she was raised, she was beaming, as bright as a beacon. She was so close to her goal now. She was the first lady of the Kingdom, and she was to go in Royal State to France, where she would be held on a level par with the Queen of the beloved land of her youth. She longed for France now, she had been yearning for it from the moment that Henry had mentioned the idea. She missed its delicate heat, its stylish, and subtle sophistication. Her excitement glittered in her eyes.

Henry had insisted that she would go to France wearing the jewels of the Queen of England, and he had guaranteed that Francois would pledge his support to their cause.

Anne's elation turned to devastation however, when news reached England that Eleanor, the new Queen of Francois, had refused to be present to greet Anne, as she was a Queen, and Anne was simply a mistress. And the only other woman at the French court with high enough a station to greet her, Francois' sister Margaret of Navarre, was diplomatically ill and unable to attend. Margaret and Anne had been friends in France, and had maintained a correspondence since she had returned to England. Henry had never seen Anne so crushed, as she collapsed into paroxysms of grief. This was a total rejection from the land she had called home for years of her life. She could not be received into the French court if there was not a woman of equal rank to greet her. Henry wept for her heartbreak, and berated the French ambassador for his master's lack of authority over the women of his court. No amount of soothing could ease the cutting pain of French rejection for Anne. She lost her enthusiasm for the visit, and it did not matter how many jewels and new dresses Henry commissioned for her, she could not make herself anticipate the visit with anything but distaste. Her melancholy had an effect on the entire court. Henry was sad because Anne was sad, and the court became subdued because of the feelings of its King. There was nothing that could be done.

And so, it was a sombre court that boarded the ships at Dover, and a sombre and sick court which arrived in Calais after a rough crossing. Waiting at the English encampment was a letter from the French King. Henry rallied a little when he read it, for he saw a chance to take Anne to the court with him after all. He had Anne brought to his private rooms, and showed her the letter. He watched in eager anticipation as she read it.

"What?" Anne asked.

"You see my love, you will be received after all."

"By his whore?" She screamed. The total loss of control shocked Henry. He had seen Anne explode before, of course, but she had always seemed in control of her anger. "He offers to have the Duchess de Vendome greet me, his whore! That is not a compliment Henry, so you can wipe the smile off your face. This is an insult. He is calling me your harlot, fit only to be greeted by another of that rank. I am a Marquis in England Henry, I am treated with respect, and I am no man's whore." The anger in her voice made Henry cringe. "So, you may write to the French and you may tell them that they have gravely offended me. You may tell them that I shall not be greeted by a woman who is so much my inferior both in station and morals. You may tell them that as soon as the tide is right I shall be returning to England for I shall not be insulted like this."

"My love." He cooed.

"No Henry, don't. Don't tell me it's alright, don't tell me no insult was intended, for I know it was. This is Francois showing he will not support our marriage. He is a fool, and he thinks with the contents of his breeches. I want to go home Henry. You must take me home. Now. This minute." Henry fell to his knees at her feet and clasped her hands in his.

"My love, Francois is a fool, and he does not think, but I am sure it is not malicious. And if you do not wish to be greeted by his lady, then you do not have to be. I had simply thought you would like to be received at any cost."

"Not that Henry. Not that. When I am your Queen I will return to France, and I will refuse to greet Francois' Spanish Queen, and I will send a common whore from Cheapside instead." She spat. The venom in her voice was somehow very attractive to Henry. He gathered her in his arms and kissed her passionately.

"I love you." He said simply. Anne held onto her anger for a moment longer, then she relaxed into his arms.

"I love you too." She whispered. They held each other in silence for a few moments, she was composing herself and he was trying to think clearly through the fog of desire that had overcome him as she had blazed. As she moved away from him her face was once more serene. "I know what should be done." She smiled.

"Anything. Anything you want I shall do." He breathed. He was entranced by her now, that passion had reignited his fantasies about life after marriage to Anne, life in their bedroom.

"No women at all shall go to the French court. And when Francois comes to dine with us he shall be permitted to bring no women from his court. That way there is no issue of finding an appropriately ranking woman for me. And Francois will be so enchanted by me that he will regret not having me at his court to show his women how to behave. He will be half in love with me before he leaves, and he will do anything we ask."

"Then let it be done." Henry sighed. He forced himself to think of the diplomatic situation in order to stop undressing her with his eyes. He needed to keep his head functioning properly during the upcoming meeting, he could not afford to be distracted by imaginings of naked thighs and taut stomachs.

Chapter Twenty-Five

October 1532

Francois immediately understood why Henry wanted to cast aside his wife for Anne. She was no longer young, up close you could see the fine lines around her eyes and her mouth that were beginning to show her advancing years, and her dark hair was becoming lightly speckled with grey, but she was still beautiful. She still had the grace of a swan, and every head still turned to follow her when she moved through a room. Her figure was still lithe, undamaged by childbirth unlike most women her age. And she was clever, she was unbelievably clever. Francois usually preferred his women much more like Anne's sister Mary, docile, pliant and perhaps a little simple, but he could see the appeal of a match of wits, as he found in Anne Boleyn. Her French was impeccable, her manners sublime, in truth he could not fault her. It was much more for enchantment with Anne than belief in the cause that made him make Henry an offer.

"Marry her here, in France." He suggested. "Once the ceremony is completed, I shall write to support your appeal to the Pope for the annulment of your first marriage, and his acceptance of your second."

"I don't think that my people would approve of my marriage abroad." Henry smiled. He was quite convinced that Francois was jesting.

"Are you not desperate to bed her?" Francois asked bluntly. "I hear she refuses you her favours until you make her Queen."

"We both wish for any issue to be legitimate, beyond a doubt."

"So, marry her here. I can provide you with a priest, and when the job is done I shall give you a chamber in my palace to cement the alliance." The thought was tantalising. An end to the waiting. Making Anne his wife. Taking her to bed at last. But of course, it was a fantasy.

"How can I? If we were to get a wedding night baby then there would be plenty to say that as my divorce has not been granted by the Pope that the baby was a bastard."

"Perhaps the child would be a girl. And then perhaps God would wait to grant you a son until the Pope had made his ruling. Surely when two of the major powers in Europe beseech him to grant you your desire, he will acquiesce." Henry was truly tempted, but he laughed the suggestion away, as if it were a joke. Although he could quickly dismiss it from conversation, he was not so quick to dismiss it from his mind. After all, what if he really were to marry Anne now, and then appeal to the Pope with Francois' support. He knew Anne didn't feel they needed the Pope's blessing, but he did. He truly needed it. But maybe if it were already a fait accompli he would have no choice but to bless the marriage. And he wouldn't be the first King to ask the Pope to bend the rules, would he. He made his mind to approach Anne on the subject at some point.

The French visit concluded, the English returned to Calais to board their ships home. Unfortunately, the vicious storms that had blighted their journey over the channel were now preventing their return. The waves crashed against the French coastline with such violence that any man standing too close would surely be lost to the sea. And so, Henry, Anne and the rest of the court were confined to the fort in Calais. It was here, on a dark, cold, wild evening, Henry slipped through the door joining his and Anne's rooms with a young priest in tow. Anne was sitting by the fire, staring into the flames. As so often happened as she watched the burning she imagines the fate of witches, and she shivered. Henry had suggested that they went through a marriage ceremony in France, and dealt with the repercussions later. She was more willing than previously to take such a risk. However, she insisted that the marriage itself must take place in England. Her concession was, that whilst they were on English soil in France, and with an English priest, they could go through a formal betrothal ceremony, a promise to marry before God. In the eyes of the church a betrothal, if it were to be consummated, would stand as if it were a valid marriage. She was unsure why this route seemed more appealing, but now she felt a sudden urgency to conceive a child. Perhaps it was her progressing years, and her fear that she was already getting a little old for childbearing.

Perhaps it was her constant fear of those around her, and her knowledge that being the mother of the Prince of Wales would be her only safety. Or perhaps it was simply that she had been desperately in love with Henry for the longest time, and she wanted nothing more than to be his wife, whatever the consequence. Whatever the reasoning, Anne and Henry pledged their love and devotion to one another right then and there, with just a priest as a witness. As soon as the ceremony was complete, Henry handed the man a purse of money, and he disappeared. No one else knew that Henry was in Anne's rooms, or that they had made a formal betrothal.

Henry extinguished the candles, leaving only the crackling fire in the grate to light the room. He had once been excessively proud of his physique, and yet as the years had progressed he had become a little more corpulent than he would have liked, and he hoped that the dim flickering of the fire would disguise some of his excess girth in Anne's eyes. He went to her and kissed her, with a growing passion. He pushed her a little forcefully onto the bed. Now that he could have her he needed to do it now. There was no time for undressing, he simply lifted her skirts, and unlaced the front of his breeches. Anne was unsure if this was truly how she wanted this to happen. She was filled with an unwilling, but desperate desire. She wanted to give in to him, but she had hoped it would be more than this. As he pushed himself into her she felt a sharp pain, which quickly dulled to an aching, throb. She wanted to enjoy the experience. She remembered the many tales Mary had tried to tell her of the pleasures of the flesh, but in reality, it was over in seconds, and then she was left feeling bruised and sticky and ashamed. As Henry pulled himself off her he grinned. It had, perhaps, not been his most prodigious performance, but his desperate desire had overcome his willpower. But she was his, totally his now. He looked at the woman on the bed, her skirts still ruffled, her hair still neatly pinned, and he smiled. She was truly his wife now, and he loved her. The divorce was no longer something he wanted, it was something he needed. Even now he could have made his heir. Anne wanted to wretch, or cry, or both. She wanted to sit in a bath of boiling water to soothe her aches. But then she looked at him. She looked at the sheer love in his face, and she calmed. She had been told before that the first time was often unpleasant, but that it didn't remain so. Henry watched her rise, with such poise it caught his breath in his throat. She seemed to float to her dresser, and began to unpin her hair. He did not see, or chose to ignore, that she was biting the insides of her cheeks to keep from flinching with the pain. As he watched the long dark hair tumble uncontrolled from the pins, rippling down her back like a river, he felt compelled to touch it. As he did he felt the stirrings of a renewed desire. But this time it was not the furious and frantic passion of a man deprived, it was the loving lust of a man already well satisfied. He moved her hair aside and kissed her neck. As he did he began to unlace her gown. Anne felt a desire growing in her that was bordering on wanton as her dress fell to her ankles. She turned to face him, and he gazed at her body, covered only in fine linen and he shuddered with longing. She raised the shift over her head and he gazed at her. And then he knew it would never be possible to desire a woman like this again. He could never look upon another form with lust after seeing the perfection that was Anne. He scooped her into his arms, as if she weighed nothing, and carried her to the bed. This time Anne began to understand why Mary had conducted herself with such little decorum once she had experienced this bliss. The passion which had built so frequently in Anne as rage was now released, she was his entirely, and she relished in it. As he watched the desire in her eyes he felt his love for her swell. Anne never did emotions by half, and now she had fully indulged her wanton side, there would be no turning back.

Chapter Twenty-Six

Winter 1532/3

Towards the end of November, the court reached Eltham Palace, to prepare for the Christmas festivities. Henry was as giddy as a school boy this year, both because of the new depths of his relationship with Anne and because he was overjoyed to be at his childhood home. As he had been born a second son, Henry had been brought up with his sisters at Eltham, under the supervision of their mother, Elizabeth of York. Henry had been truly devoted to his mother, and the childhood years with her and his sisters were perhaps the happiest of his life. Elizabeth had died, bringing a child into the world, just after Henry became heir to the throne, upon the death of his older brother Arthur. In his deepest heart Henry felt he owed his Kingship more to his mother than his father. His mother had been the oldest daughter of Edward IV, whilst his father had been the heir to the Lancastrian claim to the throne, through a mother born of a bastard line, and a father born of a Queen consort and her second husband, her master of the household. Whilst Henry Tudor's descent was shaky at best, supposing the death of her younger brothers, the Princes in the Tower, Elizabeth of York was the next heir to the York throne, and Henry had worshipped her for her royalty, for her grace, and for her beauty. In his eyes, she was everything a Queen consort should be. She had provided her husband with many children, both boys to inherit and girls to marry well. Even after the predictable infant deaths four children had survived to grow, and three of those had lived to adulthood. She had never deemed it her place in instruct her husband as to policy, but she supported him, and lead him subtly to the path she had chosen. Henry had continually held

Catherine up to his mother's example, and she had measured up well, apart from as a mother of many. He was convinced that Anne would succeed in all of his expectations.

The Christmas festivities passed in a blur for Anne, and it wasn't until mid-January that she realised she had missed her monthly course. She was filled with excitement and dread. She suddenly understood why she had felt a little uncomfortable, why her breasts had ached so much in recent weeks, and why food which she had always loved was suddenly turning her stomach. She had to tell Henry right away, something had to be done. Henry was, understandably, thrilled. His fertile lover was already carrying his child, after just a few short months. Now he had to make her his wife, and so he locked himself in conference with Cranmer, determined to find a way to marry Anne.

The conclusion was quickly reached. Henry passed a swift Act through parliament, the Act of Appeals. This Act made it illegal to try any case that occurred within the realm at a court outside the realm. That meant that the divorce would have to be tried in England, as to try it elsewhere would be illegal. The divorce would then have to be tried by the highest religious authority in England, Cranmer, Archbishop of Canterbury. Henry decided that now was the time to marry Anne, in secret, and then once Cranmer was invested as Archbishop in March he would be able to try the case of the divorce, find in favour of Henry, find his marriage to Catherine invalid, and his marriage to Anne legal and binding, giving their child all the legitimacy the church could offer.

Anne was unsure on this path, but her choice was now to take this risk, or to give birth to her child knowing him to be a bastard. And she had to decide quickly, because although she currently still looked as slender as ever, she could feel that she was beginning to swell, and it wouldn't be long before the baby became obvious, and she needed to be married before that happened. And so, the very next morning, just before dawn, Anne, her mother, and her sister in law Jane, met Henry and two of his grooms at the small chapel at court. The ceremony was simple, and short, and the pair exchanged simple rings, which they promised to keep in their pockets until their marriage was announced. Once they were finally man and wife, Anne and her mother returned to her room, and she burst into tears.

"Why are you crying child? This is your moment of glory."

"No, it isn't. This is the moment that should have been glorious, but instead, it has been a secret ceremony, that no one will know about, to cover up a pregnancy which should never have happened."

"Perhaps, but many a marriage is arranged like that my lamb, no matter how much you want to close your eyes and not see it. And you will be Queen. He will crown you Queen, and you will give him a son, and our family will be secure forever."

"Yes mother." Anne said softly.

"And now, you dry those tears, and you pinch those cheeks to give them colour, and you present yourself to the court with all the authority of a Queen born. He will not love you for crying over your union, he will want you to be jubilant at your luck."

"Yes mother." Anne replied. She sniffed.

"He is a formidable man Anne, you will have to make him happy."

"I know. I am hated. I need him to protect me."

"And don't ever let him think you need him for anything, except that you love him."

"I know." Anne snapped. "And I do love him. So much it scares me. I'm not scared about there being a day when I don't love him, that day will never come. I am scared about the day when he stops loving me."

"Well if you have given him a son, my child, it will matter little if he stops loving you, you will be safe to keep your son safe."

"So, my life rests on providing him with a son?"

"Doesn't every woman's in some way or another? Many a woman is cast aside for not providing an heir Anne, Queen or commoner." Anne bowed her head, and when she looked up she was smiling her beaming court smile. She had won, even if it was a weak victory. She was Henry's wife, and she was carrying his son, and everything hung on Cranmer declaring Henry's marriage to Catherine void before Anne's secret began to show.

Chapter Twenty-Seven

Spring 1533

"You cannot simply pass an Act of Parliament to deprive the Pope of his power."

"Cannot?" Henry boomed, his face contorted with rage.

"Should not then." Thomas More said, forcefully. "It is simply not Christian. The Pope is the descendant of St Peter and..."

"And I am the divinely appointed King of England. And no man will command my people besides me." Henry bellowed.

"No one is disputing your title as King, Harry." Thomas said, much more gently. He was the only person to call the King 'Harry', it had been what his mother had called him. Thomas More had known Henry since the death of his beloved mother, and this little familiarity became a sort of reassurance for the King, it brought his mother to mind.

"I can do what I want." Henry muttered, like a scolded toddler.

"No, you can't." More said plainly. "You are a King, you can and must be held up to a higher judgement than the common man. Harry, you have to be spotless."

"I am King." He grumbled. "I can do whatever I want, and people have to accept it."

"That is not what Kingship is about."

"Yes, it is!" Henry shouted. The sudden change shocked the older man considerably, and he placed a hand on his chest where his heart had begun to beat wildly.

"Is this really what you are going to do? Deny the Pope of his authority in England, so that you or your pet Cranmer can decide everything."

"It is my right." He declared, stubbornly.

"You must do as you see fit. As must I. And it is, therefore, with a heavy heart that I must return the Great Seal to you. I wish to resign all my posts at court with immediate effect."

"No."

"I'm sorry Harry, but my mind is made up. If you will not listen to my advice then I have no wish to inflict it upon you. If you are adamant that your way is best, then you had better appoint a man happy to oblige you, rather than me, as all I will do is challenge you."

"I don't want you to go." Henry whispered, almost as a child to his father.

"I have to. I cannot compromise my beliefs for anyone, not even for you."

"I command you to stay." But his voice was not commanding, it was weak, pleading, desperate.

"No. There has been a great friendship between us, one which I value above all things. I will not sour that by remaining, when all we could do is disagree. I shall return home to my family. You will, of course, be welcome to visit as you always have. And were you to invite me to court from time to time I would do my best to attend. But I cannot have a role here, not now." And with that, Thomas More turned and left Henry, standing there with his mouth open like a goldfish. Tears sprang to the piggy eyes, starting to become buried by cheeks which were getting plumper by the season. Henry began cursing More in his mind, damning him for disagreeing with him, for daring to nay say him, for abandoning him. Because wasn't that the main problem, Henry thought. This man had been more of a father than the former King had ever been. He had nurtured his soul from childhood. And now he was leaving him, like his mother, his older brother, his father, his grandmother, all the people whom Henry had revered had eventually abandoned him. Even Catherine had, in her own way, left him, when she had turned to God, not to Henry, for support over their lost babies. Henry was ready to collapse into self-pity with the realisation that everyone had left him, when his mind alighted on one happy thought. Anne. Anne would not leave him. Anne had married him for love, and was carrying his baby. They would never leave him. He would have Anne in his arms on the day he died, and he would leave his country to their son. So, damn Thomas More if he thought that his self-righteousness would change anything. Damn him straight to hell for his severe piety, for his condescension. Henry was King, and Anne was his Queen, and she was carrying his heir. That was what was important, not some nobody of a counsellor, he could be so easily replaced.

The next day the council met, without Thomas More, who had already left court. Henry let them deal with the petty business of the government of the realm, and, when they appeared to have exhausted their boring business, he stood to address them.

"My Lords and gentlemen, I have an announcement to make." All eyes were on Henry, unblinking, just how he liked it. "As you are already aware, I am of the belief that my marriage to Catherine, the Dowager Princess of Wales, was no true marriage." There was some mild nodding amongst the gathered men. After all, everyone knew Henry's feelings on this matter. "And as I see myself as a single man, without legitimate issue, I have taken it upon myself to marry." He paused for a moment, marvelling at the confusion bordering on shock in the eyes of his council. "I have selected as my bride, Anne Boleyn, Marquis of Pembroke. We are wedded and bedded and she is already with child." There was a stunned silence. No one moved. Henry smiled, a beaming smile that was contagious. He watched it spread around the room. Then the whispers commenced. It began as a whisper, and was soon a buzz of excitement. Although many of the men present disapproved of his choice in bride, after all, she was a mere Knight's daughter, they could not deny that they were elated that their new Queen was already carrying an heir. There were, however, a few men, enemies of the Howard family, or staunch Catholics, who were appalled by this behaviour. Their King had entered into a bigamous union with a commoner, it simply couldn't be borne. "And, therefore, I have assigned the new Archbishop of Canterbury to test the validity of my supposed marriage to my sister in law, and then the validity of my new marriage. I expect his decision soon." As the Lords filed out at the end of the meeting, Cranmer approached the King.

"Sire, about the test of your first marriage?"

"Yes?" Henry seemed jovial.

"I do not think I can come to a decision as quickly as you wish."

"What?" The note of challenge in his voice made Cranmer quake.

"Sire, there are those who disapprove of this action, both at court and in Europe. And if I make a hasty decision, they will be quick to accuse me of doing a poor job, and then they will denounce your marriage to our new Queen."

"Indeed."

"I think, therefore, it would be better if I conducted a thorough investigation, if we have a mountain of evidence to support our findings. I have no doubt that I will find exactly what you hope, but I think it would be wise to take some time over it." He held his breath, terrified that he may have angered the King.

"I agree." Cranmer let out a long, slow breath. "But just don't take too long, I would like to crown my new Queen before she goes into her confinement." He beamed at the mention of Anne's confinement, and swept from the room.

Chapter Twenty-Eight

Spring 1533

"I don't want her. Why is she in my household?" Anne asked Henry, annoyance clear in her voice. Henry had been establishing his new wife's household, filled with the most beautiful ladies of the court, mainly of the Howard affinity, but also from the greatest families in the land.

"Because she is a Seymour, my love."

"But she ruins my whole household." Anne pouted. "All my other ladies are beautiful, and graceful, and she's so, so, so, plain!" Anne shouted the last word as if it were the worst insult she could possibly give. "Her skin is pallid, and she's such a little lump. She looks like a walking corpse. I won't have her Henry, send her away or I will."

"No, my love, she won't be sent away. The Seymour's are an important family, and it is only right that their girl gets a place. And besides, she served..." Henry let the sentence hang. It was better perhaps not to mention Catherine.

"Fine." Anne sulked, and she flung herself onto a soft chair. "I'm sorry." She volunteered, in a strained voice. Anne did not like to apologise, it hurt her pride. "The baby makes me foul tempered. It is not your fault." Henry smiled. He would never have dreamed of saying that his wife was becoming grumpier by the day. He knew it was the baby, he had watched Catherine through enough pregnancies to know that the early stages filled a woman with all sorts of foul humours. Henry left Anne, and her ladies joined her.

She put her hand absent mindedly to her slightly thickening stomach and smiled to herself. What did it matter if she had the silly milk sop in her chambers? After all, she had her husband, and their unborn child, and such a plain, dull woman would never be a threat to her in any way. She put her feet on a stool and kicked off her soft shoes. Her ankles and feet were swollen and ached terribly, but it was worth it, she was suffering for her son.

"You must summon him to court." George whispered to Anne, a touch of urgency in his voice. "You simply must hear him play Annie."

"Who?" Anne was barely paying attention. It was a warm afternoon, and Anne was sitting in a window seat, half dozing in the warmth.

"Mark Smeaton. You must summon him at once."

"Why?"

"Because he plays the most enchanting music I have ever heard. Ever, Annie. I heard him play in an ale house and I swear to you I fell in love with him in an instant, for his music." Anne laughed aloud.

"My brother, in love? I didn't think you fell in love, I thought for you it was lust or nothing."

"Mock me if you must Anne, but you have to hear him. I have to bring him to you. You of all people will appreciate his talent, you will revel in his music. I swear you will not regret it for a second if you bring him."

"Oh, very well." Anne said, with a regal wave of her hand. "Have him brought to me, I must see the person who has made my brother fall in love." George left the room almost at a run to find the young musician. His playing was simply divine, it was heavenly, and he had to share this young man's gift with the world.

In April, at the Easter Sunday celebrations, Henry acknowledged Anne formally as his wife, in front of the court and the world. Anne gave generous alms to the poor, and was the image of Queenly grace, with her belly starting to round and show. Whilst the men of the court had accepted Anne with seeming good grace, the women of the country were not so accepting. Although they looked at Anne and saw beauty, and piety, and clear fertility, they were appalled that their beloved Queen Catherine had been put aside. It put a chill of fear down the spine of every woman married without a living son. If the King of England could cast aside a devoted wife, simply because he liked another woman, and his wife had given him no son, it was only a matter of time before the rest of the men of England followed suit. And those with many sons, confident in their own marriages, were shocked that the woman who had replaced their Queen was not a foreign princess, but the daughter of a simple English Knight. The people of England did not approve of any person reaching above their station. They had hated Wolsey for it, and now they would hate Anne. In spite of this, they cheerfully received the charity she was giving, and they were free with their blessings of their new, pregnant, Queen. The murmurs were just that, dissatisfied grumbles whispered under people's breath. This was not worthy enough a cause to have one's tongue split or worse, for offending the King.

After the service Cranmer announced his findings in the case of the marriage of Henry and Catherine. As expected, he announced that Henry was never married to Catherine, as she was his brother's wife, and therefore his marriage with Anne was valid and binding, and that the child growing in Anne's womb would be Henry's first legitimate heir. Within moments of this announcement, Norfolk and Suffolk were on horseback, riding full pelt towards Catherine's house at The More, under orders from the King. When they were presented to her, Catherine was seated under a cloth of gold canopy of estate, on a velvet covered throne, looking every inch the Queen. The men bowed, although not as low as they would have previously, a bow for a Princess, not a Queen.

"Has my husband sent a message?" Catherine asked, although her spies had already informed her of the nature of this visit.

"We come bearing a message from the King, madam." Suffolk began.

"His Eminence the Archbishop of Canterbury was tasked by the King to examine the validity of the supposed marriage between yourself and the King." Continued Norfolk.

"Under what authority?" Catherine asked, with regal grace.

"Under his own. Since passing the Act of Appeals it is illegal to try any internal issue outside of the realm, and therefore the King gave Cranmer the commission." Explained Suffolk.

"Fool. I know of the Act that Henry passed to disempower the Pope. That does not mean that he has the right to have his pet try my marriage."

"Cranmer has announced his conclusion madam. He has found that the marriage between yourself and the King is void, on the grounds that you were first married to the King's brother, Arthur." Norfolk said, with gentle tact.

"And the Pope himself issued a dispensation as my first marriage was not consummated." Catherine boomed. She stood, and neither man could deny she looked every inch a Queen.

"Madam, he is not your husband. He is the husband of another. And their child will be the only legitimate claimant to the King's throne. And the court prays daily that the child is a boy."

"I hope God forgives you all for your wicked ways." She said simply, and she walked from the room. Norfolk and Suffolk looked at each other with frustration, and followed.

"Unfortunately, madam, the Archbishop has ruled that the Pope was mistaken to grant a dispensation as the degree of affinity was too close, and therefore was an insurmountable barrier to your marriage. It has therefore been decided that you will hereby be known as The Dowager Princess of Wales, and your daughter will be the Lady Mary, the King's bastard daughter." Finished Suffolk. Catherine's eyes flashed, and the men were suddenly fearful that she would launch into a tirade against them. Instead, she took a steadying breath, and spoke very calmly.

"I shall, of course pray for my husband."

"He has ordered," Norfolk interrupted, coolly, "That your household will be significantly reduced, as will your income from the crown, and your lands, as is befitting your new status."

"If my husband wishes me to live elsewhere, that is his prerogative, and I shall, of course, follow his request without question. I am sure he will soon tire of his latest whore and join me at whichever palace he commands me to." Her calmness shook Suffolk. He had to break the cool veneer of peace. It was almost as though she didn't understand, like she was a simpleton.

"Madam, the King has remarried. He has taken Anne Boleyn as his wife. She is carrying his child already, and will be crowned next month in a grand ceremony. He is not your husband. He will not return to you. You should take this change with dignity, but accept it none the less."

"I shall pray for the King my husband, for if he has taken marriage vows with another whilst I still live he is a bigamist and in need of God's mercy. And I shall pray for Mistress Boleyn, as a whore, and I shall pray for the baby, as another of my husband's bastards."

"This baby will replace your daughter in the line of succession." Norfolk said bluntly.

"No one will replace my daughter in her place as heiress of England, save a son born of my body, or if I should die before my husband, a son born of a second marriage." Suffolk wanted to shake her.

Chapter Twenty-Nine

May/June 1533

Anne awoke and wished she hadn't. Every morning she awoke filled with such an exhaustion she couldn't bear to move. She was up three of four times in the night to use the pot, and the baby inside her was active, especially during the hours she was trying to sleep. She knew that this morning she had to get up. She knew she had to be dressed elaborately, and smile enchantingly. This was the morning she had dreaded, but her supporters had eagerly anticipated. It was the first day of the four day celebrations that would mark her coronation. Anne was terrified about the entire affair. She simply wanted to be Henry's wife, mother of his baby, the idea of being crowned as Queen was so intimidating. She was afraid she would be reaching too high to have the crown placed on her head. She tried to reassure herself that Elizabeth Woodville had been no greater than her when she had been elevated to Queen of Edward IV, and she sat, with grace and dignity, on the throne in the Abbey, and wore the crown, held the sceptre, and was anointed by the holy oil. This made her relax a little, but then she thought of the Queens who had followed Elizabeth, first her eldest daughter, born and bred a Princess of England, and then Catherine, born an Infanta of Spain. Elizabeth Woodville was the exception, not the rule, as far as the monarchy of England was concerned. Kings were not supposed to marry for love. They were not supposed to crown their subjects. They were supposed to marry to seal treaties, and their wives were supposed to be raised to be Queens. Anne pulled the furs over her head. She wanted to disappear off to a quiet manor with Henry and have her baby. She wasn't sure she was ready for this.

But regardless of her feelings on the matter, within hours she found herself dressed in the height of fashion, in the most sumptuous fabrics, sitting under a canopy of estate on a boat on the river Thames. Her elegant royal barge was surrounded by fifty other boats representing the guilds of London, and they moved slowly together, downriver, towards the Tower of London. The river banks were crammed with the citizens of London, and even from further afield, come to catch a glimpse of their new Queen. To those on the banks Anne looked small, and haughty. Her belly protruding in clear statement of her fertility, contrasting greatly with her hair cascading loosely down her back, symbolising virginity. Those who could see Anne closely saw, however, that the easy grace seen from the river bank was concealing clenched jaws, and hands clasped so tightly together in her lap that her nails were digging into the soft flesh of her palms. As the flotilla moved towards the tower, they were given the slightly intimidating view of a great carved dragon, belching fire over the river. Whilst the crowds on the bank called out in amazement, Anne blanched white with terror. She could almost feel the flames licking at her skin, she could almost smell singed hair and burning flesh. She focused her eyes directly ahead of her, biting hard on her lower lip, and straining to smile. The people were waiting for her to look at them, to smile, to wave as good Queen Catherine used to. Queen Anne, however, appeared steely, cold, and aloof. It did not help the common people warm to her. The kinder amongst the women commented that perhaps the baby was causing her pain, perhaps it was making her sick, or making her back ache, but the majority of the crowd thought their new Queen an austere and haughty woman.

Anne had never in her life been so grateful to see the Tower of London. Standing at the landing dock was Henry, who helped her out of the barge himself, and kissed her warmly on the lips, and ran his hand over the curve of her belly, to the wild applause of the crowd. He introduced her quickly to Sir William Kingston, constable of the Tower, and his lieutenant Sir Edmund Walsingham. Then, finally, he led her to the Royal apartments. It felt like she had been travelling for hours, when in fact only thirty minutes had passed. She begged leave of Henry to rest as soon as they were shut away, and he tenderly helped his wife onto the grand bed, and stroked her hair as she fell, almost instantly, into a deep sleep.

There were no celebrations for Anne to attend the next day and she was glad of it. She chose to stay in her bed chamber all day, something unheard of for a Queen. She was served by only one woman, and she laid upon her bed all day. In response to Henry's imploring message, desperately concerned about her, she simply replied that she wanted to conserve her energy for her state entrance to London the next day, and the baby was tiring her. Henry left her be, and Anne spent most of the day staring at the canopy above her bed. She desperately wanted to sleep, but her mind kept running over the things which were to happen over the next two days, and her stomach churned. She blamed the baby when she brought up bile, although it was nothing to do with her pregnancy. Anne was filled with a fear that clenched at her very soul and wouldn't let go. She was terrified that she would do something wrong, terrified she would betray herself as unworthy. And if she did that, would Henry cast her off as he had done Catherine? He was nothing but solicitous now, but his ardour had cooled from the moment she had told him she had missed her course. His kisses had lost their heat, and although he tenderly stroked her stomach as it expanded, he no longer showed any signs of desire towards her. Although she knew he would not lie with her for fear of hurting the baby, she had hoped that he would still want to, and it seemed that he did not.

The following morning Anne was awoken at dawn, and there was already a steaming bath waiting for her. As she soaked in the rose scented water, feeling the heat taking away the constant aches she had been plagued with since falling pregnant, she thought in wonderment of how she had arrived here, from the little girl who was scolded for running wild at Hever to Queen of England, beloved of the King and carrying his child. The baby kicked reassuringly, causing a little ripple in the water, and she giggled to herself. She had a charmed life, and if the payment for this was having to go through this ridiculous display when all she wanted was to rest, then so be it. She allowed the women to dry her, and dress her in white cloth of gold edged in ermine. She looked spectacular. The cut of the gown emphasised her growing bump, the colour made her pale complexion look like freshly churned cream, and her hair, that tempting dark hair, surrounded her like the silhouette of a halo. She walked down the stairs to the waiting litter looking every inch a Queen. As the procession set off she looked behind her. Following her were seven ladies on horseback, then two chariots filled with the matriarchs of the noble families of the Kingdom. In the first of these she saw her mother, smiling softly with pride. Behind the chariots were another twelve ladies on horseback, and a final carriage, where she could just see her sister, Mary. Anne smiled, delighted to see her sister, sat in quiet conversation with George's wife, Jane. Mary barely acknowledged her. Anne felt tears spring to her eyes, Mary still hadn't forgiven her for humiliating her in her desperation to shame Henry. She felt an urge to stand, to shout her apologies to her sister but she knew that not only would she make a fool of herself, that was not how to make Mary forgive her. Public displays of emotions were not enough for Mary, she would need to look into Anne's eyes and see the earnestness in them. There would be time enough for that later. Now she had to focus on the procession. She turned her head back to face forwards, looking at the back of the pair of white palfreys pulling her litter. The procession was going to take a long time, with frequent stops for pageants and presentations by the various guilds and merchants of the district.

The first stop was at Fenchurch street, where the men read to her in English and in French. She tried to ignore the clumsy translations, performed by labourers instead of scholars, and pretending the accents were flawless, when in fact she struggled enough to understand the English. When they stopped at St Paul's there was a group of children, dressed angelically, to read her poetry. She could barely hear the words above the cries and cheers of the crowd, but she smiled and applauded politely as if they had given her the most beautiful presentation she had ever heard. There was music at St Martin's Cross, and at Eleanor's Cross there was a ceremony of presentation, where the City of London presented her with a purse of one thousand gold marks. They then moved on to the Steelyard, for a tableau of Mount Olympus designed by Holbein, and by the time they reached Leadhall, where an angel was crowned by a falcon, Anne's symbol, Anne was stifling a yawn, and was eager to kick off her silk slippers and lay down. Her cheeks ached from smiling, and her entire body hurt from the jerking of the litter and the constant movements of the baby. After what felt like a lifetime, they reached Westminster Hall, where she was spending the night. Without even thinking of eating, Anne went to her bed, and fell asleep, fully clothed, within seconds.

It was around eight in the morning when Anne emerged from Westminster Hall. She was dressed in purple and crimson velvet, again edged in ermine, and her long hair was twisted under a jewelled coif. The Dowager Duchess of Norfolk carried her train as she walked, slowly, and carefully along a blue striped carpet through West Gate and into St Peter's. The Earl of Oxford carried her crown, and the Earl of Arundel her rod and sceptre. Henry had arranged a greater honour for Anne than had been afforded any previous Queen consort. She was seated on St Edwards chair, and crowned with St

Edwards crown, the crown of the reigning monarch. Henry had, in that little act, given Anne all the symbolic power of a King. Anne was overwhelmed. She was close to weeping as they anointed her with the holy oil, and she felt her slender neck tremble under the crown's weight as the Te Deum was sung. Then, finally, thankfully, the heavy crown was replaced with a much lighter one, one designed for a consort, made especially for Anne. The gold and precious stones twinkled in the candle light and Anne breathed a shaking breath. She was Queen, crowned and anointed. She was the true Queen of England.

Although Anne was weak with exhaustion after the build-up and the ceremony, she then had to move back to Westminster Hall for the coronation banquet. Henry did not attend, by tradition, to ensure Anne was the centre of attention. She sat, with Queenly precision, and looked above the heads of the crowds. She barely ate at all, sending the dishes to favourites as soon as she had tasted the merest morsel. She took only a few sips of wine. She desperately wanted to collapse and cry. The worse she felt, the more she tried to appear regal, and the harder she tried to look like a true Queen, the more she looked as if she were unimpressed by the effort put in for her, the more she appeared to turn up her dainty nose at the people of London, and her court. If Anne had shown some humanity, if she had hung her head for a moment, if she had allowed a tear to fall, if she had given the slightest inclination that she was overwhelmed by the situation, she would have been loved for it, but her terror of appearing human, of appearing less than a Queen, made the people surrounding her resent her, for she clearly saw herself as above them.

Chapter Thirty

Summer 1533

"Excommunicated?" Henry whispered, disbelieving.

"We knew that he would make some gesture or other." Anne dismissed, gently.

"But excommunicated?"

"He can only excommunicate you from his corrupt church. You are beloved by God."

"Am I?"

"Henry." Anne said softly. "We are married, I am crowned, I am pregnant. We are blessed. You surely cannot deny that it is a sign of God's favour that we have won."

"When you have had my heir, I shall feel much more secure."

"You are secure now." Anne said, her voice serene. Henry had been so pleased, that after the stress of the coronation, Anne had settled into the peaceful, mellow role of Queen. She sewed, she read, she sat and daydreamed about the baby growing inside her. The satisfaction of the conclusion of all of her plans had finally curbed Anne's spiky temper, and made her the Queen Henry had known she would be.

"You are right my love. Of course, you are right. If God was displeased with me, I would not have you, and our son." He kissed her tenderly, then knelt before her to kiss her stomach. Anne giggled like a girl, and Henry, gazing up at her, thought she looked younger than she ever had. Her face had plumped out in a very attractive way, her breasts were bursting out of her gown, and the satisfyingly large swell of her stomach had him convinced that his beautiful wife was carrying a son for him.

"Have you asked Catherine yet?" Anne asked. She had told Henry over a week ago that she wanted her baby to be christened in the gown that the Princess Mary was christened in, as a symbol of her child's place.

"I asked." Henry said, slowly. "But she sent me such a refusal that I should have had her arrested were she not a Princess. She says that the gown was brought from Spain with her to christen her children in, and no others."

"Oh. I understand." Anne said, though her face fell, and Henry saw the glimmer of tears in her eyes. "I had just wanted our children to be as beautifully attired as hers were."

"Oh, my love." Henry murmured, running his thumb over her lower lashes, wiping the budding tears before they had time to fall. "Our children shall be much more richly dressed than her cursed brats ever were. She could barely hand me a child she brought into the world who survived. The woman is cursed, and our children, blessed by God, will not wear the robe of a cursed one. Our children, our legitimate children, will be draped in lace and satin and anything else you wish my love." Anne looked into his eyes, and saw love there, and it made her glad.

At the end of August, Anne took her formal leave of the court, and moved into the secluded confinement chamber at Greenwich. After the magnificent church service, where the whole court prayed for the safe delivery of a Prince, Anne drank the spiced wine, and was then shut in, away from the rest of the court, in the darkened realm of women. Until she heard the heavy door shut behind her, and she looked around at the dark room, Anne had not thought of the baby being born, she had thought only of life once she had him. She was suddenly filled with fear. She recalled her one experience of a birthing chamber, when Mary had forced Catherine into the world. She remembered the blood, the screams, the nails pulling at her flesh, drawing blood. She recalled the smell of stale sweat and the revolting stench of the burning afterbirth. She was scared to death, and fear made her angry, and disagreeable. Within a few hours she was snapping at her women, who were all being so insipidly serene, and so mind numbingly dull. She wanted George to amuse her, or Mark Smeaton to play for her, but she was not allowed to see them for three long months, six weeks before, and six weeks after the birth. She instead must tolerate the inane prattle of her women, and await the arrival of her baby.

Chapter Thirty-One

September 1533

Anne's pains started in the late afternoon of the sixth of September. At first, she wondered what it was that women complained about, she couldn't understand the fuss. She felt light cramps, but nothing more than she might experience during her course. She felt sure that within an hour she would have a son in her arms without breaking a sweat. She calmly said to her women that she had felt a pain, and that she was sure the baby was coming. The older women laughed at her. She looked at them, haughtily.

"Your Grace, excuse us." Said one woman hurriedly, "But if you are standing upright and talking, the baby is nowhere near. I suggest you walk a while, and try to hurry him along." Anne was mortified about being laughed at, the woman would be punished when she was released from this prison, she would see to that. But she allowed her women to pace her around the room. She wished she had granted her mother's request to come to the birthing chamber. She had specifically refused the request, and had sent letter after letter to Mary, without a response. As evening fell her women urged her into bed, telling her to sleep as much as she could because the pain was going to get a lot worse, and she would need her strength. Anne meekly allowed them to lead her to bed, but she laid staring at the canopy, without sleeping. Stubbornly, Anne refused to sleep, even though the room was soon filled with the sounds of gentle, sleeping breaths, and the occasional snuffling snore. She must have dozed off eventually, as a little before dawn she was awoken by a pain unlike anything she had ever felt before. It felt as though her child was being clawed out of her by invisible hands. She screamed aloud, and the women jumped to attention, boiling water, and mulling the birthing ale. The pains rippled through her body progressing painfully slowly. The women were beginning to look at one another with worry. The baby should be out already. The baby was taking too long. Maybe it was the wrong way around. And then, as the afternoon was drawing in, just as they were preparing to toss the Queen in her blanket to try and turn the baby, Anne changed. Her face, which had been contorted with pain, blanched white with shock. Her waters broke, and within seconds they saw her bearing down. A woman grabbed each of her arms and tried to guide her to the bed, but Anne was beyond moving. She sank to her knees, and leant her chest on a chair. The room was filled with her raw, animal, grunting as she pushed, forcing the baby into the world. In Anne's mind, she was pushing for a week, she was running out of energy. She panted over and over again, "I can't, make it stop, I can't." But the women kept rubbing the small of her back, and sponging her neck with cool water. Suddenly, after a moment of the most searing pain where she thought she might be cleaved in two, she felt a wet slithering between her thighs, and the most almighty sense of peace. There was a split second when she didn't know for sure what had happened, and then the room as filled with the unmistakeable cry of a new baby. Anne felt the tears flowing down her cheeks. She collapsed, and finally let the women half guide, half carry her onto the birthing bed. They stripped her of her bloodstained linens, and put her in a fresh, dry, clean satin nightgown. Then they passed her the pink screaming bundle, with a shock of bright red hair. She held her baby close to her, and her breasts ached with the desire to feed. She brought the baby towards her and immediately a woman snatched it from her.

"A Queen does not feed her own child." And from the corner of the room came a buxom country woman. She cradled the baby in one arm, like it was nothing more precious than a loaf of bread, and began unlacing her bodice with the other hand. In moments, the baby was latched on to the wet nurse, and Anne felt her breasts throb and begin to leak.

"We will bind you, tightly, every day, until your milk has dried up." A midwife whispered to her. Anne couldn't see any face in the room except the round, ruddy face of the wet nurse, and the tiny little baby nuzzled close into her.

"Someone should tell the King." Anne said, aiming at an imperious tone, but sounding more like a pathetic whine, so filled with exhaustion was her voice.

"Someone has been sent your Grace."

"Has the King sent a name for him?"

"Him? Your Grace, the baby is a girl."

"A girl?" Anne felt tears swimming in her eyes, she suddenly felt drunk from the birthing ale they had forced down her, and she wanted to vomit. In the fuzzy haze that followed the birth she hadn't even thought to ask, she had been so convinced the baby was a boy. "All of that, for a girl?"

"A healthy girl. A strong, healthy girl. And there is no damage that would make it hard for you to have another child." Anne felt ill. She couldn't bear the idea of going through that pain again. And what if she bore another daughter? Or a still born child. She was more afraid now than she had ever been. Having a son was all she needed to keep her safe. Suddenly the doors burst open, and in came the King, a spring in his step.

"Where is he? Where is my son?" He asked, his eyes glittering.

"I am sorry, my Lord." Anne said, her voice strained, trying in vain to hold back tears. "I have given you a daughter." Anne dissolved into tears.

"Oh, my love." He murmured, but turned instead to the wet nurse and the midwives. "Is the baby strong?"

"Very strong your Grace. She is sucking well, and she is a good size. We have every reason to expect her to thrive. And she is beautiful. Absolutely beautiful." The wet nurse placed her little finger in the baby's mouth, breaking the latch, and held up the little bundle to her father. Henry scooped her up, and opened the sheet wrapped around the tiny body. To everyone's surprise his voice was filled with emotion.

"She is the most perfect baby I have ever seen." The little girl reached up and clenched her whole fist around her father's thumb. "Elizabeth." He said, softly, "This is Princess Elizabeth, named for my beloved mother and grandmother." He turned to his wife, and sat beside her on the bed, passing the tiny naked baby to her. "We may have wanted a son, my love, but how could I be anything but delighted with this perfect child. And this child, our Elizabeth, is so strong, and you fell pregnant with such ease, we have nothing to fear. We are both young, and I am sure once you are churched I shall get you with child again. And the next child shall be our little Prince of Wales. You must not fret, my love. God has given you a daughter to love. A son is for England, a daughter is for you. And when He is ready, He will send her a brother." He kissed her with true passion, and left. As he shut the door on the birthing chamber, that smelt so stale and was so airless, he leant against the door and a few silent tears rolled down the cheeks of the giant of a monarch. He loved his wife, and he was glad of a healthy daughter, but he needed a son so desperately. Why had God denied him again? But Henry couldn't collapse and weep like a woman, he was a King. And now he had to order the plans for the elaborate christening he had planned for his Prince to be carried out for his Princess. The Royal scribes set about changing the word Prince, on the pre-written birth notifications, to Princess, to tell the important people of the country and of Europe that the King had yet another useless daughter.

The christening was indeed grand, it far surpassed anything seen in England before. The Princess Elizabeth was to be treated as the heir to the throne. Henry and Anne did not attend the ceremony. Instead they sat in Anne's birthing chambers, dressed elaborately, and were seen by those in attendance, whispering sweetly in each other's ears. Henry was whispering of his renewed desire for his wife, and she was giggling, and replying of her eagerness to be churched so she could return to his bed. The pair barely noticed when the grand christening procession reached them, and the whole court was struck by how in love their Royal couple were. This promoted some spontaneous cheers, and finally they tore their eyes from one another to greet their baby. Anne was glowing, and she looked more beautiful than she ever had before. Motherhood suited her. Elizabeth was handed to her mother, and for the first time since she was born Anne looked at her without feeling disappointment at her gender. Instead, she was filled with love for the precious little bundle she had carried safe in her womb for nine months, and in that moment, she made a silent pledge to her daughter, that whatever happened, she would be the most important Princess to ever be born, the most beloved daughter, and a jewel of womanhood.

After the christening, Henry sent his daughter Mary a curt note. He informed her that she had a half-sister, a legitimate half-sister, and that she had been officially displaced as the first in line to the throne. She was told to no longer style herself as Princess, and she was to be officially barred from the succession as a bastard. When the former Princess received the letter, she threw it straight in the fire. She then threw the book she had been reading cross the room, and screamed.

"That whore! That whore has given him a filthy bastard daughter and he thinks to put her before me! I am the only true Princess in England, and the whore and her bastard will burn in hell for their sins." Mary was inflamed.

She worshipped her father like a God, and worshipped his crown as her birth right. She would have begrudgingly given it up to a son of her mother, and maybe even for a son of a second marriage if her mother had died first, but she would never give up her claim to the daughter of a witch, a witch who had ensnared her sainted father away from her beloved mother. "That whore will never be satisfied with her bigamous marriage and her bastard in the Royal cradle. She will not rest until I am dead. She will not rest until my mother is dead. Because while we are alive she will be nothing, and her daughter will be less than nothing." Then Mary began to laugh, a humourless, cold laugh. "But after all, the bitch only gave him a daughter. She is nothing. She will never be anything. She is another bastard daughter of a King with too many bastards to count. Maybe she can wait upon my mother, or upon me. She will learn her place." Everyone who heard that harsh laugh thought that on that day, the Lady Mary had lost her mind.

Chapter Thirty-Two

Winter 1533/4

Once Anne had gone through the ritual of churching she returned to her place as the leading lady of the court, and as the warmer of Henry's bed. The two were, perhaps, now even more in love, and now that they did not have to meet in secret they took every opportunity to be in each other's company, and in each other's bed. The more knowing ladies and gentlemen of the court looked at each other with a knowing gaze when the King and Queen were both nowhere to be found in the middle of the day. It was clear that they could not get enough of each other. But for Anne, this was heightened by the fact that she was desperate to fall pregnant again. She hadn't enjoyed pregnancy much, she had found it uncomfortable and she had felt excessively large and unattractive, and the birthing had been the thing of nightmares but she simply must conceive again, she had to have a son to make herself and her daughter safe. Henry could not criticise his wife's increased libido, but he was a little disappointed to find that now she was no longer carrying a baby, she had lost the calm serenity that he had adored, and was once again the spiky and tempestuous woman whom he had known originally. Whilst her fire was unbelievably desirable in a mistress, it wasn't becoming in a wife. But when he thought of it Henry smiled to himself, he would just have to ensure she spent the majority of the rest of their married life either carrying a child or in the birthing chamber.

Things came to a head, however, when the issue of the marriage of Henry's only recognised illegitimate son, Henry Fitzroy, was raised. The match which had been proposed was with Mary Howard, the daughter of the Duke of Norfolk. Anne was hugely in favour of the match with her kinswoman, and now she was Henry's wife she was not afraid of telling him so.

"That match must go ahead Henry."

"Anne, I can't just agree to a marriage because you want me to."

"It's not just me who thinks this is an advantageous match."

"It is advantageous to the Howard's, they are marrying into the Royal family."

"It is advantageous for your bastard, as he would be marrying a legitimate woman of the Royal affinity."

"Anne, he is my son, I cannot just marry him to your kinswoman."

"He is your bastard Henry. I wouldn't expect you to marry a pure blood son to a commoner, but your bastard can be married wherever we see fit."

"I am not sure a Howard match is fit."

"I am from the Howard family. My mother is sister to the Duke. Do you think I am no longer a fit match?" Anne was blazing.

"Regardless of what I think of your birth Anne, you are my wife, and you will do as I command, that is your role. You do as you are told and you give me sons, woman, that is all you are good for, if you can even do that!" He was spitting in her face as he yelled. Anne trembled. Her eyes filled with tears and she backed away from him, collapsing into a chair, and pulling her knees up to her chest, protecting herself. Henry looked ready to beat her, and she was sure he could kill her with his bare hands when his mood flared like this. Henry saw the terror in her eyes. It shocked him out of his temper, and he moved towards her slowly. He reached his hand out to touch her knee, and she flinched and pulled away.

"Annie, my Annie I am so sorry."

"I didn't mean to give you a daughter." She whispered. "I wanted to give you a son. It wasn't my fault." Her voice was thin and cracking with tears.

"I know, I know. I should not have lost my temper. I said things I didn't mean. And I am so sorry." She was still shaking. "Anne, sometimes I say things before I think, and then I hurt people. Please forgive me." Anne remained silent. "Annie, I beg of you, please say you forgive me. Tell me that you are not afraid of me, please. I beg of you." Still Anne didn't speak, the tears just rolled silently down her white cheeks. "And of course, it is a good match for Fitzroy to marry the Howard girl. If it will make you happy I will give my consent today." She remained silent. She was still scared. "After all, I hear the two of them are quite attached. I could not deny my own son a love match when I married you. And besides, I raised you to Queen, the Howard's could not get any mightier simply by the raising of one more girl. " He took her hand, and helped her from the chair. He wrapped his arms around her, and pretended not to feel her delicate body trembling.

Within a month, Henry Fitzroy and Mary Howard were married. It was indeed a love match, and it could plainly be seen by the beaming smiles on both faces as they were joined together. Henry felt a touch of misgivings, he had planned to legitimise Fitzroy if he and Anne failed to have a surviving son, and he was not sure he wanted to create another Howard Queen. But he looked at the joy in his son's face, and he saw Anne's genuine happiness during the ceremony, and he was sure he had made the right decision. The romance of the occasion led Henry and Anne to retire early, and spend an intensely passionate night together. Anne felt sure that night they had made a son.

The following month Anne missed her course, and she felt a familiar ache in her breasts and her belly which told her that she was once again with child. She could not wait to tell Henry. After dinner that night, the whole court was dancing in the great hall. Henry always chose Anne as his partner, and tonight was no exception. During the dance, she whispered in his ear that she was sure that she was carrying his son. Henry swept her off her feet in the middle of the dance, and when he placed her gently back on her feet he knelt before her and kissed her hands. "Thank you, my sweet, sweet love, for this great gift." He said, loudly enough for all those around them to hear, and understand that once again, just four months after giving birth, their Queen was once again with child.

Anne's happiness was marred a little the next day, however, when her sister May, who had been at court since the birth of the Princess, asked for a private conversation with her. She gladly took her sister into her private chambers, and faced her, beaming. "I am pregnant again Mary. I am sure this one is a boy. I have kept down no food in over a week, and they tell me that is a sure sign!"

"I too, am with child Annie." Mary said, softly, looking at the ground.

"What?"

"I am about four months into my time." She murmured.

"But you are widowed!"

"I am married again Anne."

"Married? To whom?"

"William Stafford. He is in the service of our uncle. We have a small amount of land in the country. I love him very much."

"You married again? To a commoner? Without my consent? You stupid foolish girl. I could have had you married to a Duke, or a foreign Prince, and yet you throw yourself away on a common man?"

"I fell in love Annie, surely you understand that?"

"You may call me Your Grace, as I am your Queen." Anne said, imperiously. She was unsure why she was so angry, that Mary had thrown herself away on a lowly marriage when she could have had anyone as the sister of the Queen of England, or perhaps she was so angry because her sister had fallen in love, and had married, and hadn't told her. Her sister no longer cared for her opinion. Anne knew that she had ruined their sisterly relationship, but she manifested her hurt through a cold, austere attitude. "You will leave my court, and not return until you are sent for. Consider yourself in disgrace."

"Yes, Your Grace." Mary said, softly, her eyes on the ground. She swept an excessively low curtsey, and left the room. She would not cry, she could not cry. Anne had ceased to be her sister years before, and she could not love her as a Queen. She could not respect her. And she was glad she no longer had to serve her. She happily packed her belongings, and she and her husband moved quietly to their small country estate.

Anne intended to tell Henry of Mary's marriage that night. Although he was no longer sharing her bed, for fear for the child, Henry came to her rooms every night after dinner with small ale, and the two would sit alone by the fire and talk of nothings until Anne was too tired to do anything but sleep. Her ankles were just as swollen with this baby, and Henry often took her feet onto his knee and gently rubbed them until the pain had gone away. But tonight, Henry seemed preoccupied.

"Anne, my love, I have something to tell you." She looked up at him through her lashes. She was already half dozing. Henry thought this may be the perfect time to tell her the news that was going to crush her. "Elizabeth is to be given her own household."

"So she should be, she is a princess after all."

"Anne, she is going to move to Hatfield, to have her own household."

"Hatfield? It is a little small for the court my dear." Anne murmured.

"No Anne, the court is not going, we are not going, just the Princess and her household." Anne's eyes snapped open.

"What?"

"It is the Royal way. The Royal children are always raised in the country."

"She is only a baby."

"The country air is better for a growing baby."

"But she is my baby!"

"Anne, the baby you must focus on is the one growing inside you. Elizabeth is safe and well, and will be treated like a Princess in her own household."

"But Henry!"

"No, Anne, no buts. She is going. By the end of the month."

"But, I don't want her to go."

"Anne, you are Queen of England, not a fish wife. You do not get to raise your children. You can order her clothes, dictate her education, and visit her regularly, but she is not yours to bring up, you have other responsibilities. Besides, the nursery must be made ready for the Prince you are giving me." Anne got up, wordlessly, and went to bed. She cried to herself that night. She cried at the loss of Elizabeth, she cried with fear that this baby would not be a Prince, and she cried that she had given up everything to be Queen, and she had no control of her own life.

Chapter Thirty-Three

Spring 1534

A few months after moving Elizabeth to Hatfield, the Royal couple went to visit her. Anne was rapidly expanding with her latest pregnancy, and despite only being in her fourth month, she was already finding walking uncomfortable, and was hardly riding. The progress by litter was slow, but Anne was so excited to see her daughter that Henry could not deny her the pleasure. Despite being desperate to see her daughter, whom she missed more than she had ever expected, Anne had a second motive in going to the house at Hatfield. When setting up the little Princess' household, Henry had requested his daughter Mary go to wait upon her sister, to remind her of her place. Anne had felt a little uncomfortable with this, and had a plan. If she befriended Mary, she could request her return to court, perhaps first as one of her ladies, and then in her own right. Henry had sworn he would not speak to Mary throughout the visit, and had sent ahead to have her kept in her rooms. He was livid that Mary had so far refused to congratulate him on his new marriage or the birth of the Princess. Mary still stubbornly refused to answer to anything other than her original title of Princess. She had acknowledged that Elizabeth was her half-sister, but would not accept her legitimacy. Whilst Henry was discussing the arrangements for redecorating a set of rooms at Hatfield, Anne crept upstairs and found the Lady Mary.

"My Lady?" Anne said, softly, smiling in the sweetly serene way she could only achieve when in the peace of pregnancy.

"Madam?" Mary responded, coolly.

"I have come to speak with you, I am hoping to repair your relationship with your father." Mary stepped forward eagerly.

"If you could do that, madam, I would find myself in your debt."

"I am sure that I can convince him to have you back at court."

"Then I owe you a debt of gratitude." Mary smiled, and Anne saw in that smile that she was her father's daughter, quick to love and quick to hate.

"I would, of course, need you to do something for me." The smile froze on Mary's face.

"And what is that that you would require of me?"

"The King will not have you at court unless you accept our marriage, and acknowledge me as Queen." Mary looked shocked. "I would not expect anything from you other than a brief statement of acceptance, and that you walk behind me, only slightly." Anne knew that she had overplayed her hand. Perhaps she should have brought Mary to court, taught her to be her friend and then she might have respected her as Queen without needing to be asked.

"I can accept no marriage between you and my father. I am aware that you are his whore. I am aware that he has got a second bastard on you. And I am aware that my sainted mother is cast aside so you can wear her jewels and sit in her place. I cannot and will not accept you as Queen. There is no Queen in England except my mother, and there is no Princess except me." Her eyes had gone small and piggy in her rounded face, she looked exactly like her father, and Anne was sure her temper would be just as violent. "Of course, I wish to be brought back into my father's good graces, and would, of course, appreciate any efforts you might make."

"I am sorry, Lady Mary." Anne said carefully. She had no desire to further inflame the temper that was bubbling within the young woman. "But if you refuse to accept your father's remarriage there is nothing I can do. He will not have anyone at court who does not accept his marriage."

"Then I shall stay here, and mind your bastard for you." Anne took in a deep, steadying breath. Mary saw her eyes open a little wider, she saw the smile falter for a second, and then Anne swept from the room. When she returned to the group she looked pale and ill. Henry, assuming she had walked too far, insisted she sat and drank small ale and ate a little bread and cheese before they returned to court. Anne knew she had made an enemy of the Lady Mary today. Little did she know that it would not have mattered what she had said, what she had done, what she had promised, the Lady Mary already despised her with all of her being, and would never have accepted her as a stepmother.

Lady Mary was not the only person struggling to accept the change, not only in the Royal marriage bed, but in the line of succession. Henry wanted no debate as to who was Queen, and who Princess, and so he swiftly passed a new act through parliament, the Act of Succession. This officially barred Mary from the succession of England as a bastard. It stated very clearly that the heir to the throne would be any son born to him and Anne, and if there was no son, the succession would pass to the Princess Elizabeth. This Act was swiftly followed by the Act of Supremacy, to ascertain in the minds of the people that Henry was the supreme head of the Church in England. Henry felt that it was not good enough for these Acts to simply become law, he made it compulsory for every citizen to sign their support for the Act, denying his marriage to Catherine, accepting his new powers and his new heir. The majority of the court and the country signed the Act freely, without complaint or hesitation. Unfortunately, Henry was devastated to hear of the relatively small number of people who refused to accept his terms, and therefore refused to sign. There was a large population in Kent who refused to sign the Act, after hearing the prophecies of a nun named Elizabeth Barton. The Holy Maid of Kent, as she was known, claimed to have foreseen the King's death, as a punishment from God for marrying Anne. Henry had her arrested, and tortured, and before her eventual execution she confessed that she had never had a seeing, and that she was simply stirring up trouble for the woman who she felt had stolen the crown. After hearing her confession, many flocked to sign the act, worried that they would be punished for having believed her. Henry was, however, merciful. Anyone who would sign would be forgiven. After all, he simply wanted people to agree to the truth as he saw it.

At Easter, The Lady Mary came to court along with the Princess Elizabeth's household. On the way into the church for the Easter Sunday ceremony, Mary not only failed to curtsey to Anne, she swept in ahead of her, as if she had precedence. Anne was unsure how to react. She could hardly reprimand the girl in church, and she felt like perhaps she would look petty for bringing it up at all. After all, perhaps Mary hadn't noticed her, perhaps she hadn't recognised her. She did not want to tell Henry of the snub, as she was still hoping to repair her relationship with Mary, eventually. She would have felt like a child going to Henry to complain of her. But it did play on her mind. She barely concentrated through the service, and was clearly distracted throughout the dinner that followed it. Henry knew there was something wrong, and spent the duration of the meal gently pushing her to tell him what had caused her trouble. Eventually Anne confessed, and before she could ask Henry not to make a scene about it, he was on his feet.

"Lady Mary." He bellowed, his voice purple with rage. "Get yourself here, now, girl." Mary slowly, deliberately, calmly, walked towards the dais, and curtseyed low, looking directly at her father, making it clear that the sign of deference was for him alone, and not for Anne.

"Father?" Her voice was soft, and she looked at him with a defiant air.

"Curtsey to the Queen."

"I am sorry, father, but my mother is not present."

"Your mother is the Dowager Princess of Wales!" He shouted. She did not flinch from his rage. Anne had to admit it, she was every inch a Princess, she was every inch her mother's daughter.

"In the eyes of God, my mother is Queen, and I shall show respect to no woman who pretends at that position." Anne put her hand on Henry's forearm, trying to urge him to regain control, and to be seated. He ignored her.

"You are an unnatural daughter, and I am ashamed of you."

"I am sorry you feel that way father."

"You are banished from court. I do not wish to see your face until you can accept your wrong doings."

"I have done nothing wrong your Grace." Mary said with an icy coolness that was reminiscent of her mother. "But I shall, of course, absent myself from court for as long as you desire." And then, without any chance for Henry to reply, she turned her back on him, in a hugely obvious sign of disrespect, and walked with deliberate grace from the hall.

As if the defiance of his daughter was not enough, Henry then heard of another betrayal. When examining the lists of those who had refused to sign the oath, Henry came across a painfully familiar name. Thomas More. He felt the bile rise in his throat. He could not allow More to refuse to sign. He

178

would become a rallying point for so many others. He had to be given the same consequences as all the others. He was arrested and thrown in the tower. Henry was careful to send a man to More every day, sometimes twice a day, asking him to sign. More refused. Henry was livid. If his oldest friend and adviser was prepared to defy him, who else was plotting against him?

Chapter Thirty-Four

Summer 1534

The court was spending a hot, lazy, summer at Hampton Court Palace. With Anne being so heavy with child it was decided not to take the court away from London. They spent their days picnicking by the river, and sitting in the shade of trees reading poetry. Anne was content. This baby, she was sure, was going to be a boy. One afternoon, as Anne and Henry were walking along the riverbank, disaster struck. They were just discussing plans for new trees in the gardens, when Anne felt a ripping, wrenching pain, low in her stomach. She doubled over and shouted out in shock. The pain was sickeningly familiar. But it was too soon, she was not quite into her seventh month of pregnancy, the baby was not ready. And yet the sudden gush of liquid between her legs told her that he was coming, regardless of whether it was his time or not.

"The Queen! Someone help the Queen." Henry called, in panic. He had never seen a woman in labour, despite the many children that he had conceived, and he was afraid. Anne's women rushed towards her, and scooped her into the palace. Henry shouted behind them, "Save my wife, please, keep my wife safe." Everyone was touched by the tenderness of his tone, but they also read the subtle undertone. He did not expect a baby not yet seven months in the womb to survive, and he needed his wife alive and well to get another child. Henry followed the women up to the Palace, and paced outside the door, listening to the anguished cries of his wife. Anne was in turmoil. She clenched her thighs together so tight it took three of her women to part them. She was hoping in vain if she held her legs tightly together her baby could not come out. The older women could see her thoughts, but knew that she could not save the baby. Perhaps if there had just been pain, they might have stopped it with rest and herbs, but she had lost her waters, and there was no doubt that the baby was coming. The pain came quickly, and in less than half an hour Anne felt the familiar urge to bear down. She tried to fight her body's needs, but she could not help it, and the baby slipped out of her after just two pushes. Silence. A deafening, painful silence.

"My baby!" Anne wailed.

"It is a boy, your Grace, but he isn't breathing."

"Save him." She begged. "Please, save my Prince, oh please God save the Prince." She continued talking, begging, praying, but her words were indecipherable through her agony. She didn't register the pain in her body, all she could feel was the emptiness in her belly, and in her arms, and the heart-breaking knowledge that no matter how much she prayed, her son was dead. Slowly, the sobs subsided, and she turned to face the wall. She did not let them change her from her bloodstained clothes, she just lay, facing the wall, refusing to speak. The grief was overcoming her in waves, and she felt as if she were drowning. She had failed her husband. Her son was dead and it was her fault. She was not sure what she had done to cause it, but she had killed her baby boy, her saviour, her Prince. How could she ever look at Henry again, after what she had done.

He sent six notes over the rest of that day. Her women read them to her, but she made no reply. He sent her jewels, and food and wine, but she didn't turn away from the wall. Anne was sick with fear. What if this was God's judgement? What if she was cursed, what if she would never have a son? What if she was going to end up like Catherine? What if Henry realised his mistake and left her? What if he went back to Catherine, as the Pope had demanded? Anne barely listened to the consoling words of love that Henry sent her every hour.

A week later, Henry sent a note saying he had moved to Windsor. It was where they had been planning to go for her confinement. She had wanted to give birth to her Prince there. And now Henry had gone without her. Anne sat up, for the first time in days. She was trembling. He had left her. Without saying goodbye. He had done this to Catherine. She had failed him, and he had left. For the first time since the loss of her son, she cried.

She was unsure if she would ever be able to stop crying. She had lost her son, her husband had left, and she had nothing left, nothing at all. She barely understood that Henry was still writing words of love to her three or four times a day. His letters begged her to come to Windsor as soon as she felt strong enough. They spoke of his need to see her, and that he had only gone because of the expense his courtiers had already gone to in order to make the road to Windsor ready for him, and to provide food and accommodation for his courtiers outside the castle.

As the days passed, Anne began to listen to the letters a little more. She began to believe him, and she began, finally, to recover enough of her strength to consider the short ride to Windsor.

She moved her small household to Windsor two weeks after Henry, and she fell into his arms, collapsed in her grief. Seeing the devastation lined so clearly in the face he loved so tenderly made Henry's heart melt in agony for her. He could not be angry with her. He could not blame her. She had done nothing wrong, God had chosen to take their son. His soul ached for the loss of yet another son, but he knew it was not Anne's fault, and he knew she was in agony too. Catherine had always borne her grief with dignity, but Anne's raw emotion was so much more endearing. Catherine had prayed constantly, Anne simply looked deflated. He wanted to console Anne, whilst he had only ever wanted to leave Catherine to her devotion.

"It is not your fault my love." He whispered gently into her hair. He felt her whole body convulse with grief.

"I lost our son. He is dead, and it is my fault." Her beautiful voice was strained.

"God took him, my love. God took our Prince into his keeping. He came too early. There is no blame in a baby coming too soon." His voice was soothing, but Anne could not believe him. "We will make a new son, my love. God wanted this boy for his own, and the next one will be ours. I have every faith my love." But Henry was feigning his conviction. Later that day, he fell to his knees in the chapel to beseech God to withdraw the curse that killed his sons. He begged God to forgive his sins, to forgive his carnal desire that had led him to bed Mary Boleyn, in case that had blighted his marriage to Anne. The tears rolled down his cheeks as he thought of the civil war that would follow his death if he did not have a legitimate, surviving son. The country would divide between Mary, Elizabeth and Fitzroy, bastard though he was. He needed a son more than ever. He was getting desperate.

Chapter Thirty-Five

Winter 1534/5

"The Pope is dead? Are you sure?" Anne asked her brother, excitement filling her voice.

"I am sure. And I am sure the King already knows." He called after her as Anne half walked, half ran to Henry's apartments. She burst in to find Henry encircled by members of his council.

"Is it true? He's dead?" Anne asked.

"Yes." Henry said slowly. "But it solves nothing. The new Pope is not sympathetic to our case."

"What?"

"He has sent me a notification that I must return to Catherine. He has as good as declared you a whore, and Elizabeth a bastard."

"What?"

"He has declared to the world that you and I are not married in the eyes of Rome, regardless of what the Church of England says. This makes Elizabeth a bastard, not a Princess."

"He can't do that."

"Yes, he can."

"But we can ignore his foolish prattle. Why should it matter to us?"

"It matters because now no one will want to marry Elizabeth. She had the taint of a bastard. Maybe if we had a son the Pope would be more sympathetic, but two wives and two daughters does not make a very convincing argument Anne." He barked, and then went back to his advisers. Anne was shocked. He had been so loving about the death of their baby, the baby she had named Edward in her own mind, and for him to now use it against her was hurtful and cruel. She turned on her heel, and left his apartments. She was scared. What if he followed the Pope's advice? What if that is what his advisers were recommending. She had to become pregnant again, and quickly. Henry still visited her bed most nights, and his attentions to her were just as loving and diligent, so she had plenty of reason to hope for another baby. But since the loss of her son, she had cried every time her course had arrived, as it reminded her very clearly that she was not having a baby, that she was still failing in her role.

On the first day of the twelve night celebrations, Anne had good news for Henry.

"Are you sure?" He asked, his face lighting up with excitement.

"I have missed my course, I am swelling, and, well, I know. We are having a baby." The delight rippled over his face.

"When?"

"August, I think."

"Oh, my love." He buried his face in her neck, and sighed with happiness. Anne was determined that this baby would be a boy, and that he would thrive. She would take no risks. She would not ride at all, she would eat whatever her physicians recommended. She would not lose this child.

In the first week of the new year it became clear that Anne was not the only one worried about a miscarriage. Jane Boleyn, George's wife, ran frantically into Henry's presence in such a state of panic that Henry grabbed her by the elbow and led her to a window.

"Is it the Queen? Is it the baby?" He demanded.

"No. Not exactly. It is Purkoy, the Queen's favourite dog." Henry relaxed his tight grip and looked a little annoyed that he was being interrupted for something so trivial. "He has fallen out of a window. He is dead your Majesty. No one dares tell the Queen, no one wants to distress her, in case, in case." Jane could not say the words, but Henry understood her panic.

"I shall tell her. I shall go to her at once and break the news." Anne was lying on her bed, resting. Pregnancy always made her lethargic, and this one was worse than the previous two. She barely registered the door opening, and her husband coming in, and sitting on the bed next to her. It was only when he raised her to sitting and held her hands that she began to worry.

"What has happened?"

"Annie, my love. I have bad news. I do not want you to distress yourself, for the sake of the baby."

"Tell me quickly Henry, is it my mother, my brother?"

"No, no. Be still angel. It is Purkoy. I'm afraid he has had an accident. They could not save him." Anne shook. Henry caught her up in his arms and rocked her gently as she wept.

"Oh no. He was my little joy." She sobbed.

"I know my angel, I know."

"I do not get to hold my daughter every day, Purkoy was my substitute, I loved him so dearly."

"I know. Would you like me to buy you another dog? Would that make the loss less great?"

"No. I cannot replace him. He was too special."

"Then what can I do? I will do anything to make you smile again, to make you easy in your mind." Anne paused.

"I want Elizabeth at court. Not now, but when I have had this baby, I want Elizabeth to come to court and live with us."

"Anne, you know why she is in the country."

"We can keep her safe Henry. It is the only thing I want in the world, except for the safe delivery of our son. Please."

"Annie, I don't know."

"Please, Henry. When I have given you your son, please let me have my daughter with me. Please. I beg you."

"I. Well. When you have had the baby, then we shall come to an arrangement. Perhaps Elizabeth could spend some months at court, and you could spend some at Hatfield with her?"

"Oh, my love, I thank you." Anne fell on his hands with kisses. Henry turned his face from her gratitude. She did not know he was lying. She did not know that he would say anything she wanted to hear, just to keep her still and calm and keep the baby safe. He would do anything to keep this baby safe.

Chapter Thirty-Six

Spring 1535

It was an unusually warm spring morning. Alice, one of Anne's young maids, woke up with an ugly rash on her usually pale skin. She was terrified that the young Knight she had been courting would see it, and be repelled, so she quickly covered her face in thick layer of white lead paste. While the other women commented to each other that such a young, pretty girl needn't paint herself up like that, they largely ignored it. Anne smiled to herself when she saw Alice's face. The poor girl was looking moon eyed at a young man in Henry's service, she was obviously trying very hard to impress him. She dismissed the thought, and went back to sewing tiny lace hats for the baby. She felt him wriggle about, and she rested her hand on her belly. She was sure that this baby would be fine, he was so strong, she marvelled at it.

As the day went on, Alice began to feel hot, and dizzy, and her limbs ached like she had ridden for three days straight. She tried to dismiss it, and to continue serving. She needed to be there when the King's men came, and surely it would not be long. She got up to fetch a glass of cool small ale from a jug on the side, and her world went black. There was a small scream when the ladies saw Alice fall. Anne jumped to her feet and knelt by the girl. She touched her face and felt it burning.

"Bring me water and cloths, she has a fever." Anne called, and she lifted

Alice's head onto her knees, and gently patted her face with cool wet linens until the girl came around. "Now, you are to go to bed. I will hear no arguments. You will go to bed, and I will have a physician sent for. You gave us quite a scare."

"I'm sorry, your Grace." Alice whispered.

"Can you stand?"

"I am not sure." Anne beckoned forwards her mother and Jane Boleyn.

"Take her to her bed, and see that she rests. Once she is settled, fetch her a physician." The women nodded, and set about following their orders.

The following morning, three other women woke with the rash. It was then, when it could be clearly seen that this was a contagion and not an isolated case, the King had to be informed.

"You must shut yourself away from your women." Henry insisted.

"Oh Henry, I cannot do that and you know it."

"Then those infected must be sent from court until they are recovered. You cannot be in a room with them. It may harm the baby."

"I am sure the baby is fine Henry. He kicks me readily enough."

"I must insist Anne, I will send the women from court until they are well again. We cannot risk this baby."

But it was too late. That night, Anne was awoken by an all too familiar pain. As she moved her sheets she saw they were stained with her blood. In her heart, she knew she was losing the baby, but she could not move for terror. The tears rolled down her cheeks. Still she didn't call out. Even though she felt the regular pulsing pain rippling through her body, even though she knew that the baby was already lost. As the intensity of the pain increased she called out, and her women ran in and sat with her, as the tiny baby, no longer than from her fingertips to wrist, came easily out of her body. Someone must have awoken the King, because he strode in, his face furious, thick furs over his nightshirt.

"You stupid, common, fool!" He bellowed. "You risk the life of our Prince to soothe a servant? She is not your equal Anne. You ought to remember that any child of ours is more important than any other person in this entire court. You cannot just risk our child like that Anne. It is irresponsible. It is stupid. It proves that you are not worthy of the title of Queen." Anne was still in her bloodstained sheets, the baby was bundled in a corner, wrapped in linen. Anne was silent. She curled into a ball, rolled in her own blood, and Henry saw her shoulders shake. At first, he did not care. "I should cast you off for your blasted foolishness. Do you care nothing for our babies, for my succession? You have killed two of our children Anne, from your own foolishness." His words hit Anne like a physical blow. She gasped, and then she began to rock, slowly and gently. It was then, when Henry saw the raw anguish on his wife's face that he realised that berating her would not bring back their baby. Shouting would not fix the problem, and in fact, all he was doing was scaring his wife, and hurting the one person who could feel his pain. He sat next to her, careless of the sticky blood that was bound to ruin his expensive furs.

"Oh Annie, I'm sorry. My grief took over me. Of course you were going to tend to someone you care for. And perhaps you had already contracted the illness before you even knew it. I am so sorry." She stared past him at the wall. "There will be more babies."

"I have killed our sons." She whispered.

"No, no my love, it's not your fault."

"You just said it. You said I killed them."

"You know that when I am distressed I say things I don't mean."

"You blame me. You think I chose for our sons to die."

"No." She looked him in the eye, tears streaming down her face, barely able to see him.

"I had to feel my body repel those babies, Henry. I had to go through a birth for both of our lost sons. I felt them leave my body, and I didn't hear a cry, and I knew that our boys were dead. I knew that they were dead the moment I felt the pains and I could do nothing to prevent it. I could not stop them from being born, any more than I could have stopped Elizabeth. At night, I dream about the tiny face of our boy who came too soon, and now I shall dream of this baby too. I see them in my dreams Henry, every night, I see the dead face of the boy I lost, and now I shall see two dead faces. Am I not punished enough? Does God not punish me enough by stealing my sons away and making me see their faces. Must you punish me too?"

"Oh, my Annie I am sorry." He held her close. She kept her body rigid. She let him hold her, but she did not relax in to him, she did not take support from him, nor did she give any out. "There will be more babies. We will have many sons. We are both young."

"I am not young Henry. I am very old. You have taken my youth." And with that she turned to the wall to experience her grief in the only way she knew, alone, and silent.

Henry returned to his bedchamber, and dismissed the page who normally slept in a pallet bed at the foot of his bed. When he was quite alone, Henry wept for the loss of yet another baby. And he wept for the pain he had caused his wife, and he wept because he feared she no longer loved him as she once did.

When the sun rose the next morning Henry summoned Cromwell to him. He had decided in the dark hours of the early morning that his sons were blighted because of his rift with Rome. He needed Cromwell to heal the wounds with Rome, so that he and Anne could have a living son. He was becoming desperate.

"Your Grace, I beg your pardon, but God is not displeased with your break from Rome."

"Are you sure?"

"Yes. If he were, he would have taken your daughter too."

"Then why do my sons keep dying? Why do they emerge from the womb before they are ready? Why?" His voice cracked.

"My King, may I be frank?"

"Of course."

"God may be displeased because although you have distanced yourself from the corruption of the Roman church, there are still many ungodly practices going on in your churches."

"Oh?"

"It is my opinion that God is not punishing you for things you have done, but is showing you that you have much left to do before his church is pure." Henry nodded, thinking.

Anne was still curled in a ball on her bed. The women had managed to change the sheets, but she would not allow them to remove her bloodstained shift. She was in agony. Her insides were burning from the birth, and her heart was breaking. She was grieving the loss of her baby, and she was grieving for what she was sure was the end of her marriage. For how could Henry love her after she had lost two of his sons.

Chapter Thirty-Seven

Summer 1535

"A Cardinal." Henry spat, his voice filled with venom. "He has made that old fool a Cardinal? Has the Pope lost his mind?"

"It appears so." Cromwell responded, calmly.

"He's in the Tower. He is in the Tower for treason, he refused to sign the oath."

"I would guess, your Majesty, that that is the reason Rome has promoted him from Bishop Fisher to Cardinal. I think it is another attack against your marriage, and your supremacy."

"Well by the time they send his damned Cardinal's hat he will have no head to put it on, mark my words. I want every traitor in the tower tried. Immediately. If they are found guilty, I want them dead. Do you hear me?"

"Yes, of course. You do remember that Thomas More is also imprisoned, on the same charge."

"He is a traitor. Traitors deserve to die. That is all there is to it." Henry roared in rage. "Set the trial dates. Do it, Cromwell, or the next trial of a traitor will be yours." Crowell scuttled off to the Tower, to arrange the trials, and to have a new scaffold build on Tower Hill. There would be a lot of bloodshed. Henry was becoming more and more ready with the axe and the noose for those who disagreed with him, he was becoming vicious and ruthless as he aged. It was almost as though the less secure he felt, the longer he was without an heir, the more worried he was about being usurped, the more he wanted to punish those who disagreed with him. Maybe it wouldn't matter that he had no son to follow him, maybe he would have no people to rule by the time he died anyway.

Fisher was found guilty of treason quickly, just as Henry wished, and was beheaded before his Cardinal's hat arrived from Rome. He was quickly followed to the scaffold by Thomas More. On the morning of his execution, Anne went to Henry's rooms.

"You will send him a pardon, wont you?"

"Why?"

"Because you love him like a father. Because he is one man. Because you don't want him to die."

"He is a traitor. He denies my supremacy. He denies our marriage. He denies our daughters right to the throne. You should wish him dead."

"Henry, I could not wish any man dead. He has a family, he has a life. Why are you taking it?"

"Because he is a traitor." His voice was edged in steel. "And you should, perhaps, be more concerned with making another baby to inherit the throne, than with saving the life of a man who has no love for you. I shall come to your chamber tonight."

"No." Anne could not bear the idea of him touching her whilst More's blood was on his hands. "It is my time, I cannot admit you." He nodded, he was barely listening. Anne might be returned to his good graces after the death of their baby, but he was more preoccupied with his fascination with death than he was with her at the moment. Anne walked back to her rooms with grace, and spent the day sewing and acting as though she had no cares in the world. She ignored the booming cannons from the Tower that told her that More had died, that a good man had died. After dinner, she went straight to her bedchamber. She sat up in bed all that night, crying silently, so as not to wake the maid lying at the foot of her bed. She had been right to fear Henry in the beginning. She knew now that all those times she had thought his anger was so great he might kill her, that he was truly capable of it. The man she loved so intensely it hurt, was becoming a monster. He was becoming a monster, and she could not make herself stop loving him.

Chapter Thirty-Eight

Autumn 1535

"I hate it here Madge." Anne confided to her cousin, Madge Shelton. "There is an awful atmosphere." The court was on progress, and was staying at Wolfe Hall in Wiltshire, home of the Seymour family. "Henry seems to love it though."

"Have you not heard the rumours?" Madge asked, her eyes gleaming. She loved nothing more than a gossip.

"I have not. But I suppose I will now." Anne tried to act like she wasn't interested, but she was eager to hear. The Seymours were no friend to the Howard family, and she wanted to know what the court was saying about them.

"They say that Edward Seymour's wife was playing him for a fool."

"Oh, many a foolish wife betrays her husband. It is unseemly, but still."

"Wait. The man she betrayed her husband with was," She paused for dramatic effect, "his father."

"What?"

"Edward Seymour has found that the two sons he thought were his, might in fact be his half-brothers. She had been cast aside, as I am sure you can understand, and the whole house is filled with unspoken anger at the affair." Anne laughed aloud.

"And the Seymour's were so self-righteous when Henry began courting me. And they are there sharing women around the family." She laughed out loud. She looked to the corner of her chamber where little Jane Seymour was sitting, sewing, apparently oblivious both to the conversation and the awkward atmosphere in her family home.

"Edward has just remarried. A lady called Anne, with an unspotted reputation."

"He best keep her on a dog's leash, in case he finds her in bed with some other member of his family." Anne laughed cattily. "Why did I not know if this?"

"The rumour surfaced whilst you were, well, after you, when you were still..." Madge was floundering.

"When I lost my baby." Anne said, softly.

"Yes. And then when you emerged from your rooms there was such a spree of executions that no one remembered the Seymour scandal."

The court stayed at Wolfe Hall only a few days, and then moved on to Winchester, and finally arrived at Windsor at the end of October. The court went for a great deer hunt, but Anne chose to stay at court. Henry looked at her with concern, but was far too busy wanting to try a new horse he had acquired over the course of his progress, so he left his wife with just her mother in attendance and went for the hunt. Anne spent the day sat in the padded window seat of her presence chamber, looking lazily out of the window. She had sewing on her lap, but was not attending to it. Mark Smeaton was sitting in one corner of the room, playing melodies on his lute that should make her weep, but she could barely keep enough focus to listen to them. Her mother guessed the secret Anne was holding tight in her heart. After all, there was only one reason that Anne would opt to miss a hunt, there was only one time she would sit in quiet contemplation when she could be being active. But a mother also knows not to speak of the reason for the change in behaviour, not to mention that her daughter had slipped off her shoes and was absentmindedly rubbing at swollen feet and ankles. A mother doesn't mention the extra strain in her daughter's bodice, or the fact that she has struggled to keep any food down for days. A mother knows that her daughter would want to tell her husband before the rest of the world. So, Elizabeth Boleyn sat quietly, and watched her daughter with hope in her heart.

The hunt returned an hour or so before dinner. Henry bounded straight up to Anne's chamber to tell her of the kills of the day. Anne listened to him without interrupting, with a slightly glazed expression on her face.

"Are you quite well my love?" He asked, in a panic, touching her face to see if she had a fever.

"Oh, I am very well." She smiled a soft smile. Henry looked confused. She shifted her gaze from his face, to her stomach, and back again.

"Are you?"

"I am."

"And it will be?"

"I am sure."

"And it will come?"

"In the early summer." He kissed her tenderly. Gone were the days when a jubilant Henry would scoop his wife of her feet for announcing a new baby had stirred within her. Now he showed her affection in a much gentler way. He was so scared that any wrong move by him would cause damage to the baby, and so he treated Anne like glass.

Chapter Thirty-Nine

Winter 1535/6

In early January, Catherine of Aragon, alone, and abandoned, died in her bed. When the news reached court, Anne went straight to her privy chamber and began to write a letter of condolence to her stepdaughter. She beseeched Mary, yet again, to simply accept her marriage, and she could come to court with all the honours of the daughter of the King. Anne hoped with all her heart that the poor motherless girl would want her father in her life so desperately she would give in to his one request, and accept the marriage.

That afternoon Henry summoned all the foreign ambassadors to the Great Hall. He had Elizabeth brought from her nursery, where she had been staying over the Christmas season, to show off to them all.

"This is the Princess Elizabeth. My one true heir. The death of the woman who had claimed to be my wife for so many years has made this little girl safe in her inheritance. She is a perfectly formed child, and she would be a perfect bride for any Prince of Europe." The ambassadors stood shocked. "And now, there is no 'other Queen', and you can no longer deny this Princess her legitimacy." They all felt that perhaps this was in poor taste, and they all looked, covertly, at the Spanish ambassador, a close personal friend of Catherine. He looked horrified, Henry seemed to be glorying in the death of a great woman who had shared his life, his throne, and his bed for twenty years. "And what is more, in one week's time there shall be a grand tournament, to celebrate England's freedom from the prospect of civil war." He was grinning broadly as he left the room, handing Elizabeth to her nurses as he went.

Anne was mortified at the prospect of a tournament to celebrate a woman's death. It was, to her, the most gaudy and macabre spectacle that could be imagined. But she did as she was bidden by Henry, and she helped to make the arrangements, organise the challengers, and sent orders to the kitchens to arrange a spectacular feast. It was agreed between Henry and Anne that she would not attend the joust. She felt that there was far too much excitement involved, and that it might be bad for the baby. Instead, she would preside over the feast, and present the prizes later on. Henry had sworn to Anne he would not fight in the lists, until they had an heir it was not safe for him to risk his life. Henry agreed willingly, he was starting to feel a little too old to compete against the young men of court. However, the ever-changeable King had decided, by the time he arrived at the arena, that in fact he was going to ride, and he sent a page running back to fetch his horse and his armour. Henry rode out against Sir Francis Bryan. He was oblivious to the shouts around him as he set off for his run, he assumed he was being cheered by his adoring people. If he had listened he might have heard them shout that his visor was still up. And if he hadn't left his visor up, perhaps he would have been safe. As it was, Bryan's lance hit him straight in the face. Henry was knocked from his horse, and was unconscious before he hit the ground. They brought him back to the palace on a stretcher. Maybe Anne would have been prepared if she had been looking out of the window, but she was dozing on her bed, waiting for the trumpets which would announce the end of the joust, when she would need to prepare herself for the feast. Instead, she was awoken with a start by her uncle, the Duke of Norfolk, storming into her bedchamber.

"Anne, get up. Now. The King is hurt, he might be dead, get up you stupid girl." Anne stood, but the world span around her. She could not focus, she could not balance, and she fell to the floor, hard.

Anne came to on the floor of her chamber, women flocking around her. She knew something was wrong. Their faces were so pained, it could not be good news.

"The King." She whispered. "Is the King alright?"

"He is slightly better, we think." Madge Shelton said, softly. No one would meet her eye. She didn't understand. And no one seemed prepared to explain. Anne sat herself up, and looked around the room. Her eyes fell on a pile in a corner, a pile of bloodstained linen. Her hand went straight to her belly.

"No." She moaned, softly. "Someone, please tell me. My baby? No!" She struggled to breathe, she was taking great gasping breaths but her head was swimming. "Is my baby? My baby?" She gasped.

"I am so sorry, my love." Whispered her mother. She clung to her mother's arm like a child and wailed. "It was a son." Her mother murmured into her hair. "The King is awake, he knows." Anne moaned, this was true intense pain that was running through her body. Her tiny baby, born after only fifteen weeks in the womb, had no chance of survival. It had been so small that he had come without enough pain to wake her from her faint. She held her empty stomach, willing the baby to move, to kick, to prove them wrong, but another look at the bloody pile that was being quickly bundled into the fire told her otherwise. The chamber doors were flung open, and in walked Henry. his face was bloodied, and he was limping heavily, using George Boleyn's arm to steady him.

"My love." He whispered.

"I am so sorry." She said brokenly. "They told me you were hurt, that it looked life threatening. I fainted. I came around and, and, oh Henry our baby." She dissolved into tears. Henry got, awkwardly, to the ground and held her. He could not find words to say to console her. He understood. In his heart, he knew that the shock of the news could have brought the baby on, well before his time, but he could not admit to himself that this was his third child by Anne who had come too early. His third son Anne had failed to provide. "At least you are alive. I was so afraid." Anne mumbled into his chest. Henry did not trust himself to speak. He was sure if he did, the emotion would pour out like a wave, and he would not be able to take back the words that might erupt. Henry left Anne to her women, they needed to change her from her clothes into a nightdress, and give her a draught to make her sleep. He summoned Cromwell to his rooms. Cromwell pretended he could not see that Henry's eyes were red with tears. He pretended not to hear the quaver in his voice.

"The Queen heard of my accident and went into a dead faint. The baby came. There was nothing they could do."

"Yes, your Grace."

"I believe you were right. God is punishing me for the appalling state of the Church in my country. Tell me what to do. I must fix the problem. I must have a son. Do whatever you have to do, Cromwell. Fix it. Please." Cromwell bowed himself out of Henry's presence. He called his man servant to him straight away.

"The King has given us the go ahead. Send out the men. Investigate every religious house. I want to know it all. We will root out the old ways, and we will have the King destroy them, until all that is left is the new faith." The man nodded, silently, and went off to follow his master's instructions.

Chapter Forty

March 1536

Whilst Henry sat in peace talks with the Imperial ambassador, Cromwell was shut in his offices, working alone, on his latest obsession. Although he started with honest intentions, since rising at court Cromwell had become obsessed with honours, with position, and with income. He was jealously protective over his own, and lusted after that of others. After having watched the fall of several men over his years at court, he had seen that their honours were divided up between those in favour with the King. Currently, Cromwell was high in favour, and perhaps he could profit if some noble was to fall from power. He had started working on a list of who owned what within the realm, and used that to work out who was vulnerable. And then it came to him, a delicious idea, one which, if he pulled it off, would not only leave him with the pickings of vast estates, but would also put him in a position to supply the most influential person with the King. If he were to topple the Boleyn family, he could choose the next Queen. At first, the idea seemed far-fetched, after all, Henry was wildly in love with Anne, but then he started to see a chink in her seemingly infallible armour. Anne had failed to provide Henry with a son. The King, so obsessed with God's will, could be persuaded to believe that the death of their sons, before they were even born, was a blight by God. And he was sure he could find something that would convince Henry to abandon the marriage he made for love, to start the fall of her family, and Cromwell, the devoted servant who showed him the light, could reap the rewards.

When the peace negotiations took a break, Henry went for a walk with the newest member of his privy council, Edward Seymour. Seymour was witty, and amusing, and very intelligent, and he appealed to Henry. Of course, Henry, blinded by the dazzling young man, didn't realise that Seymour was flattering him for his own advantage. Henry was always sure people loved him for himself, although mainly, they loved him for what he could provide for them. It was a well-known fact that the most important and influential woman at court was the one in the King's bed. A Royal mistress was the most powerful woman at court, and every family sought to place their daughters, sisters and cousins into the King's bed. Edward Seymour was exactly the same. His sister, Jane, was no beauty, that was plain to see, but she was malleable, she was mild, and she was adoring. He had seen, quite rightly, that Henry's beloved Queen was still just as fiery, and just as wild as she had always been. He knew that Henry was getting older, and that sometimes Anne's energy was too much for him. He rightly assumed that this meant that if Henry was going to take a mistress, she would be the antithesis of his wife, and that was where Jane came in. Jane worshipped her brother, and was such an obedient girl that she would have followed him to the end of the earth if he asked. He had no doubt that if he were to ask her to go to Henry's bed she would do it, blithely and without passion. But the women who bedded Henry with ease were the quickest to be discarded, the ones who lasted were those he had to pursue. The ones who achieved most for their family were the ones who refused at first. And this was what Edward was coaching his sister to do. To deny, whilst encouraging, to withhold, whilst offering, to shy away, whilst enticing. He was in short, following the example of Anne, he was going to use her own tactics to supplant her in the King's mind, and in his bed. It mattered not that she was Queen, all that mattered was that Henry could be distracted, and then Anne would lose her political power, and her faction would be in decline.

When Henry met Jane, he couldn't help but be pulled in by her. If he thought objectively, he knew that he didn't find her even slightly physically attractive, and she had little by way of dazzling conversation. But she was peaceful, and she sat at his feet staring up at him with loving eyes. Anne looked at him with furious passion, with eyes that could devour him. Anne challenged him, Anne inflamed him, Anne exhausted him. Jane was simply a meek girl who would sit and adore him. He enjoyed that, he appreciated the contrast. It took none of the passion from his love for Anne, but he found himself drawn to Jane, he wanted her company more and more, and was keeping company with Edward more frequently so he might bring his sister into his presence. He decided to send her a gift, a gift of money was ordinarily enough to ensure a girl would drop her guard and part her thighs. He would enjoy it with her, he was sure. She would lie beneath him and gaze at him with those adoring eyes, she would let him do his business without question and then she would leave when asked. Anne had no trouble conceiving, and he was sure that she would soon be with child again. With a pregnant wife whose bed he couldn't visit, no one could blame him for taking a mistress. Especially one like Jane, who would ask for nothing, and who would readily relinquish her place when the Queen was once again ready to rejoin the King in bed. He sent a purse of money, and a letter, and sat, smiling to himself, wondering how she would express her gratitude. He was not expecting the purse returned, still full, and the letter still sealed. The messenger was quaking.

"What is this?" Henry asked.

"The Lady returned it Your Majesty, with a message."

"What was the message."

"She said that she cannot accept a gift or a letter from you, and she could only receive gifts and letters from a man once God has provided her with a husband." The man gabbled his message. He was terrified of the King's reaction. He was confused, however, as the King began to laugh. A full bellied, booming laugh. She was playing coy. She wanted a good marriage before she would join him in bed. He began to list noblemen in his mind, who might be amenable to a promotion in exchange for his wife's favours.

Edward Seymour absent mindedly stroked his sister's hair.

"Well done, little sister. You are doing something great for your family." Jane didn't speak. She bowed her head. She had been a little neglected as a child, by everyone other than Edward. She was plain, the only plain sibling in a brood of enormously bright and attractive children. She had been taught humility and timidity, so that she had at least that to recommend her in marriage. Her family had expected little Jane to marry a nobody, a third son, perhaps, with little fortune, and little ambition. All except Edward. Edward had known from a young age that his plain, ignored little sister would outshine them all. He petted her, and fuelled her adoration for him, because he knew one day she would be in a position to reward him. "I knew that you would do well, little Jane Seymour. Maybe one day you will give the King a son, a half Tudor, half Seymour would be a formidable child. You could match your child with the nobility of Europe, a King's bastard is nothing to be sneered at. Jane gazed up at her brother with the same devoted adoration with which she looked at her King. Edward softly stroked her cheek and kissed her forehead. "Do as I tell you moppet, and you will have jewels to rival a Duchess I'd wager, and he will make you a Countess for sure." Jane had no ambition, she cared not about jewels, and about titles.

"And I would give them all to you, readily, brother." Her true devotion was to Edward alone, her admiration for Henry was all at Edwards command.

As the court gathered at Greenwich for Easter, Edward Seymour and his wife were given Cromwell's usual rooms. He happily gave them up, for he knew it was so the King could meet with Jane Seymour without causing a scandal on her name. If the King took a mistress, the hold of his wife would be weakened, and he could set about his plan to bring down the Boleyn's, they would be begging him for favours. He forgot that Anne had been his friend, he forgot he had supported her. His greed overtook any loyalty he might have had. Anne had not given him enough rewards, and so he would turn to those who might.

Anne was devastated at the new arrangement of rooms. Cromwell's rooms adjoined the Kings, she knew that Henry would only order that change of rooms so he could pursue an affair with the Seymour girl.

"I will not be disrespected in this way Henry."

"Leave us." Henry barked to Anne's ladies who filled her presence chamber. "Now!" There was a scurrying as the women left the room. The gossip was already starting. "My love, I did not mean to cause offence. I simply..."

"You simply want to make Jane Seymour your whore. Could you not have even picked a pretty girl Henry. There will be talk. If you choose such a plain girl to take to your bed then there must be something hugely lacking in our marriage."

"There is nothing lacking my love."

"Except a son. Which the world keeps reminding me."

"And I would only take a mistress once you are again with child."

"Oh Henry, you are making excuses. Admit it. You no longer desire me. I have carried four children, and my body is ruined. You no longer want me."

"Don't be ridiculous. I still want you as much as I did the first time I saw you."

"Don't lie to me Henry." Anne screeched. She flew at him, trying to claw at his face. He caught her wrists and threw her away from him. She landed on the floor.

"Put away your claws, you cat." He snarled. "Do not forget that I am your King."

"You may be a King, but you are also a faithless husband."

"I have given you everything I promised. I put aside my wife and I married you. I made you Queen. It is you who has yet to fulfil your promises."

"I do my best. What can I do if you are more interested in some milky faced cow than your wife. How can I make a baby on my own!"

"Anne, you sound pathetic."

"I love you." She screamed like a curse. "And it crushes my heart to see you so blatant in your affection for another woman. For one of my ladies."

"You forget yourself madam." Henry's tone was warning, but Anne was beyond caring. She flew at him again. This time he caught her tight in his arms. He held her against him as she tried to beat his chest. She pulled her face away to look at him. He kissed her, hard, and within moments the two were on the floor, her skirts around her waist, his breeches unlaced. The passion between them was even more intense than it had ever been previously. The fight had inflamed them both to such a point of desire that they could not even make it to a bed. Once he had finished, Henry laced up, and went to the door.

"Business to attend to, my love." He flashed her a cheeky grin. Anne righted her skirts, and smiling herself, let him go. It wasn't until he was gone that she realised that she had not obtained a promise that his mistress would be dismissed. And as Henry went to his own rooms, panting slightly with exhaustion, he could not help but wish he could go and rest his head on the lap of little Jane Seymour, have her stroke his hair and calm him. He was amazed to find that he could not resist her.

Chapter Forty-One

April 1536

Anne could barely control her laughter, as she sat in a window seat with her brother. "That cursed Imperial ambassador Chapuys refused to have me in the peace talks."

"Why is that funny, Anne? It is a serious snub."

"So, Henry arranged for them to take a walk, and manipulated the walk so they crossed my path on the way back from chapel. Chapuys had to either bow to me, and therefore acknowledge my position as Queen, or risk infuriating Henry." Anne could barely breathe with laughter. George finally saw the humour.

"So, what did he old goat do?"

"Oh, he made me a weak little bow, but he glared at me like he hated me."

"You seem a little too amused, what is the private joke?" George whispered, bowing his head towards his sister. She leant in so their foreheads were almost touching.

"The whole court is whispering that the King is losing his love for me in favour of that soppy Seymour girl. And he has just caused such discomfort in such an important ambassador in order to make him show respect to me, and to amuse me. He might look at that pathetic little thing with lust, but it is still I who holds his heart. And as the word of that slips around the court, those who have been circling around her as if she is the rising sun will have to beg my forgiveness of bended knee, for I am still the beloved Queen, and she is a barely cared for mistress." Anne's laughter was close to hysterical. George laughed a little in response. He understood that his sister felt she was walking a fine line, attempting to keep Henry's favour. Anne had always laughed most emphatically when she was dying inside. He understood at once that his sister was glad to have Henry's love still, but was scared that next time the mistress would win out, because Henry showed no sign of giving up on his love for her either. George and Anne both knew how close love and hate were, and they were both acutely aware that if Anne did not fulfil her promise to give Henry a son, the love that had led him to humiliate an ambassador would be used to belittle the Queen herself, as it warped into hate.

It was only three days later that Anne worried her influence was, in fact, in the decline. Anne had requested the newly vacant position of Knight of the Garter for her precious brother, but instead it had gone to Sir Nicholas Carew, a great friend of the Seymours. Anne knew that Jane had asked for it, and it had been granted. She knelt before Henry that night when he came to her bedchamber. Her hair was loose around her shoulders, and she was wearing only her linen shift. She looked like an angel, Henry thought.

"My Lord, I had begged that my brother George be honoured with the garter. I must know why he was denied?" Her voice wasn't hard, or angry, and that made Henry feel guilty. He had simply succumbed to the asking of Jane Seymour. George had probably deserved the position more. Now he needed to reassure his wife, who was kneeling before him beseechingly. He loved her. He still loved her, in spite of everything. And the tears rolling down her white cheeks filled him with compassion. He sank to his knees in front of her, and wiped away her tears.

"Shh my love, please don't cry. I know you wanted the position for George, but I couldn't give it to him."

"Why?" She whispered. Anne was so afraid that she was losing Henry, and he could see it in her eyes. He wanted desperately to reassure her. He could not take back his decision, it had been foolish, but he had done it now.

"Because." His pause was only for the briefest of moments, and then the solution came to him. "Because I have something else in mind for George."

"What?" Her face looked hopeful. He had to make her smile. It broke his heart every second she was not smiling.

"Well, I have to make the arrangements, but I felt it was time that your brother received a promotion in his own right, rather than receiving your father's titles as he casts them aside for new ones."

"You would make George an Earl?" Her eyes sparkled, she was radiant. He wanted her. There was no more to it. He kissed her. He had not thought of making George an Earl, he was already a Viscount, he did not need more positions, but if it made his wife glow with such happiness he would give her brother anything.

"To bed, my love." He murmured into her kiss. She smiled, and rose up. She prayed that tonight she would conceive the son she so desperately needed, and that he would finally stay in her womb until the right time for his birth.

"Daughter, I must speak with you." Thomas Boleyn whispered, with such urgency that Anne immediately followed him away from the crowds in the Great Hall.

"What is it father? Is everyone well? Is it mother? Or Mary?" Anne was anxious.

"We are all well. But there are rumours."

"Rumours?"

"Cromwell. I have been lead to believe he is planning to overthrow our families power."

"How can he do that?"

"The King loves Cromwell, and Cromwell loves power." Thomas said, simply. "Do not do anything to cause either Cromwell's rage or the King's suspicion. Now is not the time to take the King to task about anything. Now is not the time to deny a request of Cromwell's. Do you understand child."

"Yes father." Thomas backed away, back into the throng of people, and Anne rested her forehead against the cool stone wall. Cromwell had far too much influence with her husband. And Henry was far too easy to manipulate. After all, hadn't she played her part in manipulating him against

Wolsey? And Wolsey had ended up dead. Her fear was paralysing. And then her mind went to Elizabeth, and panic filled her. What would happen to Princess Elizabeth if something happened to her? She would need a protector.

Anne mulled over her worries for the next few days. She thought about what would happen if Cromwell poisoned the King against her. She worried about who would take her side against the all-powerful Cromwell. She worried about Elizabeth. She worried about what Cromwell would do to her, to her family, to her friends. He could not topple the Boleyn's without there being ripples. Who would Cromwell bring down to achieve his goal. Anne was barely sleeping, and had hardly touched food in days. She looked drawn, she looked haunted. Her mind kept coming back to the thought that whatever happened to her, she needed to find someone to keep Elizabeth safe. And there was only one person she could think of who would remain safe during a Boleyn cull, but would be faithful enough to protect her child. Cranmer.

"I need your help, Cranmer." Anne said, bluntly.

"Of course, my Queen."

"I am afraid. I am afraid for my life."

"Why would you fear that?"

"I hear that Cromwell is no longer my friend, and I am afraid."

"What do you need?" Cranmer had known Anne for a long time, he loved her deeply, and would do anything in his power to protect her. "Do you need sanctuary?"

"No. Nothing like that. I will not give in and hide. But if something happens, if something terrible happens and I cannot protect my daughter, you must do it for me. As a friend, I ask you to take care of Elizabeth. I think that I will find myself compelled to a nunnery, and have my marriage declared invalid. They have cancelled our trip to Calais, have you heard? I think it is because Cromwell want a new Queen when they go to France." This was the first time Anne had voiced aloud the fear that had been running through her mind as she had watched the Seymour faction rise, and that had been plaguing her almost constantly since her father's words. Now she knew that Cromwell was against her, she felt sure she was in danger. "Cromwell will want to find a new wife for the King, one who he can control. You must protect Elizabeth." Cranmer looked into the familiar eyes, wracked with anxiety and now surrounded by the fine lines of age and worry. He saw she was genuinely afraid, and that she was, perhaps, not fully in control of herself. She appeared a little manic, and he was worried that she had nothing to fear, but was going to cause her own downfall by her crazed rantings.

"Of course, my Lady, of course I will guard her. But I think you are mistaken. And I think you need rest, my Queen. Perhaps you should take a short break from the demands of court. I think you are seeing problems where there are none." Anne nodded, vaguely, and turned from Cranmer to return to the Great Hall, to return to her husband. As she entered, she saw Jane Seymour, standing in the centre of a circle of courtiers, looking like she was a Queen. She was, indeed, the new Royal mistress, and was wielding the power of the role. Stood close behind her, whispering in her ear, was her brother, the leader of her faction. Anne felt her mind racing. She had not thought much about losing her place at court, even when Henry's new infatuation had started. But suddenly, all the little worries in the back of her mind were screaming at her. She was sure she was in danger, but she had no one to trust. She did not know why this was suddenly overwhelming her, but she could not cope. What if her father was right, if Cromwell was against her then she had no protectors other than her kin. She had nothing. And she had no son. Her head was swimming with the worries, she had no idea what to do, and then, almost as if her body was desperate to give her release, Anne's world went black.

Chapter Forty-Two

April 30th, 1536

"Bring Mark to me." Anne said to her women, she was still very pale, and looking very ill after her fainting fit the night before.

"He isn't at court." Madge Shelton replied. "We sent for him first thing this morning, we thought you would want his music, but he is not here. He is not in his rooms. I think he has a sweetheart in town."

"Send again, will you." Mark Smeaton, just as George had assured her, played the most spectacular music, and he was in Anne's rooms every day. Often, she did not even speak two words to him, but a day without his music seemed longer, darker and simply less enjoyable.

Mark Smeaton bowed shakily as he was presented to the Queen. Her own brother was stood there, speaking of the wonder of the music Mark played. He felt sick with nerves. He was nothing special to look at. He was thin, and his limbs seemed overly long. His skin was sallow, and his hair was dark, and he was often mistaken for a Spaniard. His siblings, all golden and blonde, had joked that their mother had cuckolded their father with a foreigner to make Mark. He may not be attractive, but he could make even the crudest instrument create the most beautiful music. He had reduced many a grown man to tears simply by his playing, and his singing voice was exquisite. He had been singing at an alehouse in Cheapside when George Boleyn had seen him. He was more than a little bemused to be here, in the Queen's chambers, but it was clearly God's will. He played his lute for her, and the Queen cried, the tears streaming down her face whilst her smile beamed. She was radiant. She was the most beautiful woman he had seen in his life. His heart leapt when she said she wanted him to stay at court, to be her musician. He came every day to her rooms, in hope of the faintest of smiles. He knew she was too far above him for him to seek to speak with her, but on those days when she granted him her glowing smile he felt like the richest man alive.

"Tell me about the Queen." The sickly-sweet voice of Thomas Crowell broke through the burning, ringing in Mark's ears.

"I don't know anything." Mark cried. His lips were dry, and cracked, his voice was hoarse from screaming.

"Another turn." Cromwell said, lazily. There was the unmistakeable sickening crunch of breaking bones. The wrenching pain made Mark sick. He had heard about the rack, he had always known that it was the most intense pain a man could imagine. He was not sure he could endure it. He passed out. The scent of vinegar brought him round. As they moved the rag from his nose he could smell blood and piss and vomit. He hoped that the pain would fade, but every second his poor body was prostrated across the rack it was becoming more intense. The next turn wrenched his arms from their sockets. They kept the vinegar on hand, he could not handle the pain.

"Tell me about the Queen." Cromwell asked again. There was no compassion in him as he looked at the broken man before him.

"What do you want to know?" Mark asked. He could take the pain no longer. There was nothing else he could do.

"Do you love the Queen?"

"Of course, I love the Queen. Please, a little water." Cromwell nodded to the man turning the crank, he moistened Mark's cracked and bleeding lips with a little water.

"Does your love go beyond that which would be considered seemly?"

"No!" Mark wailed.

"Another turn."

"Please, please no. I've done nothing wrong."

"Of course you haven't." Cromwell raised his hand to stop the turning. "We do not think you have done wrong Mark, and if you help us, if you will testify for us, we will keep you safe. You can go back to your family, you will live the rest of your life as you were supposed to. Perhaps you will marry a farm girl, and have lots of babies. Just tell us what we want to know. The Queen seduced you, didn't she."? It wasn't a question, it was a statement. His heart cried out for him to tell the truth, to shout that the Queen was honourable. That he worshipped her but that she never so much as glanced his way other than to thank him for his music, or to give him the occasional gold coin. But his body, his poor, crippled, broken body could take no more torture. He was afraid, and he had no choice but to trust Cromwell. He had to tell Crowell what he wanted.

"Yes." He said. Immediately, unseen hands untied his wrists and ankles. He found he could not move them, they were too broken and warped, but someone helped him sit, and they held a cup of wine to his lips. He drank greedily.

"And the Queen enticed you into her bed, didn't she."? He still felt guilt, but he had to save himself.

"Yes."

"More than once?"

"Yes."

"Thank you, Mister Smeaton. You shall be returned to your cell now. You have been very helpful." The men carried Smeaton to his cell. He was left on the straw on the floor, unable to move. As he heard the key turn in the lock, the tears began to fall.

"I'm sorry, my Queen." He whispered, over and over again. He felt like a failure as a man. He should have taken the pain, he should have upheld the Queen's honour. He should have died before he lied, before he besmirched the Queen's good name. But the pain had been so intense. He looked at the arms hanging limply at his side and the tears flowed more freely. "I have failed you my Queen. And may God forgive me, for I shall never forgive myself."

Cromwell put his feet up on the rack and smiled. He had known that the poor musician who frequented the Queen's rooms would be easy to manipulate into a confession. He would leave him for an hour and then he would bring him to him, he would feed him, he would treat him with care, and he would coerce him into revealing names of other men who came into the Queen's rooms. Maybe he had seen the Queen go privately to her bedchamber with some of these men. Infidelity in a Queen was treason. If he could have Anne Boleyn tried for treason, the taint would tar her entire house, and he would have the pickings of their offices, and the power to choose a Queen who would favour him above all others.

Chapter Forty-Three

May 1st, 1536

"Have you heard anything of my musician, Mark Smeaton?" Anne asked Henry. They were seated on a dais, awaiting the start of the May Day jousting. Henry was not riding out this time, after his near miss he had vowed not to joust again.

"No, my love. Why?"

"He hasn't been seen for over a day. He is not in his rooms, and no one knows where he is. I wondered if you knew anything? I have missed his music."

"Then tonight I shall send you one of my own musicians, and I shall have someone search the city for Smeaton." He kissed her lightly. "Do you have any news for me, my love." He whispered, touching her stomach.

"Not yet. But I am expecting my course in a week or so, I shall let you know if it arrives, I am hoping this month…" They smiled to each other, so engrossed in each other's eyes that it was as though the rest of the court had melted away. They had been like newlyweds recently. Anne had seemed so vulnerable, and Henry had taken great pride in being her protector. For a few weeks, she had seemed shaken and distressed. She would not tell him what was wrong, but she clung to him every night, and she was so meek when he joined her in her room that his desire for her multiplied, and the face of Jane Seymour was beginning to blur in his mind. He wished he could tell Anne he did not love Jane, not like he loved Anne, but the mention of her name sent Anne into hysterics. He had chosen, instead, to look after his weakened wife, and hope that a son conceived in peace, rather than passion, would thrive.

"Sire, I must speak with you." Cromwell appeared at Henry's shoulder. Henry vaguely inclined his head towards Cromwell. He began to whisper frantically in his King's ear. Anne could not hear what was being said, try as she might, but she watched as Henry's jovial countenance turned pale, then red. His eyes darkened, and his mouth screwed up into a pout. The thunder in his face was clear. Anne felt sick. She wished she could hear what Cromwell was murmuring into the King's ear. Without notice, Henry rose.

"There will be no jousting here today. Go home." Henry snapped. And with that he turned to his groom, Henry Norris. "With me." He said, beckoning. He did not even say goodbye to Anne, or offer an explanation, he simply left the pavilion. Anne watched her husband go, she saw him mount a horse, which Cromwell had waiting, and she saw the cloud of dust down the London Road as he sped away, with just Cromwell, Norris and a few guards. Anne was confused, and she was afraid. She felt sure that she was about to have to fight for her marriage, but she did not know what Cromwell was levelling against her, so she could prepare no defence. She gritted her teeth, and stood, showing her widest court smile. She turned and walked back to the palace, followed by her ladies. She called for music, and sat with her sewing as if she was unconcerned. But her mind was not on the idle conversation of her women, but instead was thinking of the many fictitious charges Cromwell could lay against her, and how she would counteract them. Once Henry returned to court she would go to his rooms. Her sexuality held much sway over the King, even as she aged, and she would try to seduce her way back into her husband's good graces.

Chapter Forty-Four

May 2nd, 1536

The guards did not knock, they simply walked into the Queen's apartments a little after breakfast.

"What is the meaning of this?" Anne stood and spoke in her most imperious tone. She needed to appear every inch the Queen now, more than ever.

"My Queen." The guard looked at her with sympathy. She could not remember his name, though he had stood outside her door since before she was crowned. "I am sorry."

"What do you want?" She asked coldly.

"I, that is to say we. We have come to. We have orders to arrest you my Lady." Anne fell back into her seat.

"On what charge?"

"On the order of the King."

"On what charge?" She tried, and failed, to keep her voice level and calm.

"I do not know. But we are to escort you to the Tower."

"Madge, gather my dresses I might need for a visit to the Tower, Annie, fetch my sewing, Lizzie, I will need my..."

"No madam, we are to take you now, before we miss the tide. You can bring nothing with you. None of your ladies will accompany you." Anne blanched. She was truly under arrest. She stood, trying to control her shaking limbs, and followed the men out of the palace, and into a small, waiting boat.

The journey to the Tower was a slow one. The people of London lined the streets, watching the Queen being taken to the Tower under arrest. No one knew what she was charged with. But they felt sympathy. They could see, even from the banks, that she was shaking, they knew she was afraid. She may have stolen the place of another, and she may not have been a Princess by birth, but in their own way the people of London had become accustomed to Queen Anne. The women had sympathised with the loss of her children, and the men were entranced by her face, and the remarkably slender figure after so many pregnancies. The little boat bobbed through traitors' gate and Anne felt icy fingers up her spine. She had the sudden fear that she would not leave this place. Waiting on the little dock was William Kingston, the man who had greeted her for her coronation. He took her hand and helped her from the little boat. She did her best to stay upright.

"Master Kingston, are you taking me to a dungeon?" Anne asked. Her voice, once so controlled, was shaking as much as her hands. It was clear she was straining to hold in her tears.

"No, madam. You will be going to the Royal rooms, where you stayed before your coronation." She wasn't sure if that was better. This seemed like a cruel mockery of her coronation visit, when she had been rounded with Elizabeth in her belly, she had been beloved by the King, and the people were disinterested. Now her husband was disinterested, and perhaps now, in her hour of need, the people of London might love her. She allowed the men to lead her to the rooms, and when the doors were opened she was shocked to see some of her clothes, and her belongings were already there. This had been planned then. The women sitting in the room were not of her choosing, but women who were friends and kin to Cromwell. They were spies, pretending to serve her. As the key turned in the lock, Anne felt the laugh bubbling inside her. She was so very afraid, and she had no idea what was going to happen, and yet she wanted to laugh. Laugh that her husband, so powerful and so commanding, would follow any man, puppy like, if they offered him something that would placate his ever-present conscience, or would satisfy his endless greed and gluttony. The women looked at each other as the Queen laughed quite hysterically. Her eyes looked hollow, and the laugh was almost a cackle. They all crossed their fingers in their pockets, in the old sign against witchcraft.

No one would tell Anne what they were charging her with, no one seemed to know. If Anne had remained calm, all that Cromwell would have against her would be the word of a musician, obtained under torture. But Anne was desperate to know what was being said against her. And in her panic, she began to rant, forgetting that every word that came out of her mouth would be reported to Cromwell. She spoke at random about people she had favoured, people she had spurned, times she had not behaved as a Queen should, and finally, crucially, about the courtly romances that went on in her rooms. Cromwell was outside her door, and he heard her list names of men who had been in love with her, men who would support her in times of need. He smiled. This was gold. This was exactly what he needed.

Chapter Forty-Five

May 3rd, 1536

"May I ask the charges against the Queen?" Cranmer asked, on his knees in Henry's presence chamber.

"Treason." Henry's voice was strained. He had barely slept in days, his eyes were red and puffy from crying, they had almost disappeared into his rounded face all together.

"Treason?"

"It has come to my attention that she had been, that she was, that, oh Cranmer, there were men." Henry began to weep.

"Are you sure?"

"Her musician has confessed. I made her a Queen and she took a musician to her bed." He sobbed. Cranmer stood and put his arm around Henry's shoulders, leading him gently to a chair.

"And it is just the musician who is accused?"

"No. Henry Norris. He denies everything. I promised him a pardon if he confessed, but he denies it. And Cromwell says there are others. He is conducting interviews now."

"And is he conducting these interviews in the Tower? On the rack?" Cranmer asked gently.

"I don't know." Henry said, gruffly. "Does it matter? She has taken other men to her bed. My children. The children I mourned, and my daughter, were they even mine. Maybe they were children of her lovers?" Henry's breaths were coming in great gulping gasps. Cranmer felt sick. He was quite sure that the accusations against Anne were false. He was sure that Cromwell's 'confession' was wrought on the rack, and was the crying's of a broken man hoping for respite. Men would confess to anything if tortured for long enough. He desperately wanted to tell Henry this, but he was afraid. The King was like a lion with a thorn in its paw, whilst it might appreciate help, it might also rail and roar against anyone coming too close.

"I must beg for mercy for the Queen."

"You would plead for a traitor? Are you traitor yourself Cranmer?"

"No, your Grace. It is only that I find it hard to believe the accusations. I do not question them, of course, but I know that the Queen loves you deeply, and it shocks me that she could have done such things." He cringed internally. He wished he had the strength to stand up for Anne, to protect her reputation which was being slandered and ruined to bring more power to Cromwell. He felt sick. She had been right. Cromwell was behind this, and she had known him to be her enemy. He should have done something then. He should have spoken to the King. Perhaps he could have saved Anne by damning Cromwell. But Crowell was clever. He had manipulated the King's love for her by giving the appearance that she hadn't loved him. Henry was broken, like a child, and he would adhere to anything Cromwell said.

"Do not beg me to spare her. I cannot spare her. There is only one punishment for traitors."

"I know, your Grace. But if I may, I would like to remind you that you are King, and you can punish her any way you see fit. If she has betrayed you, you could exile her. She could declare your marriage null, she could go to France, and you could be free, without spilling the blood of the woman you have loved so deeply."

"Do not beg me Cranmer. I cannot do anything. She is a traitor. And I will have to live with that for the rest of my life. The woman I love, the only woman I will ever love, pretended affection to gain my crown, and betrayed me." His tears were so great after this that Cranmer could only bow and retire, leaving the King to his raw, agonised grief. Cranmer wished he was a strong man, a powerful man, but he was simply a man wanting to survive. He daren't go against Cromwell now, he valued his own head more than he valued Anne's. He went straight to the chapel to pray, for his soul as well as hers.

Chapter Forty-Six

May 4th, 1536

As the water gate opened to admit yet another person embroiled in the downfall of the Queen, the Londoners around the Tower shouted their support for the poor prisoners. They called for God to save their good Queen Anne, they called for the King to come to his senses. Anne heard them, from her apartments in the Tower. She felt a little wave of irony, the Londoners who had hated her when she was on the ascent now loved her in her decline.

"Who has been arrested now?" Anne asked the man who brought her meals. He didn't answer. He looked at Anne with sad eyes.

"My Lady, many men have fallen with your star." He said softly. "And I pray for you." His voice was barely above a whisper. Even the keenest eared of Anne's spy ladies couldn't not hear him. Anne felt very alone, and she was terrified of who might be in the Tower with her. She ignored the food on the table, and laid on her bed, staring at the ceiling.

"You must eat madam." One of the women said softly.

"Why? He will kill me anyway, why should I bother to keep myself alive." Her voice was cold. The women didn't know how to react. They knew that she would be killed for her crimes. And despite themselves, they all knew that she had done nothing wrong, except being bold, and bright, and careless.

Whore

The key turned in the lock of William Brereton's cell. He was accused of being the Queen's lover. It was absurd, he thought, he barely even visited the Queen's rooms, and only when he was with the King. He didn't know which other men were here, but he had heard that George Boleyn was missing from his rooms. Maybe he had run away, to avoid the taint of his sister, or maybe Cromwell had named him amongst the lovers of the Queen. Any man who had influence with the King, any man he loved, was finding their way to the Tower.

When he had decided that the Queen would be brought down by her beauty, Cromwell had seen an opportunity to clear his way to being the King's only trusted adviser. He would have accused Edward Seymour if he thought it would stick, but not even the King, gullible as he was, would believe that she would take Seymour to her bed. He could deal with Seymour later, but he could take care of George Boleyn, Brereton, Norris, Thomas Wyatt and Francis Weston, with ease. The young men who surrounded the King. It had been gloriously easy to convince the King that the men so many years his junior who appeared to be his devoted friends, loved him only for the favours of his wife. It was easy to twist the outgoing and flirtatious Queen into a harlot, ensnaring man after man into her chambers. Cromwell couldn't help but laugh to himself at the ease with which he had brought down all those standing in the way of his power. Even Norfolk and Thomas Boleyn could not escape the stain of Anne's downfall. They had already withdrawn from the court, and were at their country estates. He was sure they would stay there. They dare not speak out for anyone accused, because they would be imprisoned too. He felt a slight twinge of guilt for adding George Boleyn to the list of lovers. His original intention had been to name him as her pimp, her procurer of men to satisfy her appetites. But when Henry had so willingly accepted the charge of incest, sobbing as he did so, it had been so easy. Everyone knew that the marriage of George and Jane Boleyn was strained to say the least, and he was sure that with a little persuasion he could elicit a testimony from George's own wife that would damn him to hell. The moment of guilt passed. It would all be worth it. After all, what had any of them ever done for him.

Francis Weston's wife left Henry's presence in tears. Her pleas to ransom her husband had fallen on deaf ears. She knew in her heart the accusations were false. Everyone knew they were false. Her husband was collateral damage in a plot to kill the Queen.

Chapter Forty-Seven

May 6th, 1536

"A letter for the King." The messenger said to Cromwell.

"From?" He asked, not looking up.

"The Queen." He held out his hand and the messenger placed the letter in it. He waved the man out, and when the heavy door had shut Cromwell broke the seal and unfolded the letter. It was a very long letter, written in Anne's unmistakeable, elegant handwriting. It pleaded her innocence in a very convincing way. She spoke elaborately about her love for Henry, and she had quite succinctly summarised the plot against her. It appeared that despite imprisonment, and the fear of death, Anne was still a powerful personality. It was fortunate that the letter had come here, rather than to the King, because poor Henry, so heartbroken and so desperate to be loved, would believe every word, and would release Anne and throw Cromwell in the Tower. And he knew that Anne would be ruthless if the tables were ever turned. He would lose his head. He gulped, then balled up the letter and threw it deliberately into the heart of the fire. He stood, watching the paper catch, crackle and eventually crumble into ash. He smiled. She would not be allowed to write again, he would make sure of that.

Once every scrap of the letter was burned into nothingness Cromwell went to see Henry. He had to press Henry into a trial, he had to make sure Henry was prepared to kill Anne. If he spared her, if he showed even the slightest drop of compassion, Anne would turn the tables. She knew him to be her enemy, and now one of them must die. Henry was sitting alone, in silence, staring out of the window. He did not look up as Cromwell walked in. He didn't speak, he waited for Cromwell to make his point.

"Sire. I wanted to speak to you about setting a date for a trial. And commissioning gallows and a pyre."

"What?" Henry's head jerked up.

"My King, it is only right that the accused be tried for their crimes, but the whole country knows that they will be found guilty. I simply thought you would prefer to have the places of execution ready so that justice could be done quickly."

"But a pyre?"

"Well, burning is the usual punishment for a female traitor."

"No. I won't burn her." Henry's voice was tired, it lacked its usual force. He sat for a moment. He remembered the beautiful day when he and Anne had been riding, and she had told him of her fear of fire. Despite it all, he still loved her enough to refuse to have her burnt. "She isn't a witch. And she is afraid of fire. I will have her beheaded if I must."

"My Lord, I am not sure that would be possible."

"Why not? I am King, I can do as I please."

"Of course. But it would be hard to find an Englishman who would do the job. To behead an anointed Queen. There would be those prepared to put a lighted taper to kindling, but to strike the death blow with an axe."

"Well then find a man who is not English." Henry was weary, and it was when he felt like this he was at his most malleable. Cromwell smiled.

"I could send to France. I hear there are executioners there beyond compare."

"Yes, yes if you must." Henry was distracted. He was thinking about Anne's neck, her beautiful neck, severed and bleeding. He had often fantasised about killing her, it had scared him and aroused him in equal measures. Now there was nothing sexual in it, it sickened him. The idea of her perfect body crumpled on the floor, or her long hair knotted in the executioner's fingers as he displayed her perfect face to the world. Could he really order that? But then his mind was filled with the image of her riding other men, lots of other men and he felt the bile rise in his throat. "Just see to it Cromwell. Now go!" Cromwell backed out of the room, leaving Henry to his macabre fantasies. Cromwell almost laughed as the door shut behind him. What delicious irony. The woman made so alluring by the French, the woman who loved the French and acted French would be killed by a French man. He scurried away to send for the executioner, feeling no compunction that he was summoning the man to kill her before she had even had a trial.

Chapter Forty-Eight

May 12th, 1536

There was clear unease in the courtroom on the morning that the men were brought in for trial. The jury were afraid. It had been made very clear to them by Cromwell that the King wanted a guilty verdict. Not a single man believed that the accusations were true, not a single man wanted to jeopardise his immortal soul by condemning innocent men to death, but not one of them wanted to defy the King. The evidence presented was very shaky. No one was convinced at all. Cromwell panicked as he watched. He had made a fatal error. An error which could prove to be his undoing. He had not accused any other women as complicit. In fact, he had no women to testify that they had even the slightest hint of anything improper. But if there were no women involved, then how would the men get in and out of the Queen's most private rooms, where she was never alone. It was too late now to choose a woman to fit up for being the Queen's assistant in her infidelity. He held his breath and hoped no one would emphasise this point.

When Mark Smeaton was brought to the stand, half carried on clearly broken limbs, he readily confessed. He sobbed as he told the court he had been intimate with the Queen on many occasions, and at many times. He accused the men who surrounded him in the witness box, Weston, Brereton and Norris, of sharing the Queens affections. He was trembling when he spoke, and his words were barely audible above his sobs. The men of the jury looked straight ahead, not daring to catch the eye of any other. Each man had been picked with care, they were not sympathetic to the Boleyn family, or they held grudges against the men accused. Even so, watching the poor man, broken and ruined by the rack, sobbing confessions, they felt sure he had been coerced. They all knew if they had caught the eye of another man they might have given up, they might have fought for what was right, they might have won, and then they would have died. So all eyes were focused on the man on the stand.

After they helped Mark down, they brought up each man in turn. Each man denied the accusations. Henry Norris even went so far as to highlight that on the date he was accused of having lain with the Queen she was in confinement after the birth of the Princess Elizabeth, and there would have been no way for the King to visit her bed, let alone another man. But the prosecution wove a tale of such alarming depravity it went beyond belief. The men needn't have protested their innocence, as nothing proved it more clearly than the frankly ridiculous stories told by Cromwell. He spoke of men hiding in chests when the King came in to visit his wife, he spoke of men willingly sharing her, he spoke of her enticing men during court dances, or her beckoning them from the jousting field to come to her rooms. He spoke of her as such a whore that no man could fail but be convinced of her purity.

But Cromwell was a powerful man. It mattered very little that his accusations were clearly fiction, that men on his hand-picked jury were in fear of their lives. As each man came back with a guilty verdict the gathered crowd shouted their disbelief. Each man was sentenced to death by beheading. Mark Smeaton was the only man to react, the only man to be shocked. The others had known from the moment they were arrested that they would die. They understood why they would die. But Mark had been promised his freedom. He had lied under oath, he had betrayed his Queen and her friends, under the impression that he would be released. As the men dragged him from the courtroom he screamed "I lied. The Queen is innocent, she is innocent! You promised me I would be safe Cromwell, you promised me if I lied I would be safe." But it didn't matter. The Queen had not yet been tried, but she couldn't be found anything but guilty. Her executioner had already been sent for, her household had been abandoned, she was spoken of as a dead woman.

Anne heard, finally, who had been accused when the news was brought to her that they had all been found guilty. She laughed, a hollow, mirthless laugh. Their guilt would be used to prove hers. It was a sickening perversion of justice. But, as always happened when Anne was most afraid, she could not help but laugh. The women who surrounded her were concerned for her sanity, she was laughing like she was a mad woman. And perhaps, Anne thought, she was. She had fallen in love with a man so fickle, and so powerful, and she had known fear of him, and still she had carried on her path. Perhaps that was, in truth, madness.

Chapter Forty-Nine

May 15th, 1536

As the peers of the realm assembled to play jury in the spectacle of the trial of Anne and George there was a distinct uneasiness Although their father had been excused, the foreman of the jury was their Uncle, the Duke of Norfolk, and Henry Percy, Anne's former betrothed, was there as well. No one spoke. No one knew what to say. They knew the verdict of the previous trial. They knew there was only one possible verdict today. Not one of them felt easy about it, even those who hated the Boleyn's and their rise to power. They could not condone killing half the court because they had power and influence, not on such ridiculous charges. But there was nothing they could do. The verdict was decided before the accused siblings were even brought into the court room.

George was first to be tried. The prosecution threw slander after slander at him, and George, ever the relaxed man, rebuffed every accusation with simultaneous wit and a dismissive tone that showed distain for the entire proceeding. Every member of the jury was inclined towards acquittal. There was no evidence against George, and he was a very affable young man. They felt to a man that they could probably let him go, to live in obscurity, without any repercussions upon themselves. But George, as he so often did at cards, overplayed his hand. A small slip of paper was handed to him, and he was asked to answer whether or not he had discussed that matter on the paper with his sister. George laughed aloud looking at the paper. Every member of the jury tensed, and every spectator held their breath, desperate to know what was on the paper.

"You wish to know," George said, in his carrying, clear voice, "whether I ever discussed with my sister the fact that the King is inadequate as a lover, and that he often fails to perform." There was a hushed silence. He had taken things too far. His arrogance had just signed his death warrant. He could not be allowed to speak about the King like that in public. So sensitive was the issue it had been decided to write it down, to ensure that the masses did not hear any questions about the King's virility. It was only a matter of minutes for the entire jury to find George guilty. He couldn't have known that had he shown some humility when presented with his final accusation he could have kept his head. But as it was, the axe was pointed towards him, in the symbol that he was to die. George took it with grace, and shrugged his strong young shoulders, as if those shoulders weren't soon to be without a head.

Anne walked into the courtroom every inch the Queen. There was a sudden awkwardness amongst the jury, as regardless of what she was accused of, Anne was Queen and they should stand as she entered the room. The masses stood, as one, and Anne acknowledged them gracefully, and tactfully ignored the slight of the peers, who all remained seated. Until this point Anne had no idea exactly what she was charged of, only that her co-conspirators had been found guilty.

"Anne, Queen of England," Started her Uncle Norfolk, "You come before this court accused of treason. The accusation is that you wilfully and deliberately took lovers whilst married to the King, and that you attempted to foist children of these unions onto the King, claiming them to be his lawfully begotten offspring. You also stand accused of incest, with your brother Viscount Rochford, and of ill wishing the King." Anne staggered. She had not realised the charges against her were so carnal. She had imagined charges of witchcraft, she had imagined charges of plots, but not of this, never of this. No one would believe this of her.

"My Lords, if I may speak." Anne said. Despite the fact that her stomach was turning somersaults, Anne's voice was calm, filled with the poise she had so often lacked. "I staunchly deny the accusations made of me. Anyone who knows me even a small amount knows that I love the King with an affection that has never waned, even when I stand here, on his orders. I love him as a man, and as a husband. All that I have to confess is that sometimes I forgot he was also my King. Sometimes I spoke unguardedly, sometimes I did not show enough respect or deference, and I certainly was not grateful enough for the high estate he brought me to. I know, as I have always known, that I am not worthy of the crown, and that I only gained it through the love of the King. I have never betrayed the King in any way. I have spent three years as the Queen of England. I do not have a moment of my life when I am alone. When I go to bed, if the King is not joining me, a maid sleeps in my bed. If I walk anywhere, I am watched, if I am in my chambers, I am never alone. This is why I look on the accusations of infidelity as sheer nonsense. If I had committed any indiscretions, the entire court would have known within the hour. And as for the accusations of any impropriety between my brother and I, I wholeheartedly admit to loving my brother, but only as any sister loves her brother. We shared our childhood, we were the best of friends. He has stood by my side through every difficulty I have faced in my life, he is my baby brother, and I will love him to the end of time. It makes me sick to my stomach that anyone could twist and pervert such a pure love as exists between siblings, simply to bring me down. And as to the final accusation, I have never ill wished the King. As I have previously stated, I love the King with all of my heart. That is, perhaps, my undoing. I never guarded myself, I let my affections run free, and maybe this is what has led me to this place. I understand that you have already found the others accused alongside me to be guilty. I understand that this leaves you with no choice but to find me guilty also. I shall speak no more, you may say what you will, and you may come to the verdict that you feel you are obliged to, rather than the one you feel is right. With all my heart, I forgive every one of you. God bless the King." And Anne sat down. There was a ripple of applause. She could see Henry Percy's hands twitch.

"I think perhaps it is time to make our votes." Said Norfolk. His voice trembled. One by one, every man called out guilty. Henry Percy's voice wavered as he said the word, and he fainted.

Anne was taken back to her rooms in the Tower. She had been told that she was to be beheaded, and she smiled despite herself that Henry, after everything, had saved her from burning. He still loved her, in spite of it all.

Chapter Fifty

May 15th, 1536

As soon as the verdict was reached, a small boat was on its way to the court to let the King know what he already assumed, that his wife had been found guilty of betraying him in the most personal way. Henry was inconsolable with his grief. Part of him had hoped, against all of Cromwell's insistence, that they would find her innocent, that they would say it had all been a mistake, she would come back into his arms, and they would laugh together, and then they would roll into bed together like they always had. He was still aching for Anne to carry his son, he could barely move with the loss of it all.

As Henry was crying in his private chambers, Cranmer was on a mission from his King. He shivered as he walked through the gateway to the Tower. There were a lot of ghosts in this place, a lot of good men had breathed their last here. He hoped that if his mission here was successful he could save one soul from the eternal torment of the Tower. As he was let into Anne's rooms he was struck by how thin she had become in the past fortnight. She looked ill, he could see her collarbones, sharp against her paper-thin skin.

"Anne, you look..."

"I look horrendous, I know, old friend. But if I am going to die, I suppose it doesn't matter if I die a beauty or a hag." She laughed.

"Perhaps, you may not have to die at all."

"Then they did not tell you, I have been found guilty. The Queen of England is a traitor, and will be killed thusly."

"No, Anne. I have come with salvation."

"There is no salvation for me now."

"Yes, yes there is." Cranmer looked eager. "I have here a paper, repudiating your marriage to Henry. It says that you were never married to the King because he had a prior relationship with your sister."

"Just like they offered Catherine."

"No, not like that. It will save your life. If you were never married to the King, then any infidelity they have found you guilty of would be an example of loose morals, but not treason." He paused to allow this to sink in. "You would be branded a whore, and Elizabeth would be bastardised."

"Then why would I agree to that? Why would I disinherit my own daughter, and brand myself a whore? Now I understand why Catherine would not back down on her marriage."

"Because, if you were simply Henry's mistress he could not kill you. He might choose to send you into exile. Perhaps you could go to France? And with Elizabeth excluded from the succession there would be no reason she couldn't go too." Anne was tempted. After all she had been through it would be so demeaning to call herself a whore, but if she could live, if she could go away with Elizabeth maybe it would be worth it.

"But I wouldn't have Henry."

"No. I do not see a solution where you and Henry can go back to how you were."

"I know."

"I know you still love him, and he still loves you, desperately. He is heartbroken. That is why he will let you do this. All you have to do is sign. There is nothing wrong with calling yourself a whore to save your life. You could always confess and repent when you are safely in France." Anne was tempted. Her mind went to her precious daughter, not yet three years old. It would be wrong to make her grow up without a mother. And if they went to France she would be able to bring her up herself, and maybe when

Henry came back to France for treaties, she might be able to see him, to touch him, to convince him to take her back. It might work. It was her only hope. And, although she wasn't convinced that it was going to work, she signed.

Henry barely noticed the paper Cranmer handed to him. "How did she look?" He asked, weakly.

"Ill, your Majesty. She says if she must die it doesn't matter if she has lost her looks."

"Oh, my Annie." He moaned.

"Your Majesty, she signed a declaration, invalidating your marriage. She was never your wife, so she cannot have committed treason, even if everything she is accused of is true. You could send her into exile? You could send her daughter too? You could be merciful?"

"I could?"

"If she were not your wife, she could not have been unfaithful to her King."

"She could go to France? She would be alive, in France?"

"Yes. I know that you love her Sire. I know that it will break your heart to sign her death warrant. I have found you a way out."

"Yes. Yes, you have Cranmer. How can I ever repay you? I will write to her now. I will command her to France, and after a time, if she keeps herself in an honourable way, I will send Elizabeth to join her mother. You are a good man Cranmer, you have a good soul." Cranmer bowed, and almost skipped as he left Henry's presence. He had saved her life.

Henry wrote in a fever. He was exultant that Cranmer had given him a way to save the life of the woman he loved without looking weak, he could save the men too. None of his friends would have to die, they would just go into disgrace. Maybe he could bring them back, one by one, over time. Then he would have back all of his friends, and it would be as though none of this had ever happened. He still struggled to believe it had happened. He tried not to think about it. Thinking about her with other men made him want to cry again. Cromwell burst into the room just as Henry was signing his name, with a flourish.

"Majesty, I have heard that you are set to forgive the Queen."

"She is not the Queen. She had renounced the marriage. If she was never Queen it was never treason." Cromwell ran cold. In a technical sense, it was true. Henry had found a loop hole to save the lives of everyone Cromwell had worked so hard to bring down. If they were pardoned, he would be a dead man.

"The verdict has already been given your Majesty."

"I am King, I can be merciful."

"You wish to have mercy on them? Truly?"

"Yes."

"You wish to be merciful to the woman who shamed you, who made you grieve for dead babies that were probably not yours. You wish to be merciful to the men who went to your wife's bed. You want to forgive the people who committed the most carnal of sins in the bed you bought for her, on the sheets you lay in. You want to forgive her for taking her own brother into her bed, for enticing him, and caressing him, and letting him have her, whilst they laughed at you for your lack of sons. You crowned her, regardless of a piece of paper signed in a desperate plea for forgiveness. If she needs to do this, is it not proof that she is guilty?" Henry felt sick. His stomach churned, his head span and his eyes watered. Cromwell knew he had almost sealed their deaths. "Do you not feel obliged to purge yourself of this woman entirely, this woman who beckoned your friends into her bed, who gave them what she denied you for so long. This is the woman who gloried in her crown, whilst taking her pleasure with any man who would go to her. She has implied to the world that you could not satisfy her, she needed a string of courtiers to do the job you failed to." Henry trembled. Cromwell was right. Of course, he was right. She had betrayed him. What did it matter if they were man and wife or not. She had been crowned Queen, and then she had done those disgusting things, with so many men, with her own brother. She couldn't live. He loved her, but she had to die. He had always known, from maybe the moment he first fell for her. Anne Boleyn was never going to live to be an old woman. She was too full of life for it to drag on. She would be a short-lived candle, snuffed out whilst it was still burning bright, never guttering and fading. Anne had to die. He balled up the letter promising her freedom, and throwing it into the fire. He sat by the fire, on the floor, watching the flames eat the words of love and forgiveness. He cried, self-indulgent, noisy, gasping sobs. He cried for the love he had once had, for the love he thought he had.

There was a gentle tap on the door, and a pageboy entered. He wiped his face roughly with the back on his hand. The boy delicately pretended not to have seen his all-powerful King sobbing on the floor like a child.

"What?" Henry snapped.

"A message from Mistress Seymour your Majesty. She would like you to join her for dinner tonight, at the London house of her father." Henry felt lighter. Jane was exactly the person he needed to see. Her cool, calming presence would ease his worries.

"Tell her I shall come." He waved the page out. Absent mindedly, he wiped the remaining tears from his cheeks. Why was he wasting tears on the woman who had betrayed him when there was dinner with a woman who worshipped him to contemplate?

Chapter Fifty-One

May 17th, 1536

The sun was pale in the sky the morning of the first executions. Anne looked out of her window, imagining she could see all the way up to Tower Hill. Imagining she could see her brother one last time. George stood alongside the other convicted men, tightly held in by guards, awaiting his turn at the scaffold. There was an enormous crowd around the raised platform, but for once, the crowd was silent. Ordinarily the crowd at the execution of a traitor would be screaming and spitting, berating the sinner for his crimes. Today it was silent. Ordinarily, no one truly heard a man's last words, there was too much chatter. Today, they heard every breath.

Smeaton was first. They carried him, and laid his head on the block. He merely sobbed, "I'm sorry." before the axe fell.

George watched, as one by one men he had known and counted as his friends had their heads taken from their bodies. And then it was his turn. As he climbed the steps he heard a few people muttering blessings for him. He had thought long and hard about what he was going to say on the scaffold. He was an innocent man, but protesting innocence to the end proves nothing. He stood at the front of the platform. The air itself seemed to be still for him, to hear the last words of George Boleyn.

"I am not a good man." He started. "I am a wretched sinner. And I have always known that death was coming for me. I love my sister, as any man should, and I followed her as my Queen. I will not apologise for that. I am sorry for the hurt that this will cause to my family, and I am sorry I was not a better husband to my wife. My sins are the sins of a young man, a man not yet in full understanding of the world, but they are sins none the less. And so, I take my leave of this world of sinners, to join the angels. I hope that you will pray for me." He knelt at the block, and collected to the last, he flung out his arms as the signal of ascent. The final thing he heard was the swoosh as the axe dropped.

Anne heard the canons, and she knew her brother was dead. She did not cry. She simply stood at the window and whispered into the air, "I shall join you tomorrow, my sweet brother. Save me room, just one night." Then she laid upon her bed, gently stroking her long, slender, elegant neck.

Chapter Fifty-Two

May 18th, 1536

Anne dressed with care that morning. She may not care about the lines on her face, or the extra grey hairs marring her darkened locks, but if she had to die, if Cranmer had failed as he must have, and if she was to die, she would die a Queen. She did not know that throughout the land her marriage had already been declared null. She did not know that there had been uprisings, women infuriated that Henry was disposing of another wife for no reason. She did not know that Jane Seymour had been spat at whenever she ventured out of her father's home, for all of London knew Henry visited her at night. Anne was preparing to die a Queen. In spite of this, when she heard the key turn in the door she trembled. Sir William Kinston walked in, looking grave.

"Is it time?" She asked, solemnly.

"I am afraid, my Lady, that the weather has delayed your executioner. He is in the country, riding as fast as he can, and we hope that we shall only be postponing until noon."

"So, I shall die at noon."

"Yes, my Lady. You have a few hours reprise." Anne looked sad.

"I had hoped to be beyond my misery by then, and to be with my brother in Heaven." Kingston hung his head. He liked this woman whom he had seen crowned as Queen and then brought so low. He did not wish to see her die.

"And also, you will not be executed at Tower Hill. They will do it here in the Tower, on the Green."

"Why?"

"There will be no crowd, there will only be a few courtiers to bear witness."

"Henry is afraid that I will speak against him." She whispered. Henry had feared that, but more than that he feared the people of London. They had united in sympathy for Anne. What if they stormed the scaffold, what if they took her, hid her, got her away. Or what if they were so enraged by her death that they went after him, or Jane. Henry could not take that risk. Anne was glad of it. "I had not wanted to have all eyes upon me when I drew my last breath. This, at least, is a comfort." She sat herself on a hard, wooden stool, looking every inch the Queen. Kingston felt the urge to bow to her as he left the room, and he only barely suppressed it. As he locked the door his eyes smarted with tears. If only he could leave the door unlocked, let her melt away. But he would be hung for it. His family would be disgraced, and he had children to think of.

Midday came and went, and still there was no summoning to her death. Anne knew that the executioner had not arrived. She knew, that despite her preparations, this would not be the day she died.

Chapter Fifty-Three

May 19th, 1536

As she walked to the block Anne felt the sunshine on her face, and relished in its delicate kiss on her cheeks. Kingston has been right, there was next to no one there. And there was a simple stool placed in the centre of the Green. That would be where her last breath would be taken. She stood before the small crowd to impart her last message to the world.

"I have come before you this morning to die. It is the will of the King, and therefore the will of God, and so I shall not speak against it. I have not always behaved as I ought, and I have committed many sins for which I beg forgiveness. I beg all of you here present to be loyal to your King, for he is the finest King in the world, and you could not ask for a kinder, more loving ruler. I beg you to pray for my wretched soul." Her voice was so calm, and yet so earnest, that even the courtiers who were her sworn enemies felt lumps in their throats. She stepped back and allowed her women to take off her outer dress and her head dress. She handed a small purse of money to the executioner, and she gave him her forgiveness. Slowly, she seated herself on the stool. She looked ahead, and began to pray. She did not hear the executioner raise his sword, and she barely heard the soft hiss as it swung through the air. There was a collective gasp as the beautiful head of Anne Boleyn was struck off in a single blow. The crowd backed away from the head as it rolled. The body collapsed upon itself. As the executioner held up the severed head of the poor Queen, the canon roared.

Far away at Greenwich Henry heard the canons, and he crossed himself. "Lord forgive me for what I have done." He murmured. Then he called for his horse, he was going to visit Jane Seymour.

Epilogue

May 30th, 1536

After a private wedding to Anne, Henry felt compelled to have a much more public wedding to Jane Seymour, the woman who had stolen his heart. But the crowds did not cheer. They did not look upon her with love, because he was marrying her less than two weeks after murdering his Queen. Henry pretended not to notice the eerie quiet everywhere he turned. The jubilant cheers of his people were, it seemed, no more. The people of England might not have liked Anne, but they had seen her anointed as Queen, and they were appalled at her death. Never again would the people of England look at Henry as their golden King, he was tainted now with the blood of his beautiful wife and the men whose only crimes were being her friends.

Princess Elizabeth lost her title the moment her mother lost her head. The Lady Elizabeth was kept out of sight, watched over by Archbishop Cranmer as she grew. She would never remember her mother, apart from a vague smell of lavender, and a swirling of skirts. She was too young to understand what had happened, but she knew her mother was never coming back, and that her father had a new Queen. Elizabeth's mother slipped from her mind, and her world became focussed on her giant of a father. And she dreamt that one day, she would be as great a Queen as her father was King.

ABOUT THE AUTHOR

Emma L. Fenton is a mum of two, a singing teacher, and a keen historian. She has written stories for as long as she can remember, and being an author has been a dream since childhood. She lives in Surrey with her family.

Visit www.emmalfenton.com or follow me on social media
@emmalfenton

23700818R00153

Printed in Poland
by Amazon Fulfillment
Poland Sp. z o.o., Wrocław